he spiralling figures locked into position, spell-casters blossoming into light.
"Stand aside, Kieri."

Kieri gritted her teeth until they ached, and slid her arm around Rathen's side. He lowered his head, as if already defeated. Arkan's wrist flicked downward, and his spell-caster released a scarlet plume of disablers. Rathen's breath hissed between his teeth. A hook arced through the muscle of his forearm, its barb deeply anchored. Rathen spread his fingers in a counter-spell and broke the stream of fire attached to it. But its tail lashed around his wrist, burning deep.

"No," Kieri sobbed.

Spells whined around her. On reflex, she swung in front of Rathen's body, her back to the sparkling flares. Fire burned up her spine. She muffled a cry against Rathen's chest. His heartbeat thudded under her cheek. His undamaged hand swept down her back, the ice of an air spell chilling the pain. The void of spell-craft stopped Kieri's breath before wind rushed inward, balancing the energies unleashed.

Keep him on the ground! Adien's urgent cry grated through Kieri before the man hazed in the corner of her sight, spell-caster flailing. Rathen's head snapped up, and he ducked sideways. Instead of shearing through his pinions, the spell hit the upper surface of his coverlet feathers. A cloud of black down swirled into the air and he gasped.

Rathen, fly...

ELF LOVE

An anthology

Edited by
Josie Brown,
Rose Mambert,
& Bill Racicot

PINK
NARCISSUS
PRESS

ELF LOVE: An Anthology.

Cover illustration and design by Duncan Eagleson

Published by Pink Narcissus Press
P.O. Box 303
Auburn, MA 01501
www.pinknarc.com

Library of Congress Control Number: 2010938236
ISBN: 978-0-9829913-0-5

First trade paperback edition: February 2011.
Printed in the United States of America

This book is dedicated
to the memories of
J.R.R. Tolkien
and Gary Gygax...

...without whom no one
would give a damn
about elves.

Acknowledgments

I would like to give special thanks to the following people, without whom neither this book nor my sanity would exist. First, I would like to thank Duncan Eagleson, whose unwavering support and enthusiasm has kept me from throwing in the towel on this project on more than one occasion. I would also like to thank him for supplying such beautiful artwork both inside and on the cover of this book. Second, I would like to thank Chris LaFond for all his work copy-editing the book for no payment – other than chocolate and sushi – under such a short deadline. Third, I would like to thank Dr. Bill and Sweet Josie Brown for some very lively discussions and their work editing the anthology. And finally, I would like to thank the writers for sending us such great stories. It was delightful working with you and I hope we can do it again soon!

Rose Mambert
Editor-in-Chief
Pink Narcissus Press

Contents

Introduction

When my friend Rose approached Sweet Josie Brown and me about setting up a press, I was out of work, so I said "SURE!" While we talked about the kinds of books and stories we like to read, and by extension the kind of stuff we'd like to publish, we used terms like "fine fantasy" and "good books" and "things that don't suck." It's been fun looking back on those conversations and realizing how very little actual meaning is denoted in words like "good" and "fine" and "doesn't suck." I think we've each learned a lot about what the others like to read.

We also talked, in those initial conversations, about genre. Rose and I are fantasy readers from way back, and Josie likes – let's say a more *mature* style of reading material. I get the impression that Josie's favorite dragons come in tattoo form. But what is fantasy anyhow and really, who cares? We figured out pretty fast that the kinds of material we like best defy the boundaries of genre, and we made that one of our informal goals.

I think this book reflects that goal pretty well. We've

collected here stories that approach the elf love theme from all angles and directions: some traditional fantasy, sure, but also a noir piece, some urban/contemporary stories, and at least one story that isn't really "genre" at all.

As for that theme... Let's say that another of our informal goals was to challenge authors to come up with something unusual or offbeat. We wanted to keep people thinking. Initially, when Rose said "Elf Love," my response was "Are you kidding?" But about ten seconds later I had thought of several story ideas that read the theme ironically or that I would love to read.

It's a very broad theme on the face of it. All you need is an elf and some aspect of love, right? A talented author sees a theme like that and says "That will be terrible unless..." and what comes after the "unless" is an awesome story idea.

I'm proud of this book, and I'm proud of the stories it contains. I'm wicked excited about what comes after "unless."

Bill Racicot
Editor

"For Legolas' sake, Jason!" I yelled. "Nobody believes in this crap anymore!"

Ed Cooke works for the Methodist Church in York, UK. He writes lyrics for the progressive rock band Voyager Project; their album WHERE ANGELS FEAR TO TREAD *is available via Reverb Nation and CD Baby (CDBaby.com). Ed edits the Christian e-zine* RUBBER LEMON *(rubberlemon.co.uk). He has written half-a-dozen stage musicals and one short film,* EMBARGO *(embargo.on-the-web.tv), a summary of the history of philosophy set in a Birmingham pub.*

Despite all his activity, this is Ed's first piece of prose fiction to see print. Clocking in at only 550 words, it was the shortest story we received, but one we thought worthy to kick off the collection.

When I asked Ed his opinion of elves, he said, "I think elves are a sinister bunch, if you believe everything you read in Michael Swanwick's book The Iron Dragon's Daughter.*"*

Not an Elf Yet
Ed Cooke

By the time Jason told me he was an elf, it was too late. I was already in love with him.

"Not an elf yet, not completely," he would correct me when I introduced him to friends. "But I am on the way to becoming one." I would stroke his perfectly smooth cheek and smile indulgently.

First thing every morning, Jason would leap out of our bed (he wasn't absolutely certain elves and humans were supposed to mate, but so far there had always been *something* in my bottom drawer that silenced his objections) and read the Book. The Book was leather-bound and very thick, and its pages were edged in real gold leaf that turned red when you riffled them. I didn't riffle them very often, because the text was printed in runes. Many times Jason offered to sit down with me and teach me how to read the Book. We tried it once or twice, but there were plenty of other things I would rather have been doing than hearing all about how some English words were rendered as suffixes in Elvish. Or Elven. Or whatever the hell their stupid language is called.

I suppose it was at the end of one of these lessons that I snapped. I seized the Book and gave it a short sharp quiz in aerodynamics. Despite valiant flapping of its Rizla-thin pages, it failed abysmally.

Dismay scribbled itself across Jason's delicate features in lines I could understand all too clearly. He crossed the room to fuss and fawn over his Book, which only incensed me more.

"For Legolas' sake, Jason!" I yelled. "Nobody believes in this crap anymore!"

He winced. I crossed my arms to protect my heart from the forlorn looks he was shooting at me, and went on: "Next you'll be telling me you go to one of those meetings."

His alfheim met in the high school gym. I can't believe I agreed to go.

Two of them greeted us at the door. They looked pretty ordinary, except they wore goofy tunics and goofier grins. They gave me a flimsy photocopied sheet, with a motley parade of runes that could have meant anything and an English translation underneath. I got the gist of it as we perched on one of a set of parallel bars: some gibberish about inhabiting the southernmost end of heaven that shall survive after earth has died. I had folded it into a paper boat by the time the meeting started.

The leader stood up. Jason whispered, "That's our yngvi." I glared at Jason and he didn't try to explain anything else that happened. I didn't want to know. I just wanted to get out of there.

For Jason's sake I sat through an hour's recital in Elvic (Elvese?) and then a further hour of what I presumed was commentary in Old Norse, repeated in English. Somewhen during the third hour, when the singing started, I walked out.

Jason found me sitting at the school gate, calming my raddled nerves with a cigarette.

"It's perfectly natural to react that way," he said. "We all have trouble accepting our true nature at first." His smile was probably meant to reassure me.

"Bullshit," I said.

He stroked the points of my ears fondly and gathered me into his embrace.

"What was that?" "Is she like that all the time?"
And inevitably – "what's with the ears?"

Josie Brown is a Political Theory Ph.D student at Boston University. A native of Worcester, Massachusetts, she currently lives in Holden with her husband and two cats. "I think of myself as a Renaissance woman and am constantly looking to learn new things and find connections between disciplines and ideas – it makes life much more exciting."

As for the idea behind "Tidings of Comfort and Joy," she writes, "This story was inspired by the battle over California's Proposition 8. I'd just been so revolted by the Proposition itself and the behavior of its proponents, and so struck by the ugliness required to want to keep people from making public declarations of their love. I think that love brings joy to everyone, not just the people involved in the connection, because love is the height of human existence. To oppose it in any form requires a meanness of spirit I'm not sure I could deal with, and that's what started me thinking about what you'd do to escape that kind of inhumanity. Writing it was startlingly difficult. I drew on a lot of memories of friends and places I have loved, and I felt the distance from them intensely."

"Tidings" holds not only the distinction of being the only Christmas-themed story in the anthology, but also the only one without any actual elves in it.

Most of Josie's writing can be found on her eclectic blog: theoutlawjosie.blogspot.com

Tidings of Comfort and Joy
Josie Brown

If you think about it, it's not so weird for someone to dress up like an elf, even if they're old enough to know better. In winter, it's almost played out, and if you happen to work at one of those Christmas stores, it's dress code. When I followed the neon orange of the "Help Wanted" sign into Joyful Jingles, stomping snow off my boots and peeling back layers of wool, Jesse's bright green hat and pointy ears didn't faze me for a second. I was broke, cold and hungry, and all I really cared about was the store's willingness to cut me a check once a week.

By February, things were definitely weird.

Let's get this out up front: there's always something sad and desperate about those year-round Christmas joints. They're always in those creepy, ill-lit strip malls next to used book stores – used, not rare – and third tier fast food restaurants, clinging onto the Christmas spirit and gathering dust. The clientele is a crapshoot too. Most of them are in it for the arts and crafts, but you also get a constant stream of people who don't seem capable of happiness, who come in and stand looking at the ornaments and the plastic trees like some ray of light is going to come down and show them how to feel joy. It's even worse when they buy something after standing there for twenty minutes. But hey, for a steady paycheck, I can work up some fake cheer once in a while. For Jesse, though... man. No matter what, she'd be right there with 'em, asking how she could make their day more joyful and slinging around holiday cheer. Not a trace of irony, either. It was like working with a puppy.

When I went out for a cigarette I'd see some of the customers coming out, and that's when I'd get the questions. "What *was* that?" "Is she like that all the time?" And inevitably – "what's with the ears?" I'd just shrug off the questions, then go back inside and look at Jesse's ears. They were really a hell of a thing, these ears perfectly spackled and smoothed onto her head, with soft points rising above the braided trim of her hat. It must have taken her forever each morning to get those things just right. You couldn't even see a telltale "Made in China" anywhere, and it seemed like she could hear all right, with just a few perky "pardons" scattered through the day. No wonder people asked about them.

Normally, it was just the two of us in the store. She'd dust those damn trees and ask me Christmas trivia I didn't know or care about, and I'd wear out the mouse playing solitaire. When July rolled around, the owner sent us out into the storeroom for inventory while he rehabbed the place. Take a second to think about all the tiny parts involved with Christmas. You have the ornaments and the bells and the tiny baby Jesuses and the ornament hooks and light bulbs. Now take all of that and multiply it by a factor of someone who shops for Christmas décor all year 'round, and you have the

Joyful Jingles storeroom. It was a nightmare. After five hours of counting and dropping things all over the floor, I declared an inventory break.

We went out to the loading dock and sat quietly for a few minutes, watching the trees wave behind the dumpster and the white trails of clouds lazing across the clear blue sky. I took off my shoes to warm my feet in the summer sun, and Jesse set her hat aside and leaned back on her elbows. I sat there looking at her hat on the edge of the dock, with her curly-toed shoes swinging casually below it, and finally asked, "Jess, what's the... elf thing?" She looked at me like she was surprised I'd noticed, then looked back at the dumpster. I hadn't thought about it being a personal or private thing, but it looked like I'd stuck my finger in an open wound. Just as I went to apologize, she started to talk.

"I didn't always work here, you know," she began. "I used to live in Virginia, and I worked in Washington. I used to eat lunch in the park, and one day when I went out for lunch there was this woman there, a woman with a suit and no shoes. Her name was Ori, and I saw her every day after that. We had the same lunch, too." Jesse stopped for a minute and looked back into the storeroom. Dull thuds emanated from the front of the store. "Ori and I started meeting at the train after work," she continued, "and we'd go out to dinner, and maybe a movie, especially when they had movies on the Mall and we could lie there and watch the sky while we waited for the sun to set. After a while we started going to each other's apartments after the dinners and the movies, and eventually we saw each other all the time. I never had a lot of friends, so at first I was just excited to have this friend, someone who had room for me in her life. Sometimes you meet people and you realize that some part of you has always known them, from the first moment you drew breath.

"The first time we kissed, it was like drowning. She put her hands on the sides of my face and I felt like I was surrounded and carried away." I'd never thought about Jesse kissing anyone. "I never really bothered with loving other people, but all the ways I know how to love people now, she taught me. The one thing I did learn on my own was a way to love the city, and when I stood with Ori in the middle of this place, with all the energy of the buildings and the history and the people running electric through my feet, I just felt like I could do... anything. I could be whoever I wanted." She interrupted herself. "I know this probably sounds crazy and like it has nothing to do with the elf thing, but I swear it does." I told her it was okay even if it didn't explain the elf look, and scooted up to look at her instead of the ugly dumpster across the way.

"So anyway, we were together for a year, and on our first anniversary we took the subway to a festival downtown. When we got on the train, I saw one of my coworkers, so I had stopped to say hello to him. We finished talking and I started back towards the seat Ori'd found, and I noticed the plexiglass window that she was leaning her head on had crazed and all of the lights of the tunnel were refracting in rainbows through the spiderwebbed lines of the glass. Ori's hair fit right in, with yellow and gold shining like tiny Christmas lights in her hair, and I just remember thinking how beautiful everything was, even in those gross old subway cars with the orange carpet. We got out and spent a couple hours wandering through the fair. It was a day a lot like this, actually, but colder, getting towards the end of summer. After a while, we sat on a bench to watch the people pass by, until Ori decided she wanted to grab some apple cider and some top secret something. She wouldn't tell me what it was, but she told me I had to stay on the bench and she'd be right back."

Jesse looked down at her shoes and continued, but her voice had shifted somehow. "I watched her walk away in this long coat and long hair with that posture she had, like setting her shoulders back was the key to world domination. I don't know that she was wrong, really. Anyway, she disappeared, then popped up again at the cider stand a while later, and I watched her waiting there in the wind. I can't tell you how gorgeous she was. There's a beauty that I think only humans can have, because it's about their mind too, and the things you know they've done and how they feel about you and the world and the people in it. These guys kept talking to her, and I could see her brushing them off, but in that nice way she had about her that made guys walk away thinking her rejection was the nicest thing that had happened to them all day. She came back to me and we started walking toward the restaurant where we'd planned to have dinner."

"Those guys reappeared a couple blocks behind us, and of course they were calling after her. I never understood what makes men think it's okay to just yell at women on the street.

Does that work for anyone?" I could feel the exasperation rolling off her in waves. "We kept walking but they kept following us, and they got more and more upset as they figured out we were on a date and not just two friends out for a day in the city. We were both nervous, but Ori decided to take a back route to the restaurant to get out of there. I thought we'd lost them when we ducked into the side street, but then I felt a hand on my shoulder. As I turned to look at the owner of the hand, he shoved me off balance and into the wall. Everything lit up like that window on the train and I felt Ori's hand leave mine. I woke up a while later, clutching some piece of garbage that I'd fallen on. I saw Ori a few feet away.

"I tried to go to her, but when I moved, pain ripped through my leg and I was back in the window, full of light. I looked down and saw the white of bone coming through my calf. I took a closer look at the situation and finally noticed the glossy red pool around Ori's shoulders and the chasm in her temple. I put my necklace between my teeth and bit down hard as I dragged myself to her. The glass bead in the pendant shattered, but I managed to get to her. I could see right in to that magnificent brain of hers. I started to scream and didn't stop until we were in the emergency room and doctors pushed sedative after sedative into me."

After this, Jesse stopped talking for a long time. Even the trees were quiet, and dark clouds edged in on the bright sky.

"When I found someone to tell me what had happened, it was all over. A woman who lived above the street had heard the men screaming at Ori, calling her all kinds of names. They were furious, I guess, that she dared be gay, that she would rather be with me than sleep with them. This woman looked out to see one of them undoing his pants while the other one slung Ori against a dumpster. When her head hit the edge of the metal bin, they ran. The woman called the cops, but she never yelled or threw anything. I just never understood that.

"My leg had been broken so badly it took me months to get back on it. It's all plates and pins. I have to take a doctor's note with me to the airport now." She cracked half a smile at this. "I spent months down there working through rehab, but once I got out and went back to work, I couldn't get away from Ori not being there. She wasn't in the park or on the subway or in the city, and as long as I knew that, I couldn't... I couldn't feel the city the same way. I finally moved back to Scranton, I guess because I felt like there was so much space. When I got there I couldn't get a job like I had back down south, so I got a job at some bar down the street. That was okay, but then Ori's case went to trial and somehow people found out she'd been my girlfriend and I came home one night and someone'd painted 'Go home dyke' on my apartment building and I didn't really know what to do with that because I *was* home. I quit at the bar and moved here to Great Falls.

"I just applied everywhere, and then I got to Joyful Jingles and it was like it could be Christmas every day. I figured that would override everything. Someone's mad that you're gay, who cares, it's Christmas. Someone yells at you, who cares, it's Christmas. Everyone's happy on Christmas."

26

She took a rattling breath and continued on. "The elf thing just seemed like the perfect solution. I thought about how beautiful that day was and how hideous the violence was, and the ugliness was all human, you know? If not for humans, that would still be a beautiful, perfect day. So I thought, maybe I can opt out, so I don't ever make life ugly. I guess I just figured I could be an elf instead. I could just make Christmas all day, and not worry about being human. It probably sounds stupid to you, but it's been seven years now and it seems to be working. People just leave me alone, and now sometimes on days like this I can just look at the sky and remember that things can be beautiful.

"So that's the elf thing."

What do you say to that? If you're not me, you probably say something infinitely soothing, something that manages to apologize on behalf of humanity and close the wounds of that story. I, on the other hand, looked at Jesse and told her that her ears were really good. And that she was awesome at being an elf. I couldn't believe I said it. She just looked at me and patted my arm and said "thanks."

I looked up the story later, when the renovations were done and inventory was over. It was more and less painful in newsprint, and I wondered how Jesse managed to cling to anything beautiful about that day. I could hear her talking with customers as I read, with her voice vaulting and lifting over the Christmas music. I remembered her talking about the lights in Ori's hair and wondered if she thought about them when she strung the little white lights in the display windows. Probably. I started trying to answer those stupid trivia questions she'd call out, and I even agreed to go caroling with her when Christmas came around for real. The two of us took care of that store all through the year, together. But when I saw customers coming out shaking their heads, I just answered their questions with a short "nothin' wrong with keeping up the Christmas spirit." There's no good way to explain that being human just wasn't working out.

"Melkor's spit, Marroc. Of course he's good. The guy's an Arch-Ithron."

Duncan Eagleson is an author, painter, animator, leather sculptor, and award-winning maskmaker.

In his youth, Duncan pursued a variety of careers, including advertising copywriter, art director, trade show director, actor, stage fight choreographer, private detective, astrologer and card reader, among others. Encouraged by Joseph Campbell's remark that the best predictor of an artistic career was the number of different jobs held before age 30, he turned finally to art and writing, producing illustrations for magazines, book covers, and film and theater posters.

Does this guy ever sleep? Judging by the number of contributions he has made to this book, the answer seems to be "no." His first submission, "Goodnight, My Lady" appears on page 72. He has also supplied the art for the cover as well as for the comic scripted by Sarah Eaton on page 142.

About "Reclaiming the King," he writes, "Having submitted 'Goodnight,' I got wondering what more original stories I could come up with about elves. As I turned this over in my mind, thinking 'Elves... elves...' I suddenly remembered my younger brother, at the age of four or five, asking about Santa Claus's little helpers. At that point, 'Reclaiming the King' leapt to mind almost full blown, and I just had to hope that the King's (and Danny's) love for the human world would be enough to qualify the story for inclusion."

Reclaiming the King
Duncan Eagleson

> *And as the number of Keys on the Wheel, so were the number of the turnings of the Sun that the King endured the Great Captivity.*
>
> *– Book of Al-Vis Aeron, The Chronicle of the Teleri*

August, 1977

The green Pontiac LeMans rolled slowly down the street, its driver and passenger scanning the sidewalks and alleys carefully.

"You should have picked him up yesterday," the female in the passenger seat said.

"Relax, Mary Sue, he'll be here," said the driver. "He never leaves the area."

"Don't call me that when we're alone. My name is Sirren."

"Hell, girl, what're they teaching you kids about undercover work these days, anyway?" The man, who Sirren would have called Marroc, but who presently went by the name of Danny Fisher, made a disgusted snorting sound. "Don't you know better? You gotta stay in character at all times, never let your guard down, otherwise, you'll fuck up and let down at the wrong time."

"I've never let my guard down in front of a human. Anyway, we're almost done here. Tomorrow night, we'll be gone."

"That's the plan, but don't count your chickens, honeybunch, they're still just eggs."

"Yes, of course, you may not be able to find this guy again. Then we'll have to go hunting for another one."

For the moment, they rolled along in silence. She began to hum quietly.

"Stop that," he snapped. She complied.

Sirren was among the best operatives in the Company of the Ignotum Ambigue, the secret service of the Court of the Telerian Elves. She had graduated at the head of her class, and been decorated twice for valor. She had participated in several covert operations, one of them in Kortirion, and two in the human world (though not previously in America) before she had been assigned to partner with Marroc on this, what her case officer had called the most important op in the history of the Company.

Marroc himself was a legend in the service. Instructors at the Company training facility (commonly known as "The Form") used his infiltration of Svartalfheim as a textbook example, and he had performed more successful deep cover operations than any single agent. After working with him for several weeks, although she still respected his abilities, Sirren was finding him less intimidating than simply irritating. She sighed, scanning her side of the street.

"We'll find him," said Marroc. Then a moment later, "There. There he is."

The homeless guy rooting through the dumpster stood a good six feet, and must have weighed 270 or so. Despite her irritation, Sirren found herself nodding in approval. He already looked right. Black hair, squarish features that might have been handsome before alcohol, drugs, and fat had taken their toll. Give him a haircut, and he'd do.

The car stopped, and the two got out. They approached the homeless guy, the man humming low, the woman quietly singing.

Later, as they placed the unconscious man in the trunk of the LeMans, the man said quietly, "I hope this guy y'all are bringing over is good."

"Melkor's spit, Marroc. Of course he's good. The guy's an Arch-Ithron."

"I'm just saying. You can't always trust them Noldor."

There had been signs and portents, for those who could read them, though there were few enough in the human world who could. Thunderstorms had rolled in during the afternoon, but had broken neither the heat, nor the overcast. In the moist warmth of the evening, under a cloudy sky, strange lights were seen in the skies, and in the forested hills, folks in rural areas heard what might have been the cry of the Wampus Cat.

As midnight neared, the handful of truckers and late night drivers in the truck stop off Route 269 might have thought it strange that a figure had simply appeared near the back of the parking lot, had any of them noticed it. This figure, however, was strangely difficult to notice or focus upon. If anyone had noticed (they hadn't), or paid the figure any attention (they wouldn't), they might have seen a slightly built elderly man in jeans and T-shirt, carrying a gym bag. Had some person resisted the impulse to look away, had they also happened to be endowed with what old-timers called *the sight*, they might have seen something very different.

The man walked toward the front of the parking lot, as a green Pontiac LeMans roared in, its windows down and radio blasting (Marshall Tucker hoarsely demanding *can't you see?*). It jounced to a stop, spraying gravel. The strange man took a step back. The passenger door opened, a woman got out, pulled the seat of the 2-door coupe forward so the older man could get into the back. He did. The girl got in, and the LeMans growled and returned to the highway heading south on 269 trailing Tucker's complaints: *what that woman has done to me...*

As the car continued down the highway, the woman, ignoring the driver's protest, lowered the volume on the radio and turned in her seat. First she, then the older man in the back seat had changed appearance. Both now had pale skin, green eyes with the vertical pupils of a cat, and pointed ears. The girl was still dressed in jeans and a white cotton top, but the older man now appeared dressed in a loose cotton robe, a necklace of bones and teeth around his neck.

"Welcome, honored Ithron," she said. "I am Sirren, this

33

is Marroc."

"I am Caedryff, Arch-Ithron of Tirion," said the new-comer. He looked at the driver, whose appearance had not changed. "Your partner might have the politeness to drop the glamour now."

"Call me Danny," said the driver, "and it ain't a glamour, reverend. I ain't never been no good at that magic stuff."

"Marr—uh, Danny," Sirren explained, "has been a deep cover operative in the human world for many years. His ears have been surgically altered, his hair is dyed, and he wears a human device called a contact lens to change his eyes." Her case officer had warned her that there was a possibility that Operative Marroc had "gone native," and after working with him for the past month, she was afraid the elf had been right. "He maintains his cover persona at all times."

"I see," said Caedryff.

The woman turned to Marroc/Danny. "Slow down," she said. "We don't need to attract attention."

"I'm only five miles over the limit, ain't no po-lice gonna bother with us."

"These Poh-leese?" Caedryff inquired, "They are the human Elite Guard?"

Danny laughed. "Ain't nothing 'e-lite' about the Tennessee cops, they're just good old boys with badges," he said. "An' this baby'd leave 'em all in the dust. It's got a 455 CID V8 Engine, 4-barrel, 335 horses, zero to sixty in six seconds. It fucking rocks, pardon my French."

"That was French?" asked the newcomer. "It sounded like Greek to me."

"No," said Sirrin. "It was American."

They were changing over to Route 40, and Charlie Daniels was singing the philosophy of a long-haired country boy, when Caedryff spoke again.

"How can you stand this noise?" the Ithron asked.

"I have no idea," Sirren said. "I guess he's gotten used to it."

Country Boy gave way to *Moody Blue.*

"Me an' the King," said Danny, taking a slug from the beer bottle. "You may not feel it, reverend, but this music weaves a spell as powerful as any Teleri singer could."

They pulled off at another truck stop just outside Memphis.

"Y' always want to arrive early for an op," opined Danny, "but not too early."

There were details to discuss, and the operation was scheduled for just before dawn, several hours away yet.

In the history of the elves, there had been many changelings, elven children unknowingly fostered by human families. This time, however, it had been a royal child, placed there for protection. The war had gone on for years, and the elf-child grew up, and when the elves returned to reclaim him, they found their king enslaved by a human sorcerer. "Such was the power of the magic that human sorcerer had," said the

35

confidential report she had read, "that the best of Telerian Ithrons were unable to break it."

Now, another quarter of a century had passed. The Queen Mother, who had ruled in the missing king's stead, was dying. Finally, in desperation, the Telerian court had swallowed their pride, and appealed to the Noldor, the deep elves, whose knowledge of magic far exceeded their own. One of the Noldor, the Arch-Ithron Caedryff, assured them that he could indeed break the human sorcerer's spell.

The Arch-Ithron had visited the human world several times before, but that had been centuries ago, and he was fascinated now with the many strange changes. Settled now in the restaurant of a Memphis truck stop, Sirren ordered a cheeseburger, Marroc had chicken fried steak, but Caedryff contented himself with coffee, that beverage being the only offering in the restaurant he was already familiar with.

"Why," he asked Danny, eyeing the chicken fried steak, "would the humans disguise one meat as another? I thought they prized the flavor of steak."

"It ain't a disguise, reverend," said Danny. "It's an enrichment. You should try some. It'll put hair on your chest."

Sirren rolled her eyes, and Caedryff politely declined, indicating he had no desire to grow hair on his chest. Danny laughed.

"In that case," he said, "y'all might think twice about that truck stop coffee."

They arrived outside the mansion close to four in the

morning. Danny had killed the radio a couple of blocks away. Now he killed the engine. They got out, and Sirren led the Arch-Ithron to the trunk, which she opened. He gaped at the body in the trunk.

"What is *this*?"

"That's our Surrogate."

"This? Surely you are joking. Even with the most powerful of reshaping spells, there's simply too much of him. No one will ever take this corpulent behemoth for the King of the Teleri."

Danny walked back to join them. "Been a while since you seen the king, eh, reverend?" He chuckled. "You think *I've* changed? Brother, are you in for a surprise." He finished the beer, and nodded to the Ithron's leather bag. "Get your mojo working, reverend, we ain't got all night."

From within the limestone walls of the mansion, a piano could be faintly heard. It was playing *Blue Eyes Crying in the Rain*. Danny nodded, dropping the empty to the floor in the back of the LeMans. Now they could make out a man's voice singing. The Ithron opened his bag.

He took out a bottle of salt and one of water. With the salt he began to draw designs on the pavement, muttering as he drew. When the design had reached a certain complexity, he shifted to the bottle of water, and dribbled the water in loops and whorls that added to – and in some cases, blotted out – the original design. When he was finished, he flicked out his hands, and the whole thing burst into flame. The flame then vanished, leaving no trace of water or salt behind. Sparks and flashes of light flickered in the air about the mansion, and then vanished. The singing stopped, and the piano faltered, missing a note. The old elf nodded.

He returned the two vessels to the bag, and brought out a mummified hand, wax-coated. There were short black wicks standing up from beneath the fingernails. The Ithron gestured, and the wicks lit. Like the voice a moment before, the piano stopped.

"Okay," said Danny, grunting as he hefted the unconscious homeless man out of the trunk in a fireman's carry. "Let's do this." A large automatic pistol appeared in his hand. "Time to take care of business."

Sirren drew her own gun, the Ithron picked up the hand, and the three of them marched toward the mansion.

Sirren sang the door open, and peered inside the mansion, wondering what they would find. Surely, the king would recognize them, and aid them in their mission if he could. There had ever only been a handful of kings of the Telerian elves, each one the reincarnation of an ancient king before him. They entered their new life with full memories of their previous lives, and with the powers they had wielded in them. If this human sorcerer could imprison a Teleri king, he must be powerful indeed. Would the king even be capable of lending them aid? Was the Noldori Arch-Ithron powerful enough to break the human's spells? If so, was he trustworthy?

All Sirren's life, there had always been a certain coldness and reserve between the Teleri and the Noldor. And now here was a Noldor Arch-Ithron, following Sirren and Marroc into the mansion, carrying a hand of glory.

There were two men, one in the antechamber, and one in the hallway, both unconscious on the floor, put there by the hand's power. The three elves wound their way through the mansion, crossed a racquetball court, and came into a small (for the scale of the place) club-like parlor, all leather chairs and dark wood. The king sat at an upright piano at one side of the room, the only person in the place they'd seen awake. On the leather couch, a woman lay unconscious. The king turned and regarded the three elves warily.

"I felt the spell break," he said. "Figured it had to be you folk. And y'all found yourselves a Noldor Ithron." He looked at the old elf. "An Arch-Ithron, at that, 'less I miss my guess. My greetings, Grandfather. No wonder y'all got through the spells."

"It was harder than it should have been," said Caedryff.

The king nodded, smiling. "Hell, you don't think the Colonel managed to whup up them spells by himself, did you?" Aeron of the Teleri laughed. "That was my magic you bashed in."

Caedryff bowed. "The magic of a king."

"Your magic?" Sirren gaped at him.

"It was not, after all, a binding," explained the Ithron. "It was protection."

"Yeah, well, sorry to tell you folks this," the king held up his hands, "but you're wasting your time. I ain't coming back. I love it here. I love what I do. I got people here now, as important to me as the Teleri. More, in fact." He glanced over at the unconscious woman on the couch. "This is my home now, and these are my people."

Marroc dropped the nearly dead homeless guy in a nearby chair.

"Look, your Majesty," he said, "I hear what you're sayin'. I ain't far behind you, far as that goes. But there's things you don't know. The Queen Mother is dead..." The king's face went slack with shock. "I'm sorry to have to tell you that, but it's the truth. And the power struggle in Alqualondë has begun. You stay here, the Teleri will be split apart by civil war, and a whole lot of elvenfolk will die. You go back, you could put a stop to that. Your people here, if you leave, will they face war, bloodshed?"

The king glowered at him in silence for a moment. A single tear made its way down his cheek.

"Truth is like the sun," he said finally. "You can shut it out for a time, but it ain't goin' away." He sighed heavily, wiped away the tear, and stood. "Alright, let's do this. Don't suppose I get to say goodbye to anyone?"

"I'm afraid not, sir," said Sirren. "They wouldn't remember it anyway. Their memories of tonight have been carefully crafted."

Aeron looked at the body on the chair.

"And who is this poor sucker they're going to bury in my place?"

"A random homeless guy, happened to have the right size and shape," said Marroc.

40

"No, it is not," said the Ithron. "It is your brother." The king stared again at the older elf. "The man whose life you have lived. He is the child who was stolen, so they could put you in his place." Now the king's stare was dark and intense. "Not my idea, nor my choice." The Noldori Arch-Ithron added, "I was brought into this affair only recently, and did not know until just now."

"Me neither," said Danny. "Swear to the Havens, Majesty, I thought I was picking up a random homeless guy happened to look a little like you." He glared at Sirren. "I surely do hate when the Company pulls shit like that. They ought to have told me."

"Highest clearance, need-to-know basis," said Sirren.

"You're certain of this?" the king asked the Ithron.

"I see, I perceive. I now feel the patterns in his sluggish blood. I can assure you, his blood, his bones, his very DNA will be identified by the humans as yours."

"I don't suppose I get to say 'sorry' to this poor fucker either?"

"He is dying as we speak," said the Ithron. "He will not speak again, nor hear."

"Whoever planned this," said the king in a low voice, "is likely in Alqualondë. Guess I got some business to take care of there." He glanced at Sirren, who took an involuntary step back. He looked again at the Ithron. "Do what you have to, and let's go."

They did what was needed, arranging the body and other manufactured evidence, the Ithron implanting pre-

41

crafted memories in the minds of each of the sleeping occupants of the mansion. When they were done, they gathered on the front step of the mansion. The sky was beginning to lighten in the east. The Ithron cast a circle of salt and water, the elves stepped within it – all but Marroc.

"I can't," he said. "Somebody's got to move the car away from here. There won't be no civil war now, so the Company don't need me at home. Tell 'em they can consider this my resignation. I'm staying here."

"You son of a bitch," said the king, "I have to go, but you get to stay here?"

Marroc shrugged. "That's the way it happens sometimes, your Majesty."

The king stared a moment, then shook his head and chuckled.

"You own a guitar, elf?" he asked.

"Yes, sir."

"Learn to play it," said the king.

The elven operative Marroc, who hereafter would be only Danny Fisher, met the eyes of Al-Vis Aeron, High King of the Telerian Elves, Duke of Alqualondë, Chanter of the Song of the Ainur, Protector of the Tol Eressea. An understanding seemed to pass between them. The Ithron's circle flared up in fire, and then the three elves were gone.

In the growing light, Danny Fisher stood alone on the steps, feeling the warm damp breeze coming off the Mississippi. He looked at the mansion one last time before heading to the car, and nodded to himself.

"Ladies and gentlemen," he said, "Elvis has left the building."

Once I got angry. Thought she was going to take that knife to me and excise me from her existence the way she had all that weird blood.

In 1998, Juniper Talbot fell in love with an Elf. What follows is a true story.

Color of the Sky
Juniper Talbot

She was insane. That much was clear. I like saying things like that. "She was insane." Period. "That much was clear." Period. What do I possibly think can be clearly inferred from a statement of someone's insanity? As if sanity or insanity had any clarity.

I loved her. That much was clear. But love is far from clear, as is any emotion involving the human heart. And her heart was far from human – as is mine.

That much was clear. Here we go again.

You'll think this story is about two women. But it's not. This may or may not become clear. I suppose that's truthful. Her body was impossible, she said. She told me so. Her body was beautiful. I told her so. It didn't matter. She was determined to make it her enemy.

Our enemies kill us. Or we kill them. With her, it didn't matter. The outcome would be the same.

I remember becoming your lover. You striking my breath away. Soft in darkness – navigating past the points – white Veil creeps between us. "That kind of freak." I slip past the Veil. I slip between your sheets. Over and over. Despite the damn Veil. I slip between your sheets, between your leather and steel, navigating through the sharp points till I no longer bleed my own blood.

I am holding the key. Do I lock you back in your tower while you drop your hair down for the next searcher? Lock us in together to rot in dust balls of whiskey and tears? Do I come over and over till my life is only stairs to be climbed – coming and coming to you?

There's murder in this story. That much should be clear by now. Don't we usually start with the victim and try to sleuth out the murderer, though? This story is backwards. It's a hall of mirrors. Each and every unrecognizable reflection totally and only *you. You. You.*

The murderer is clear here in this story. It's the corpse we have yet to identify.

She wasn't always this way. It could be different depending on... Well, I don't really know what it depended on. The light? Whether or not there was too much blue in the sky? Whoever she was, she always lived in that beautiful impossible body of hers. She always looked out of those mesmerizing eyes with varying degrees of confusion, love, hatred and pain. I don't think those eyes ever really saw me. But then again this is her story, not mine. I don't really exist. She didn't really want to.

In the dark, it was all the same. *You. You. You.*

How can I tell you all that I know about her? She

fascinated me. There were a lot of things I shouldn't know. Good thing I didn't really exist. At least she didn't believe I did, and what did I know? I could no longer bleed my own blood or be called by my own name. She just kept leaking out, and I, powerless to stop the flood, had nothing to do but sop her up, till the blood in my veins was hers, and the reflection in the mirror said only *you, you, you.*

We met on the dance floor. Not really. I'm saying that because it sounds romantic, and it seems a much better way to meet than the truth. So just accept it for now as our reality, because it's the story we like to tell each other – it's the story that makes sense.

We danced every February for three years. That was it – one night each February. One night totally enamored of each other – totally in love – never allowed to touch. It was so damn hot. It was like you see in those movies, where everyone else on the dance floor fades into the background, and amazingly, that person with the spotlight who waits in the wings for just such a moment as ours, comes sailing out and shines that gorgeous filtered light right on us – us – only us. Perhaps you know what I mean. It was a great way to start the murder.

Oh that again.

That was all. Once a year. Dance. Never touch. "Always leave them wanting more," they say. I wanted more.

Then we broke the rules. It was May – the Veils were thin – and we danced. Not only that, we touched.

"Tell me your secret."

"I'll tell you *a* secret, but I won't tell you *my* secret."

"But I think I know what it is."

"Then guess."

"It's not about guessing."

"Do you really need to know?"

Pause.

"No, I guess not."

Then there were the stones. It frightened me – they way she would talk to them. I tried to pretend I didn't hear, didn't notice the precarious way she could make them balance, but I just couldn't look away after awhile. Finally I just gave in. There wasn't any death yet. Maybe I even existed for a moment at that time. I don't now.

I know what you're thinking – that I must be the corpse. You're thinking you have it all figured out here, and it's barely even a few pages into the story. But you're wrong. At least, you're not right. Not yet. It's never that simple.

She didn't exist either.

She smelled of leather and honing oil, and some otherworldly smell I can't get out of my nostrils. She was the softest hard person I had ever met, and I was enthralled by the enigma. We talked about weapons, and she showed me her stash of steel-bladed knives lining the inside of her leather jacket. It was actually a wool coat, but doesn't knives in a leather jacket create a much more memorable image? Let's keep it that way. She probably won't mind the change.

It was the second February, and although we'd danced, we still hadn't touched. No secrets unrevealed lay between us – only the heat of the dance and the frightened desire in our eyes. We sat outside my hotel room door. I thought to invite her in, but got afraid and sent her home – drunk and all.

This is going nowhere. Get to the murder, you say.

Perhaps I am. Perhaps I was describing the murder weapons. You just can't know yet.

"First I have to hate you. First I have to tear you apart in every way imaginable. First I have to test you: let down my long sensuous hair, stand in front of you fresh from the bath combing that hair like Rapunzel in her tower, cock my head just right and look at you from beneath my long dark lashes, my tight white top hugging the damp curves of my breasts. Let the odd shape of my ears show, my eyes turn golden, my skin glow white. I see you swallow. Hard. Good, I think to myself. You're uncomfortable. You didn't want to see this. You're no different, I think. Just like all the rest. You want the illusion I gave you. You don't want this. You'll reject me, and that will be good, 'cause then I don't have to think of you anymore, and I can live my world the way I understand it. The world where I am no one's. No one."

I swallowed hard, over and over again. I hadn't expected this. My god, she was beautiful. All that long Rapunzel hair, those eyes, lashes. That tight white top clinging to her small and perfectly formed breasts. The ears. The eyes of burnished gold... I swallowed hard again. I could tell she had won some sort of victory over me, but I hadn't known there was a game. Or at least I hadn't admitted it. I was already on the bed. I would have to let her in. Would my trembling hands betray me? Could I make love after all to this holy apparition? She wasn't what I expected.

But then again, what is?

"I probably wouldn't have seen you, but that blade of yours was crying out. They say those knives can cut through the Veils and perhaps that's exactly what it did. I held that blade of yours in my hands for six months until little by little you were revealed. It would be much longer before I touched your flesh, but your hard sharp blade had a lot to say, and I couldn't help but listen.

"We met across the silence of your steel blade. I know you like to say it was the dance floor, but that's your story. It's not mine. And I'm not sure you exist – even now."

I'm telling you stories.
Here's one. You can choose to believe it or not. She

can't.

It was the back seat of some late '60s model sedan with a sky-blue interior. He would slap hard as he forced himself into that tender place that a three-year-old keeps in a white paper diaper. Maybe it was once. Maybe it was many times. Maybe it never happened at all. But what does that child know who floats out of the ravaged body to the sky-blue ceiling of that drab old car?

Now she is bewildered at the sight of a blue sky. "That's not the color of the sky in my world," she tells me. No, I know that now. The sky in her world became in time the face of a different man who held her down but refused to hit when he entered that dark secret passage of hers. She called it love.

Until the sky fell down.

You think that can't happen. You say you know the story of Chicken Little. But you're wrong. At least you're not right. Her sky fell down the day that man died. Then there was nothing but that bewildering blue.

Ah Ha! you say! At last a body!

I'm telling you stories.

It wasn't like that at all. Let me tell you how it really was.

There are these beings that live in the dark secret passages of the earth – Elfkind, they are called, Alfar, Aelf, by some. They have this tendency to fall in love with extraordinarily beautiful humans. They also have a thing with extraordinarily beautiful babies. This three-year-old was exactly that. One of these otherworld Elfbeings took to that baby and couldn't be happy without it. Here's where it gets tricky. Maybe the Elfwoman stole the baby and replaced it with another from her otherworld home. But that doesn't explain anything if you think about it. Maybe that Elfwoman enveloped it and ate out its heart and its little human soul to wrap around her own, and then she and that human baby were now one thing forever joined forever separate. Forever in love. Forever at war.

And so in bewilderment, she stares now at blue sky, which in her dark, earthy passage was not blue at all – only the roots of so many blades of grass. That perhaps explains a lot more.

Perhaps it doesn't.

You can choose to believe it or not. She can't.

There's so much to tell. Why do I only want to tell about the unbelievable softness of her skin, the scent of her hair and that otherworldly smell I can't get out of my nostrils? Why do I only want to tell you about her square, pale beautiful hands and their enigmatic, ever-changing lines that finally – one day – grew a line for me? I guess at last I cut her deeply enough to leave my scar.

Why do I only want to tell you these things?

In the dark, these things were all that mattered.

Sometimes she would cry.

I wasn't the right one. She made that vividly clear. I was patient though. Patient and persistent. I could touch her skin all night long, and slowly she would come to meet me there. To meet me in the touching place. I wondered if she knew my tricks. If she knew I was subversively working all night long to get her to inhabit those long vacant sections of skin. It didn't matter.

I don't like where this is going.

Sometimes she would cry.

Mostly she would tell me stories. Her stories. Histories.

There was one thing she loved. A 1975 Duster. The heart and soul of the universe resided in that sand-colored car with the black interior. Not a speck of blue. She was fast, cool. A wild punk rebel with way too much intelligence, anger, vision and disease. A street-wise crusader with a slick car and the soul of the universe in her eaten-out heart pounding down the pavement.

"If I drove fast enough, I could rip right through those Veils," she would tell me. A black and white photograph of this magic vehicle sits on the desk, and a smoky look grows in her eyes as she says these things.

I didn't like these stories of hot cars and fast times. They didn't make sense to me, and they belonged to a world I didn't. Maybe it was too stark a reminder of my particular kind

53

of existence. You see, I had no stories. She dreamed me into her hands until I sprang, fully formed from a steel blade. Before that...

Well, it doesn't matter.

She used to cry sometimes.

There's an ancient ritual from some alien planet or perhaps from those Elf beings in the earth's black corridors. I must have learned it somewhere, or perhaps she taught it to me as she dreamed me into her world. You stand or sit by the person who is weeping. You wrap your arm around their shoulder and pat gently, rhythmically with your hand.

Then you speak the ritual incantation:

"There, there now. There, there now."

You're thinking I haven't mentioned the murder recently. Perhaps I've forgotten. Today, there's hope. Let me have my fantasy for a while.

I didn't like the stories about the cars because they were distractions. What did cars have to do with the feel of skin, that scent, those eyes, that hair? I just wanted it to be late enough to slip between those sheets and feel the place where my body becomes yours and there's no difference. For all the hardness, in the bed, in the dark, there was so much softness. Our legs would entangle so gracefully, and she would make yummy noises in her throat as she pulled me close. Am I writing a little soft porn into this story to assuage your need to get on to the murder?

No. I just want you to remember your own nights such as these with your own beautiful beloved, and nod and smile and live for a few moments in the glow of that old memory.

You do remember, don't you? It's very important. To someone.

Today I'm bleeding – menstruating. I didn't want you to know. I get ashamed of this blood. As if it somehow betrays you. I guess it's the only blood I have that's still mine. And it's the only blood I have that truly – yes, truly I wish was yours. You see, I know this is one blood you can't bleed – the blood that might say you were like me.

I didn't want you to know this about me.

Her blood is not human so they say. Drawn in gloppy vials, the phlebotomists look askance at the weird stuff and the weird body from which it came. "This is not human," they whisper or shout.

What did they expect I wonder? Elfkind.

She began to die the day I met her. That may or may not be true. The man with the face of the sky had died not long ago, but how was I to know these things? I hadn't learned the language yet, and although she dropped clues, mostly I didn't look.

It was February – that first February. I guess knife blades held in that coat lining was a way to feel the immanence of death at all times. One hug from some well-meaning, unsuspecting stranger could push those points against the skin and draw out just a little more of that inhuman blood.

And there was my blade. My rusted blade, blackened and rescued from the ashes of my burnt-out home. I placed it in those hands – you know the ones, don't you? I wrapped it in a piece of silk so it wouldn't cut. What was I thinking? What protection does silk have against the sharp edge of a knife blade? Perhaps I was already hoping to leave my mark. Perhaps that's where it all began.

When the sky-faced man died, she was alone at home. I imagine the phone ringing and that sinking feeling when you know the voice on the other end is about to change your life.

"I'm sorry to have to tell you, but..."

"Are you there?"

"Are you there?"

No. She runs along the railroad tracks. Runs faster and faster until at last she rips right through those Veils. And there he is, on the other side, waiting for her. Waiting to dance.

In the morning they find her on the grass. I understand it was a cup of coffee that enticed her back through the Veils. "There's no coffee on the other side," she tells me and laughs. It would be sweet to say she left part of her heart on the other side with the sky-faced man, but her heart had already been taken. I think I explained that.

So she takes my blade wrapped in watery silk, stuffs it in her coat lining and goes away. Not until we dance.

Moving across the dance floor I am bewildered by your beauty. I belong to this place – you are a stranger here. There is only mystery between us, and I am still blind and a little deaf. Little did I know that you would spend half a year fitting my blade into your hilt – dreaming me into places of your own creation, drawing me into your death. You were nothing to me then, and I was only a metal dream yet to unfold.

Look at us now.

They say it takes 910 degrees to make metal soft enough to bend. In only 63 seconds it can harden, ruthlessly into any old ridiculous shape. So if you have a particular shape in mind, you have to work fast. Or go back to the inferno. Over and over again.

She had already left much of her blood at the altar of the cadeuceus. She said she took herself to the emergency room, with blade in hand and one finger on the nurse call button, threatening to cut more, right there in the waiting room unless they could help her – give her different blood. What blade was that, I wonder? How many times through the inferno to become just the right shape?

Once I got angry. Thought she was going to take that knife to me and excise me from her existence the way she had all that weird blood. Thought she was going to put me back in her sheath and never let me out. Thought she was going to delete me from her computer or store me in a file from which I couldn't escape. Despite the fact I had hardly any blood to call my own, I had begun to think of myself as real.

That's when I got angry. It was the last time I saw her.

"There was this funny place where she should have been. I had the thought that it might be what others called loneliness, but I wasn't sure I knew what that meant. There were these two parts of me always vying for attention. I couldn't ever be sure I knew this idea of loneliness.

"The room was sterile and cheerless. It didn't matter. I could seldom see things like bedclothes and picture frames. My eyes just wouldn't focus on them long enough for the patterns to settle into something recognizable, let alone to determine whether or not they went well together. But there was this funny place where she should have been.

"It wasn't always there. Sometimes if I switched positions just right, or cocked my head at a certain angle, or played the music loud enough, I didn't feel it at all. That was good. And yet, when I would least expect it – there it would be again: that funny place.

"Who was she anyway? I wasn't sure I knew. Things went so easily out of focus for me. She was familiar though. I knew that much. Somehow she would always appear when I needed something and hadn't known it. There would be her footsteps on the stairs, and all that stale air would just blow right out of my lungs. I started to tell her I loved her, even though I wasn't really sure who she was, let alone who the 'I' that was saying 'love' was! But somehow it seemed the thing to do after so much familiarity.

"It seemed to make her happy. At least I noticed she kept coming back. Once or twice I actually got her face in focus. She was beautiful, I think. There was this sort of longing in her eyes – a funny sort of patient hunger. It was hard to look at so I let her go fuzzy most of the time. She was easier to look at that way. When she was fuzzy, I could just smell her and hear her voice. That was comforting somehow. It didn't seem to matter what I said, she always smelled the same, had the same voice. With so many voices in here, you can't imagine how nice that could be.

"I started talking a lot when she would come. It was a funny little dance we had. She would sit at my feet, looking up at me, and I would say anything, anything. I kept my hand on the computer mouse at all times though, just in case I needed to delete her quick, or delete what I had just said or stop the world right there in mid-sentence. I know it sounds crazy, but it was the only way I could keep any control.

"Once she was in my bed. She liked it there. I was always a little afraid of it. Well, I mean, there was no computer to control, there was no distance – there was only the darkness and her body, and my body, and I wasn't so OK with any of those things. Well, not really. But anyway, there was this one night when she was in my bed, and I was lying on my back trying to be OK with it all, and getting a little spacey like I do at times. She liked to touch me a lot. Mostly I didn't feel it, just sort of this numb awareness that her hands were on my skin. But since I had trouble identifying my skin as mine, it was that much harder to identify her hands. But anyway, I'm getting off the point. There was this time... Did I already say that? She must have had her hand on my belly. I didn't really know it I guess. But then she moved, and she took her hand away. I must have made some sort of awful noise, 'cause she got all startled and concerned, and asked me what's wrong. You see, I guess I hadn't really noticed her hand was there, but when she took it away, I just started to float right out through the place she had been holding. Like maybe I had gathered all myself right there 'cause, well I don't know, 'cause maybe it was safe there, and you know, it's not so safe all the time in the rest of my body. She took her hand away, and out I went. Like air out of a balloon. Well, that's a cliché metaphor I guess, but it's all I can think of for the moment. Luckily I caught myself before I got very far. But there was this funny feeling where she should have been.

"Something funny happened the other day. I don't really remember it; it's kind of like a taste in my mouth, more than a memory. I'm not real good with those anyway. That's what she was for. She could hold my memories, and somehow that was easier 'cause then I didn't have to hold them. But I would know they were safe now, and wouldn't start getting out of hand like they often do, and start wanting lives of their own and stuff like that. So anyway... what was I saying? Oh yeah, this taste in my mouth. I bet if I could ask her, she could tell me what happened, but there's this funny place where she should be, and she's not in it now. I think I remember her face breaking up. Maybe I let her get in focus, and it wasn't what I was used to. She was angry I think, but I couldn't hear her words. She smelled different is all I know. She smelled bad. I didn't want to be near that smell. But she had all my memories, dag it, so I couldn't just let her take those and run! And I didn't have any place to put them.

"Hell, I don't have any place to put myself. That's why I'm here in this sterile room with the out-of-focus bedspread. At least the ceiling isn't blue.

"I don't remember how I got here. Maybe she does. But I can't ask her. There's this funny place where she should be. I don't know what it is, but I wish it would go away. Maybe I'll have another drink."

They say the dead have no future, that their present is only memory. Perhaps that's why she spoke so relentlessly of her past and never of now. All I know is that I will always tremble at the thought of her enigmatic body, and she... well, she will never be at home in it until she recaptures her eaten out heart – until she finds a world that lets her mystery be. Until she finds a world whose sky is the right color. Whatever she knew of me was captured in a steel blade and a computer screen from which she could delete whatever didn't fit. It was all about cutting. And what remains of me now is a heart of steel fitted into a hilt I can't recognize. I still don't know which one of us existed. This much is true: the dead remain forever. The living do not.

I promised a tale of murder and mystery. I hope you aren't disappointed. Without a body, it becomes very tricky to sleuth out the perpetrator. And maybe now you can realize why there is no corpse to investigate. There was murder, however. That much should be clear.

And whoever she was, I did love her. Have I made that clear? But love is far from clear. I think I've already said that. I'm finding it hard to remember. And as for the human heart? Well, her heart... I think I've already explained that, too.

She imagined not getting home tonight. She imagined never seeing her mother again and her stomach felt ill.

Athena Giles is currently a high school senior who grew up reading Harry Potter and The Lord of the Rings, and finished writing her first novel which she calls "a cheesy fantasy story" in middle school. Athena says, "I always loved to read and was encouraged to write by my family and some teachers who read my work and inspired me to continue working. I decided to ignore all those people who said writing won't get me anywhere, because I feel like the only sure way to fail is not to try."

About "The Phone Booth," she writes, "I honestly don't really know how I came up with this story. I was playing around with the limited theme. I was originally working on a more traditional fantasy elf story and decided it was boring so thought I'd try something more modern and this story is what came out of that. I generally don't write fantasy as much anymore, but bring fantasy elements into a modern and non-traditional setting."

This is Athena's first publication. Her website is athenagiles.com.

The Phone Booth
Athena Giles

Holly Warren sat alone in a clear-plastic bus stop, shivering in a corner and clutching a cup of coffee that had gone cold. Around her shoulders she pulled an old jacket that had belonged to her father who had mysteriously disappeared years before. The bus stop had a permanent stench of sweat and alcohol. She could have taken the subway and been home by now, but it made her uncomfortable enough by day; by night it was nothing less than terrifying. The night was cold and dark in a way that made Holly's stomach churn and wish she was in the safety of the warm apartment she shared with her mom. A sudden noise made her jump and nearly spill her coffee on the mostly clean work shirt she wore under her father's jacket. She looked around, half-expecting an ax-murderer coming to chop her to bits, but there was nothing in the darkness.

A car passed and Holly huddled further into her corner. Being alone at night agitated Holly's nerves enough without some creep noticing her. That was the last thing she needed. She kept her eyes down and only lifted her head to be able to down the last few sips of her coffee.

"Where's that god-damned bus?" Holly muttered under her breath, looking up and down the street in hopes it would appear.

She cursed her luck. The bus usually arrived on time and it had chosen tonight of all nights when it was cloudy and starless to be late. To top it off, the only nearby streetlamp flickered on and off, taunting and threatening to plunge the street into almost total darkness. Why was it so late? Few passengers rode the bus this late at night. Holly sighed in agitation and checked the time quickly before resuming her vigilant watch of the night for any sign of something wrong.

Holly imagined men with knives and a hunger for young girls, or bloodthirsty ghosts lurking in the darkness beyond the flickering streetlamp. She sat hunched over, trying to appear small and inconspicuous. Images of someone finding her and doing terrible things to her ran rampant through her mind. She imagined not getting home tonight. She imagined never seeing her mother again and her stomach felt ill.

Holly stood up, unable to contain her impatience for the bus and apprehension for what might lurk in the shadows. She paced the length of the small bus stop, but hurried back to her corner upon accidentally meeting the gaze of a woman passing under the flickering streetlamp on the other side of the street.

A ringing broke the silence. Holly jumped, her heart beating fast from the sudden noise, and the coffee cup fell from her trembling hands, spilling the rest of its contents onto the sidewalk. Shit, Holly thought and fumbled in her bag, thinking it might be her cell phone going off. Her mom often called on nights like this, just to make sure her daughter hadn't gotten

66

mugged in the streets. She usually thought it was silly, but tonight it didn't seem too wild a fear. Holly opened her phone but there were no messages and the ringing continued despite the fact her phone was silent. She looked around and saw no one nearby – just the empty shadows and cold darkness.

Holly's eyes fell on a nearby pay phone. That phone had never seemed to work before. She had been to this bus stop many times and had never seen anyone using it. No one needed pay phones anymore. They could call from anywhere they wanted with their precious cell phones. The pay phone was useless, so why would it be ringing?

Holly tried to ignore the ringing, but for some reason she felt compelled to answer. Maybe it was some crazed killer trying to find some girl like her, lost and alone, that few would miss. She shook her head and tried to convince herself she was being silly as she walked hesitantly to the phone. She looked around. There was no one on the street. The person on the other end probably just called a wrong number. She picked up the big, clunky receiver in the dirty old booth and hesitantly muttered "Hello?" as loudly as her nerves would allow her.

"It's you..." Holly heard a weak voice crackle from the other end just as soon as she answered.

"Well... I suppose," Holly said, trying not to sound scared. "But I'm not sure if I'm the 'you' you're looking for. This is a pay phone. I think you've got the wrong number."

"No... no, it's not the wrong number," the voice said. It sounded like a boy about the same age as her, but the sound quality sucked so she couldn't quite tell. "You're Holly

Warren."

Holly shivered and looked around to make sure she was still alone. Nothing moved in the shadows, but she still eyed them with suspicion. "How do you know my name? Why would you call this number? How do you know where I am?"

"Not everything in this world makes sense by *your* standards of what makes sense and what doesn't," the voice said. "However, if you had *my* standards of sense, this would make sense."

"What are you talking about?" Holly asked, wondering if she should just hang up. But if the man on the other end knew what pay phone to call, he knew where she was. Hanging up wouldn't help her. Maybe if she kept the guy talking she could stall him until the bus showed up and she would be safe. "How do you know who I am?"

"I knew your father," the voice said. Holly frowned. Her father had disappeared without warning not long after getting her mom pregnant. Holly had never met him. All he left her mom was a battered old jacket and a baby. "He was a friend of my father's. Things were supposed to turn out differently. You're supposed to know me. I know you. I've seen you. But I've never been allowed to speak to you before."

"Are you stalking me?" Holly looked around. The shadows threatened her even more than before, if that was possible. She imagined any noise as the footsteps of the man on the phone coming to get her and do who knows what horrible things to her. Her eyes continuously swept back and forth across the street she was on, paranoid that there was someone else on the street with her.

"Well, I wish I didn't have to," the voice said. "I wish we'd grown up as friends, far away from all the nonsense of the human world. You should have been raised in my world – the world your father came from. You weren't even supposed to have any human blood. But your father never was one for the rules."

"What are you talking about?" Holly pleaded, trying get the guy to start making sense. Maybe then her heart would stop freezing at every small sound. "I'm human. Where else is there to go other than the human world?"

"Your father wasn't human," the voice said. "Neither am I. But your mother is. The rules forbade your father from being with her. He was obligated to marry one of our own kind. But he fell in love with your mother even though almost every girl hung on his every move. Our leaders were willing to forgive your father if he gave your mother up willingly, but then she gave birth to you – a half-blood – and your father refused to leave so they forced him to. I'm not allowed to talk to you because of that. I, like your father, am going to be forced to marry another pure-blood. But fate meant for us to meet. So I'm breaking every rule just to talk to you this once."

"What are you talking about!" Holly shouted. "What do you mean I'm half-blood? Half-blood what? Are you talking about my race? Because on that front I'm basically just white and I don't think it really matters what kind of white I am."

"I'm not talking about your race or what type of human you are," the voice said. "That doesn't matter. It's the fact that you're half-blood that matters. That's what's screwed everything up. If you were pure-blood we wouldn't be having this conversation in the first place."

"What else is there for me to be?" Holly asked, getting annoyed as well as scared. "I'm just human. There's nothing else I can be. There's nothing else I *want* to be! Just shut up and leave me alone!"

Holly moved to slam the receiver down, but the voice shouting out of it stopped her.

"Wait! There is something else you could be," the voice called out of the receiver. She hesitated a moment before putting the phone back to her ear. "I'm a full-blooded elf. Your father was too. You're a half-blooded elf. The human world you grew up in doesn't believe in us anymore. There are so few pure-blooded elves like me anymore. You would have been one if your mother had been an elf. But your father chose to fall love with a human."

"You're insane," Holly said. "Elves don't exist. My father disappeared before I was even born. I don't know who you are. I don't know how you got this number or how you knew I'd be here, but if you think you can fool me or scare me, you're wrong. I'm not any bit an elf and neither are you. You're just a stupid prank-caller."

Holly started to hang up the phone as the bus rolled up to the stop. She wanted to hurry to get on the bus so she could get home and lock herself safely in her room where no one but her mom could get to her. But as she reached to hang up the phone, the voice screamed out of it, begging and pleading with

70

her.

"Please wait, Holly!" he said. "My name is Rowan. Please! Don't go! I love y—"

Holly hung up the phone sharply so the boy on the other end would hear. She shook her head and laughed slightly to force away her fears. Probably just been one of her friends playing a trick on her, she thought. Elves didn't exist and no one but her mother even knew what her father's name was. Holly grabbed her things and hurried towards the open doors of the bus, glancing back at the phone booth every few seconds. She half-expected it to start ringing again any moment.

As she walked, Holly half-thought she saw a pair of bright, silvery eyes watching her from the shadows. They had a look of something like love and longing, or maybe even hurt and loss. She dashed towards the welcoming security of the bus, resisting the urge to look back to where she'd seen the eyes. When she finally did, they were gone. Was it a cat? Or just her nervous mind playing tricks on her? Holly anxiously bounded up the stairs of the bus forcing herself not to glance back at the phone booth or the mysterious shapes in the shadows.

In my experience, whenever someone said you wouldn't need a gun, you'd better bring a good one, cleaned and loaded.

About "Goodnight, My Lady," Duncan says, "Initially, I didn't think I really had any-thing to say about elves at all, let alone specifically elf love. I looked up 'elf' and discovered the word derived from the Norse root 'alf,' which seemed to be Norse mythology's version of the Fae. Okay, so fae love by another name...

"Most traditional stories of fae love seem to center on human/fae relationships, and very often the human vanishes from our world for many years (which seem only hours or days to the human involved). I wondered about turning that around, having the elf vanish, and the human searching for him or her. This immediately brought to mind one of my all-time favorite books, Raymond Chandler's Farewell, My Lovely, where Marlowe is searching for the vanished lover of an ex-con. 'Goodnight, My Lady' is essentially the Reader's Digest version of Farewell, My Lovely with elves."

More information about Duncan can be found in the introductions to his other contributions to this anthology, and at these websites: duncaneagleson.com, eaglesondesign.com, railwalkercomics.com and maskmaker.com.

Goodnight, My Lady
Duncan Eagleson

It was a year for firsts and upsets. The Ambling Alp had lost the heavyweight title to an unknown fighter named Max Baer, the U.S. Government was backing the unions for a change, and Clark Gable was getting killed at the box office by a twelve-year-old kid.

It was the year I first learned about the Alfar.

That afternoon, I was in a little bar called Pete's, listening to the Athletics wallop the Sox at Fenway. Pete's hadn't changed much since Roosevelt had signed the Repeal last year. Everybody had been expecting it, and Nicky Petros, who owned Pete's, had stopped pretending his place was a pop stand some time before. He was making more money than ever now that his liquor was legal, and you'd think he'd have bought a new radio at least, so we could hear the games clearly. Not Nicky. When the potted ferns in his front window died, he left them that way. "Truth in advertising," he said. "It warns the uptown gents away."

When the game was over, the mood in the bar was ambivalent – nobody there favored the Red Sox much, but they knew that with Jimmy Foxx batting .364 and 23 home runs so far this season, the Athletics were a threat to the Yankees' supremacy. That haunted them. I raised a glass to the Double

X and his teammates – they played a damn good game, never mind where they hailed from.

I made my farewells, and stepped out into the street while I could still depend on staying vertical. When I paused on the corner of Spring Street to light a cigarette, I noticed a guy standing on the opposite corner, looking at the door of the club there. It was hard not to notice him. He must have stood 6'7" at least, and weighed in close to 300. He was wearing a tan suit with bright green windowpane checks, and leather-wrapped buttons the size of golf balls. It was garish, but expensive – custom made. His shirt was dark green and his tie bright red, his fawn-colored snap-brim fedora nearly matched the tan of the suit, and was beaver felt, the type with the hair still on. His shoes were two-tone wing-tips, brown and white. Lantern-jawed with a single eyebrow, he needed a shave, but he was one of those guys who would always need a shave unless he waxed his face three times a day. He reminded me of a grizzly bear dressed up in a suit, an almost comic figure, except you'd never want to laugh at this guy, at least not within his hearing.

He was looking at the bar in front of him as if he were contemplating holding it up, though nobody in his right mind would pull a holdup in an outfit like that. Above the door was a neon sign that read *Fallon's*. I knew a little bit about it – Fallon's was a colored bar. As I watched, he nodded once, and then stepped through the door into the foyer.

A moment later, a thin negro in a white suit came flying – literally – out the door, and tumbled to a stop against a car parked at the curb. He groped his way to his feet using the fender of the car, dusted himself off, cursing at the scuffs and stains on his suit, and hurried off. Intrigued, I crossed the street, warily stepped through the door into the lobby. The gorilla was standing there, looking at the inner door to the club. He glanced around at me, and a hand I could have sat in descended on my shoulder. My shoulder bones ground together in a way my chiropractor would have despaired of, if I'd had a chiropractor to care.

"Coloreds in here," he said. "You seen me throw that guy out?"

"Yeah," I said. "It's a colored joint, what did you expect?"

"Yeah?" he said, looking at the door that led into the barroom. "When'd that happen?"

I searched my memory.

"Five, maybe six years back," I said. I remembered then that the new owner had either been too cheap to pay for a new sign, or else saw some humor in keeping the name of the bar. Before it was a colored place, it had been a strip joint. I guess the gorilla hadn't been here in a while.

He looked at me again. "You a cop?"

"Private," I said. I gave him my name.

Fingers the size of bananas tightened on my shoulder.

"Hmm. You could maybe help me out," he said. "Let's you and me go knock back a couple."

"I don't think they'll appreciate a couple of white guys bringing their business there." There were a couple of jazz joints up in Harlem that let white folks in to listen to the music, but generally, whites were no more welcome in colored places than the negroes were in white joints. Me, I'd never seen why it should make a difference, but that's how it was. Still, even if he'd been black as the inside of your hat, I was pretty certain they wouldn't appreciate this big lug's patronage. His suit was well tailored to cover it, but I'm used to looking for that slight bulge that told me there was iron under his arm.

The single eyebrow grew a frowning "V" in the center.

"Guy offers to buy you a drink, it ain't polite to refuse."

"Okay, okay," I said, "Just don't blame me if they don't want to serve us. And leggo my shoulder. I'm a big boy now, I go to the bathroom by myself and everything. I can walk in on my own, promise."

His lips twitched in what might have been a suggestion of a smile, and the agony in my shoulder subsided as he let go.

"My Frida used to work here," he said. "She was a singer."

That explained something, anyway. But I was betting this Frida did more than sing.

"It's a cinch she don't work here any more," I said. "When was the last time you were here?"

"Eight years."

"Eight years? That's a long time."

"I was in the can," he said. "She ain't written in six."

"This Frida got a last name?

"Valentine. Frida Valentine. You know her? She's about so high, blonde, beautiful."

"That describes half the women in New York, pal. No, I don't know her."

"Come on," he said, turning toward the door. "My Frida worked here. They must know something about her. Where she went."

"I wouldn't bet on it."

Once we were inside, it was clear I'd been right. There weren't many customers, but they all eyeballed the two of us. The bouncer felt he had something to prove. I don't know why. He looked like he could give Joe Lewis a run for his money, but the big guy he was facing had a head's height on each of us, and was wide as the two of us together. I think if he'd been polite, the hulking monster at my side might actually have left him intact. As it was, when the bouncer got pushy, my new acquaintance broke him in several pieces and tossed him across the room with less effort than I would have spent tossing aside a cigarette butt. The remaining patrons suddenly remembered they had business elsewhere. The big guy ignored them, turned to the bartender and inquired for the owner. The bartender indicated a door at the back of the room. The big guy lumbered through the door.

I looked at the bartender. He was reaching for something under the bar. I grabbed hold of his arm.

"Whatcha got down there?" I asked.

He froze, looking me in the eye for a long moment.

"Sawed-off," he said finally.

"That's illegal. Besides, I don't think it would stop him anyway."

There was a loud flat bang, and then the big guy appeared in the doorway, his hat scraping the top of the doorframe. There was a smoking revolver in his hand.

"I just wanted to know where my Frida was," he said "He tried to tell me with this." He waggled the gun in the air. "He didn't have to do that." As he came closer, I realized his own gun was still tucked away under his arm.

"That's a shame," I said. "But maybe you should beat it now. Somebody must have heard that shot, and the cops will be along soon. They might think you sorta sprained your parole."

He nodded.

"Yeah," he said, "you might have something there." He gave me the gun. Then he handed me a wad of cash. "You're hired. Want you should find my Frida."

"Hey," I started to say, "I need a little more to go on..."

He kept walking. I watched him walk out the door. I tucked the roll away on my hip, and settled myself on a bar stool to wait for the cops.

The police detective who caught the case was a sour old coot named MacNeill. I'd known him for a few years. He was unpleasant and bitter, and he didn't like me much. That was okay with me, I didn't like him right back. Among other things, he was a racist. MacNeill didn't like private detectives, and liked blacks even less. If I'd been a black private eye, he'd have been tempted to arrest me for the killing then and there, and call it good. But even though he was prejudiced against anyone didn't look like him, he was a relatively honest cop.

As it was, he was suspicious – I had come into the bar with the killer, after all, despite the fact that I didn't know the big lug from Adam. After I'd repeated my story several times, he grudgingly allowed as how it might be the truth, and left to turn his attention to other cases. The big galoot would be pretty easy to spot, but I wasn't worried about him. MacNeill wasn't going to be looking for him very hard, considering the dead guy was colored. I walked out on the street. It had cooled off as the sun disappeared behind the buildings, and the street-lights had come on.

There was a hotel across the way, the type I was all too familiar with, where you could rent a room by the week, day, or hour. Some of the girls from Fallon's, back when it was a strip joint, had probably used it. I figured it was worth a try. At the liquor store down the block, I picked up a pint of good scotch, then returned to the hotel.

At the desk was an old black man who looked like he'd been sitting there since the Taft administration. His hands were folded on the counter, his head down, and you'd have thought he was asleep, except that his hooded eyes fixed on me the moment I stepped through the door. I walked to the counter.

"What can I do you for?" he asked.

"You worked here long?"

"Twenty seven years, come next month."

"So you know the neighborhood pretty well."

"Brother, there ain't a crack on the sidewalk I don't

know by its first name."

"You remember the place across the street, Fallon's, back when it was a strip joint?"

"Might be. You a cop, or a book writer?"

"Private eye. Looking for a missing person." He said nothing. "Look," I said, "I can read you a chapter of the Bible, or buy you a drink. Your call."

"I prefer to do my Bible reading on Sundays."

I brought out the bottle of scotch, and slid it across to him. He produced two shot glasses, opened the bottle, and filled each to the brim. Lifted one, and sniffed it.

"Well," he said, "at least this hooch come out of the right bottle." He took a sip. "Yes, indeed." He smiled. "This stuff been keepin' the right company."

"They served this sort of stuff at Fallon's?"

"Mebbe they had a bottle looked like that," he said, "one of them bottomless type, got refilled every night. 'Til the label wore out, anyway. Hell, maybe it was real. They do say some of the Others was seen in there now and then. Maybe it refilled by magic."

I'd heard rumors about these Others. I wasn't sure what to make of them.

"You believe in that stuff?" I asked.

"Man up on four does. Calls 'em the 'Luminati, says they're aliens, secretly running everything behind the scenes. Old Gracie, the homeless gal, she got her own name for 'em, calls 'em the Alfar. Says they're fairies or elves or something. Me, I don't know. Who you say you were looking for?"

"Girl used to sing there, name of Frida Valentine."

"Didn't know they had names. Leastwise, not real ones."

"This girl was blonde, about 5-8 or so, good shape..."

"That describes half the girls worked there, brother."

"I was afraid of that. What about the owner? Did you know him?"

"Guy name of Fallon." He smiled, and I nodded.

"Imagine that. This Fallon have a first name?"

"Mark. Mark Fallon."

"Any idea where he is now?"

"Gathered to the Lord, a year after he sold the place."

"He leave a widow?"

"Had a wife, name of Josie. Couldn't say what become of her."

"Thanks," I said. "Keep the bottle."

"Thank you, but no sir," he said. "Man takes a drink like that too often, he ceases to appreciate its particular unique qualities. You take this here bottle with you, I imagine I'll appreciate it all the more if its cousin comes my way all unexpected-like someday."

He sat down, folded his hands on the counter exactly where they had been before, and once again appeared as if he were asleep. I took the bottle, tipped my hat to him, and left.

That following morning, I visited the Hall of Justice. It didn't take long poking through the criminal records of eight years ago to find the big guy I'd met outside Fallon's. There couldn't be many guys his size that had been sent up the river for an eight year stretch in a given year. And anyway, that mug was unmistakable, even in a bad picture. His name was Hugh "Bear" Cullen. He had been collared for a museum heist in which he pinched a bunch of silver, some antique weapons, and several paintings. That was strange lay for a character like him. I hadn't figured him for a connoisseur of art and antiques. The paintings and some of the silver had been recovered, but the weapons never were, and they never tracked down the money he'd gotten for them.

I didn't owe MacNeill any favors, so I didn't bother informing him of what I'd discovered. Maybe it was the romantic in me, but I didn't think Cullen had set out to hurt anybody that day, and I was certain he hadn't planned to kill anyone – he was just looking for his Frida. His plaintive concern for her whereabouts struck me as completely genuine.

Back at the office, I dug out my dog-eared phone book. There was no telephone listing for a Josie Fallon, but the City Directory listed her as having an address in Queens. I locked up the office and hopped the subway.

Josie Fallon's place was a shabby little one-story cottage in a shabby little neighborhood. The yard was more dirt than grass, the paint on the shake siding was dirty and peeling, and the roof was swaybacked. There was an equally dilapidated garage that hadn't housed a car for as long as it could remember, and the weeds were dividing and conquering the paving of the driveway. I was glad I'd brought the rest of the bottle of scotch with me – I had a feeling it could turn out to be my best friend.

After I'd knocked for a while on the screen door, a short round woman in a faded housecoat appeared on the other side of it, peering blearily through the fly-specked screen at me.

"Mrs. Fallon?" I asked. "Mrs. Josie Fallon?"

Her voice dragged itself out of her like a sick man dragging himself out of bed.

"What if I am? Who's asking?"

I told her my name, offered my card.

"I'm not with the cops," I said, "the feds, the city, the bank, or any collection agency. I'm a private eye working on a missing persons case. Can I come in?"

She peered at me a moment more, her head moved in what might have been a nod, then she unhooked the screen door and pushed it open. She took my card before shuffling off into a room to my left. I followed.

The furniture was overstuffed and had that vague gray color that might have been any color when it had been new, but now looked like the surface of a lichen-covered rock. Antimacassars decorated the backs of the chairs and couch. Amidst all the faded gray finery, there was a brand new radio in a shiny walnut cabinet.

"Who'd you say you was looking for?"

"Frida. Frida Valentine. I understand she used to sing at your club. Fallon's?"

She looked at me warily. I took out the bottle of scotch.

"Say," I said, "it's hot, ain't it? Leaves a person with a thirst."

Her eyes were on the bottle. "It does that."

"If you had a couple of glasses..." I said.

She popped up with more energy than I'd seen her expend so far, trundling toward the kitchen. In a moment she returned with two smeary water glasses, and I poured us each a measure. I sipped at mine, and Mrs. Fallon knocked hers back like a miner in a western movie. She smacked her lips.

"Good stuff," she said. Then she looked at me thoughtfully. "Frida, you say? Them were the days. Frida, yeah. I could sing, too, y'know. And dance. Better than her. Frida was no dancer. Of course, she did sing better than me. But I had a lot o' pep."

"I'm sure you did. Would you know where Frida is now?"

"No idea." She shook her head, and held out her glass. "When Markie died, and the place closed, I lost touch with all of them."

I poured.

"Maybe you got pictures from those days? Some with Frida in them?"

"Y'know," she said with a crafty grin, "I think I might."

Back in the office, I sank into my desk chair and took out the picture of Frida. It was a promotional shot, with her posed against a curtain, one stiletto-clad foot on a chair. She was pretty, had nice legs, and a pleasant smile. I wondered if she was still smiling.

I filed the picture away, and looked up to find a guy

framed in my office doorway who looked like a model for a men's clothing ad. Thin, handsome, with blond hair on the longish side, and, even in the stifling heat of my office, his off-white linen suit looked as crisp as a freshly minted bill. I invited him to have a seat, and he looked at the client chair as if it were a cesspit I'd asked him to jump into. He took the maroon silk show handkerchief from his breast pocket, dusted the chair seat, and gingerly sat down. The maroon silk went into a side pocket. I guessed contact with my lowly chair made it unfit for further display, and wondered if he'd donate the suit to Good-will after he left, or just throw it in the trash.

"My name is Francis Hilton," he said. "I'm here on behalf of a friend."

"We all have to make sacrifices for friendship." I nodded sympathetically.

"I beg your pardon?"

"Never mind," I said. "What's your friend's problem?"

"Ransom," he said, and looked at the floor as if his lines were written there. "She had a valuable necklace stolen, and now the thieves want to sell it back. She has charged me with recovering it. I have the money, eight thousand in small bills. I am to meet them tonight, at a rest stop off the Pallisades Parkway."

"Eight thousand, that's a lot of dough. What is this necklace, solid gold with diamonds?"

"Bronze and silver. The antiquity and workmanship make it worth many times that."

"What's it got to do with me?"

"I'm... a little bit nervous. I don't really want to meet them alone."

"You want a bodyguard, there are a dozen private eyes listed in the phone book ahead of me. Why me? Why not the Triple-A Detective Agency?"

"I liked your name. Thought it sounded strong, and honest."

"Thanks. Speaking of names, what's your friend's name?"

"I'd rather not say."

I thought that over for a minute, leaving him to spend some time thinking about how dirty his suit was getting, sitting in my chair.

"You realize," I said finally, "Your necklace-nappers might not be too thrilled at the thought of you being twins."

"They didn't specify I should come alone."

"Okay," I said, "I don't think you need me, but I'll take your money and tag along. But I carry the money, and I do the talking." He agreed. As he stood to leave, he turned back toward me.

"By the way," he asked, "do you carry a gun?"

"Sometimes."

"Well, you won't need it tonight."

I nodded, but made a mental note to arm myself for tonight. In my experience, whenever someone said you wouldn't need a gun, you'd better bring a good one, cleaned and loaded.

* * * * *

A dirt road led down the hill between the pines edging the rest area. Hilton had been instructed to drive down it, but once we arrived there, just before ten o'clock at night, it didn't look like there was room for his big late model sedan to fit between the pines and the metal fence that edged the parking area. I got out, leaving Hilton in the car as I walked down the road. Between the trees, I could see the lights of Manhattan, and occasionally the glimmer of their reflection off the surface of the Hudson. The breeze off the river smelled of low tide and dead fish, but at least it was cool, a relief from the city's heat. I walked maybe fifty, then one hundred feet down the trail. Above the black silhouettes of the trees, the sky was a dark greyish orange, that weird polluted glow that hovers above New York even on the darkest nights.

There were peepers and crickets, and no other sound. I stood and waited, but no necklace thieves stepped out of the bushes. Nothing moved, nothing made a sound except all those amphibians and insects chirping about how badly they wanted to get laid. I listened to their horny pleas for a while more. Took out my pencil flash, and scanned the dirt around me. I could just make out tire tracks in the dew-damp dirt. A car had passed this way recently, and, far as I could tell, hadn't come back. Probably they were out there somewhere, laying low, jerking my chain for having disobeyed instructions and come on foot instead of driving down. Or maybe annoyed that I wasn't Hilton. I still didn't think Hilton's car, big as it was, would make it down here without some serious scratching, but maybe he wouldn't care. I turned to head back to the car.

Without having heard anything, I knew that there was someone behind me, and my hand flew to my gun as I turned, a split
second too late. The world exploded in light, and then everything went black.

"Ten minutes," said a voice.

I blinked, and that sick grey-orange of the New York
night sky swam in my vision, edged all around by black. The
voice spoke again. It was a man's voice, and it seemed familiar.

"They sap you, and take the money. Say they walk up to
the car, talk to Hilton and maybe rough him up, walk back, and
drive out of here. Ten minutes at the most." I recognized the
voice now. It was my voice. I was talking in my sleep – or my
sap-induced stupor – trying to figure it out even as I clumsily
wove my way toward consciousness. "Look at your watch," I
said. Sometimes I do what I tell me to do, sometimes not. This
time I did. It was a little after half past ten. We'd arrived at ten,
then I'd spent ten, fifteen minutes listening to the horny
crickets, so I'd been sapped at quarter past or so, and if my
unconscious detective mind had been working properly, the
necklace thieves had been gone at least ten minutes while my
backside was still communing with the dirt.

"A little longer than that." This voice I did not
recognize. "They had to move the big car to get out. They left
about ten thirty, they've only been gone five minutes." The
light of a flashlight poked me in the eyes, and I squinted,
sitting up. "So who are you, and what are you doing here?"

A cop. Great. I rolled over and got carefully and slowly

to my feet, pain shooting down from the back of my head right to my toes, lighting up everything in between. I may have groaned, but I'm not sure. The weight of my gun was still heavy under my arm, but the pocket where the eight grand should have been felt much lighter now.

I gave him my name, and that I was a private eye.

"Tough guy, huh?" He laughed. "All hard-boiled."

"Well, my head might be a bit soft right now, considering the bashing it took."

"That's nothing to the bashing your friend took."

"Tall, thin, blond guy, looks like a model?"

"Not any more."

I moved toward the rest area and the car.

"Where do you think you're going?"

"He might still be alive."

"Trust me," he said, "he's not." But he followed me up the dirt road to the rest stop.

The cop was right. Hilton lay beside the sedan in a pool of blood that looked black under the stark arc lamp of the rest stop. He'd been beaten to death, and not with the sap that conked me – they'd used something else, a real hard blunt instrument of some sort. Another cop, this one in uniform, stood on the other side of the body.

"So you seen your playmate," said the first cop. "Talk."

I explained as much as I knew. Then we went back to the station. I stood up under a grilling from Chief Patrick and a detective named Halsey for an hour or so before they finally let me go. It was two in the a.m. before I hopped a train back to Manhattan. I stumbled into my little apartment, growled at the cockroaches who ignored me, and flopped into my lumpy bed.

In the morning, I got up late, showered and shaved, walked to the diner down the street for a leisurely breakfast of hash and eggs with plenty of coffee. That made it after eleven before I arrived at my office. I unlocked the door, flipped through the bills and junk mail, and tossed most of it in the circular file. Then I called Martin Brownstein.

Brownstein was a jeweler and sometime fence. He knew more about the jewelry business – whether legitimate, shady, or downright criminal – than anyone in Manhattan. If anybody could identify the necklace and its owner for me, it would be him. I didn't think it would be a hard case for him – how many bronze and silver necklaces worth "several times" eight grand could there be floating around New York?

"You'd be surprised," he said. "Four or five items of that description have moved through the city over the past few years. I'm going to go out on a limb here, my friend, and say the one you want is the most recent purchase, also the one that's stayed around New York. The owner is Astrid Pike."

"How you figure that?" I asked. Mrs. Astrid Pike was married to Judge Baxter Wilson Pike, one of the most politically powerful men in New York.

"Mrs. Pike purchased such a necklace from Sotheby's last year. And she was a friend of this fellow Hilton."

"You knew Hilton?"

"He'd made some purchases, I suspect on someone's behalf."

"That doesn't mean it was her necklace Hilton was ransoming."

"No, but it sure makes it likely. Also, she and her husband are tight with Laird Burns. By the way, you know your friend Hilton had a gambling jones? What I hear, anyway."

Laird Burns. I knew the name. The guy ran the *La Jolla*, an offshore gambling boat, and owned a bunch of politicians and cops. Not that he exerted his influence much in the City – from what I'd heard, he didn't really need to. As long as the city tolerated his boat, he was good. But word was he had bought the last mayoral election, just to be certain.

"And they say he's one of *them*, like the Pikes."

"Them?"

"The Others," he said, and you could hear the capital letters. "The Alfar. That's why his casino is on a ship – being on water prevents them using their powers. Proves nobody can cheat with magic, not even the House. So they say."

"You believe that stuff?" I asked.

"I don't know. Maybe. My mother saw a dybbuk once. I may have seen it myself, I was just a kid, I don't really remember. There are stranger things. I'm just saying. Watch your back."

I called the Pike estate. I got the runaround from the butler and the social secretary until I told her I was the last person to see Francis Hilton alive. That got me an appointment for three.

The Pike estate was out in the Hamptons. The house was smaller than Buckingham Palace, and probably had fewer windows than the Chrysler Building. A butler who looked like he'd only recently been embalmed escorted me down a hall you could have played basketball in, into a drawing room lined with books and hung with paintings that looked like they belonged in the Met.

If his butler looked recently embalmed, Baxter Wilson Pike looked like he'd been preserved by the ancient Egyptians, at a cut-rate shop whose work didn't stand up well over the years. His skin was moth-eaten parchment, and his handshake felt like a wrinkled silk glove with some broken sticks inside it. His wife was half his age or less, and could have been the young queen of the Nile, except for her hair, which had the burnished gold of old paintings. She had a set of curves nobody could improve on, and her green eyes sent me a look I could feel in my hip pocket. She was wearing a necklace of bronze and silver. I wondered how it had found its way home.

After I expressed my condolences about Hilton's death, and we made some pointless small talk, the Judge excused himself. His wife looked after him as he left the room.

"The judge is not a well man," she said, and turned those green eyes on me again. I felt a little like a deer in the headlights, but shook it off with an effort. "He tires easily," she added. She patted the divan beside her. "Why don't you come over and sit here," she said. It wasn't a question.

"I've been thinking about that ever since you crossed your legs," I said, and obliged. Up close she smelled like a garden – floral, but also earthy.

"You don't seem like one of Francis' friends," she said. "How did you know him?"

I put my hand on her knee. It felt nice.

Which was odd. I'm not without my urges, but I don't usually feel up a rich potential client on first meeting.

"I'm a private eye. Francis hired me to tag along when he went to ransom a friend's necklace."

"And did you redeem this necklace?" She shifted on the divan, and now my hand was on her thigh. It felt even nicer than the knee. My head was buzzing.

"No," I said, looking at the bronze and silver decoration that glowed against the bare skin of her throat. "I got sapped down, and Hilton got killed. We never saw the necklace, or the thieves."

"What a shame," she said. "Kiss me."

I did.

Her arms went around my neck, and she kissed me as if she meant it. For all her soft-looking curves, her body felt dense and hard in my arms, all muscle and bone. She was very strong.

I heard the door open. Without moving, I rolled my eyes up to look, and saw the old man back out of the room, closing the door behind him. I sat back. The buzzing in my head had stopped, and I could feel my hands and feet again.

"Who was that?" she asked.

"That was Mr. Pike."

I sat back, looked at her.

"Forget him." She reached for me again. I stood up, out of that reach.

"I know," I said. "He's sick, and tires easily."

"Well, aren't you old fashioned?" she said, sitting up and straightening her dress.

"Only from the waist up."

"How do I get in touch with you?"

"I'm in the book."

Brownstein had said there were rumors about Astrid Pike being one of these mysterious Alfar. The woman was certainly strange. Looking into her eyes had been like looking into the eyes of an alien being. Or maybe I was just letting myself get spooked by all the crazy talk I'd heard recently. I headed down Broadway toward the office of Raventer Investigations.

Oscar Raventer was the one P.I. in town I knew took the weird cases. Ghosts, UFOs, monsters, you paid him, he'd investigate, and he knew more about debunking fake mediums than anyone this side of Harry Houdini. Small and dark with a large nose, he looked at you with black eyes that seemed to have seen it all, and weren't impressed.

"So," he said, "let's skip the amenities, I know you're not here for my sterling personality. What's the rumpus?"

"What can you tell me about these people they call the Alfar?"

He snorted.

"This would be on the clock, of course. You couldn't afford it, we'd be here the next three days. What are you working on? Maybe I can give you the pieces you need."

I thought about that. The Alfar had been mentioned in both cases, so I figured I'd start at the beginning.

"You remember the Met heist? Eight years ago?"

"Sure." He nodded, looking amused. "Most important pieces never recovered were a spear and a cup."

"That so?" I hadn't known that.

"Alfar artifacts. In the Alfar tribal culture, the king or chief is called the Spear, and the queen is called the Graal – it's a kind of cup. These were sacred items to the Alfar."

"Wait a minute, you're saying these Alfar are like Indians?"

He shook his head. "No, they're not even human. Distant cousins, maybe. You know, once our monkey ancestors came out of the trees, the family split up into lots of different races. Neanderthal, Cro-magnon, Human... Alfar. Like the Neanderthals, only smarter and prettier."

"So you're saying these Alfar were behind the Met heist? Getting their sacred items back?"

"You ask my opinion, yeah. The rest of it was misdirection, to cover themselves."

I glanced at the clock. I didn't even owe him five bucks yet. I figured I could go ten.

"How are they different from us?"

"Stronger, faster, smarter, and more ruthless, you

believe what people say. Me, I've seen stronger and faster. I've also seen stupid, so I don't buy the 'smarter' part."

"Somebody mentioned magic, psychic powers..."

"Couldn't say. Heard of it second hand, haven't seen it myself."

"But you think it's possible?"

He shrugged, shook his head again. "Dunno. I've exposed thousands of frauds, but I've seen a few things I can't explain, too. Without evidence one way or the other, I wouldn't venture a guess. I'll tell you this, though... the thing about iron and steel looks to be true. At least, they believe it."

"Iron and steel?"

"They can't touch either. Burns them, or gives them serious hives or something."

"And you've seen this?"

"No. But, like I say, I know they believe it."

"What about Alfar passing themselves off as humans?"

"Happens all the time."

"Any prominent ones?"

"Like who?"

"Laird Burns."

"I've heard that one. Can't say for sure, but it seems very likely."

"Judge Baxter Wilson Pike, or his wife Astrid maybe?"

He shrugged, shook his head. "Couldn't say. Why him?"

"Something I heard. You said they were stronger than humans. The judge looks like he's at death's door, but the wife's got a grip on her like a lowland gorilla."

"Might be indicative, if you had other evidence. If it's true, it would make them doubly dangerous. Like Burns, good to steer clear of."

This was getting better by the moment.

"What about, uhm, *relations* between Alfar and human?"

"What, you mean fucking? Hell, yeah. Alfar are what MacNeill would call 'promiscuous' – they're serious fuck bunnies. What I hear, you hook up with Alfar pussy, you'll never go home again. Not that I know this from personal experience, you understand.

"Of course, they do get uptight about the Spear and the Graal. Those two take vows, they can only fuck each other. Something to do with the power of the land, or the power of the tribe. I've never been able to get a clear explanation of that."

I let Raventer talk for a while more. It was all interesting, but I didn't quite see how it fit in to what I knew. I paid him anyway.

I walked back to my office thinking it all over. Oscar had said there had been a power struggle amongst the Alfar that ended, about the time of the heist, with a new clan in charge of the east coast. Sounded to me as if the new ruling clan had used Bear to get at the artifacts, and then tossed him aside. I wondered, if they were stronger and faster than humans, why wouldn't they steal it themselves, why hire Bear? Just so they could have a fall guy? And what was Frida in all this? Did they eliminate her because she knew? It wouldn't be a big deal for them, probably they saw her as a human whore, and from what Raventer said, the Alfar didn't have a lot of compassion for human beings.

Back at the office, I fielded two phone calls – one from MacNeill, another from Laird Burns, both wanting to get in touch with Bear Cullen. Why was Burns concerned with a penny ante crook with one big job to his name? Unless Burns himself had something to do with the heist.

I was musing this over when the phone rang a third time. It was Josie Fallon. She said she'd located Frida, and the girl had agreed to come out and talk – but only to her old boyfriend, Bear Cullen. I said I'd do what I could to arrange that.

What was this? Why did they all think I knew where Cullen was? Just because he offered to buy me a drink at Fallon's? Sure, technically, he was my client, he'd hired me to find his Frida – but I hadn't mentioned that to anyone, and as far as I knew, no one knew about that except the Bear and myself.

As if my thinking about him had summoned him, the door to my office opened, and Bear Cullen wedged himself though it with little space to spare.

"I been wondering where you got to," I said. "So have a lot of other people."

"Cops?" he asked. "About the guy in Fallon's?"

"Yeah, not that the cops in this precinct care a whole

bunch about a colored guy getting killed. You ever heard of a guy named Laird Burns?" He shook his head. "No? How about Baxter Wilson Pike?"

"How many people is that?"

I sighed.

"Well," I said, "I may have a line on your Frida."

I called Mrs. Fallon and made the arrangements. She'd have Frida call Bear at my number. Twenty minutes later, the phone rang, and the big guy never gave me a chance to get near it. One look at his face and I knew who was on the line. There couldn't be another voice in the world would make this big galoot's face light up like that. I stepped into the outer office to give him a little privacy.

A moment later, he joined me.

"You got a car?" he asked. I did. I took out the picture of Frida and offered it to him.

"Guess I won't be needing this any more," I said.

"What's this?" he asked, frowning at the photo.

"What do you mean, 'what's this?' It's a picture of Frida."

"That ain't Frida," he said, tossing the picture back at me. "Quit fooling around and let's get moving."

I drove Bear out to Long Island, to a nameless no-tell motel in a little town on the southern shore. The big guy said nothing the whole way out, but you could tell he was excited by the way his knee kept bouncing. Hell, I felt like seeing Frida myself at this point. But three would definitely have been a crowd. One thing really bothered me. If Josie Fallon was going to set up a meeting with Frida, why had she given me a bogus photo?

I pulled up to the motel, and Bear stepped out. The guys waiting for us at the motel were either amateurs, or very anxious professionals, because they opened fire the minute I started to pull away. I ducked, slammed it in reverse, and backed up to cover Bear with the body of the car. He crouched behind it, his gun already out, returning their fire. I wrestled out my Browning. Bear pegged the one behind a parked car across the street, I nailed the one in the cottage window. The shooting stopped. I turned toward the motel to see the door of the room as someone opened it. It wasn't Frida. I shouted to the Bear as I fired, but the guy dodged back inside. Then Bear was up, headed for the door. Fear wasn't built into his big frame. He was looking for his Frida. I got out to follow as he stepped through the door.

There were shots; it sounded like the Bear's gun. I stepped inside. There were two of them, dead, and Bear was standing in the door to the bathroom, staring at the floor. He looked up at me.

"My Frida ain't here," he said. He shook his head. "We got to find my Frida."

"What's going on, Bear? Who are these guys, why do they want to kill you? Is it about the museum heist? Was Frida in on it?"

"We gotta find her," he said, and he stalked past me,

100

out into the street. Got into my bullet-pocked automobile.

I dropped Bear at a train station, then found a pay phone and called an honest cop I knew in Queens. He said he'd check on Josie Fallon for me, and I said I'd meet him there. When I arrived, Jimmy Kemp was still the only cop on the scene, but there would be others soon. Josie lay dead on her bed, strangled.

I filled Kemp in on what I knew.

"Josie Fallon gave me a picture that Bear says isn't really Frida. When she contacted Frida, she also called someone else. Somebody she'd been paid to call, if anyone came looking for Bear or his girl Frida. That somebody tried to kill Bear."

"Now Bear's killed her?" Kemp said, gesturing at the big black marks on her neck. I peered at them closely.

"This was somebody wearing padded gloves," I said. "Finger imprints would be clear, sharply defined. These are blurry, soft-edged."

"It's a frame."

"But why?" I asked the empty house. "What does Bear know, why does he scare them?"

"Where the missing loot is?"

"No, if they already know where it is, they've moved it by now. If they don't know where it is, and Bear does..."

"They couldn't afford to kill him."

Burns or Pike or both had to be mixed up in the

museum heist, but Bear didn't recognize their names. That meant there had to have been a go-between, their tin mittens. Hilton, probably. Bear might have recognized him. Maybe that's why they killed him. He'd have bought the new radio I'd seen in Josie Fallon's place, and plied her with liquor, promises of money, got her to call a number if anyone came around asking certain questions. Then they didn't need him any more. Or maybe he'd gotten greedy, started blackmailing them. So they set him up with the so-called necklace ransom. But Hilton got nervous, and hired me to tag along.

Why didn't they kill me too? They didn't know who I was. Far as they were concerned, I was some schmuck Hilton had hired. They knew someone was looking for Frida, but they hadn't known it was me. They must be keeping Frida some place, hoping they could use her to keep Bear silent about whatever the hell it was he knew. And so far they'd succeeded.

Burns, the Pikes, Hilton, Frida, Bear... if the Pikes were behind the museum heist, it had to have been Astrid taking the lead. Josie Fallon had made a phone call that afternoon, and then they knew my name. So Astrid Pike had tried her little hypnosis-seduction thing on me, but it hadn't worked. Frida seemed to have disappeared from the city. But if Burns was involved...

Burns' boat. That's where they'd stash her.

I called Bear, then I called MacNeill. He might be a bigoted racist bastard, but he was the closest thing I had to an honest cop with jurisdiction.

* * * * *

MacNeill met me at my office, and I laid the whole thing out for him. He didn't like it much.

"Pike?" he said. "That's bad enough, but Burns? Laird Burns pulls a lot of weight in this city."

"He's a crook."

"He keeps all that shit out on his boat, and off the streets, so we look the other way."

"And take your plain brown envelope every month."

MacNeill glowered at me.

"What the hell is it you want?" he said.

"What do I want?" I told him. "I want a drink. I want a vacation. I want a whole lot of life insurance, and a house in the country. What I got is a hat and a gun. What I got is the certainty that there's a girl being held on that boat, and I'm going out there with Bear Cullen. And I've also got a feeling that if I don't have some cops behind me, I may not be coming back."

MacNeill looked at the floor for a long time.

"Cut me own throat for a fuckin' two-bit private dickhead who thinks he's Sir Galahad. Alright. I'll give you ten minutes lead. Then I'll arrive to remove the annoying trespasser from Mr. Burns' boat. And if there's a certain lady there who would like a ride to the docks with a police escort, we'll oblige her. That's as far as I'll go. I ain't arresting Burns, or even suggesting in public he done something wrong."

It was the best I could hope for from MacNeill.

The water taxi was out, we didn't want Burns knowing

we were coming, so we hired our own boat. The boatman's name was Latham, he was nearly as big as me, with red hair. When I said we wanted a discreet ride to the *La Jolla*, he looked from me to Bear Cullen and back again.

"You got a good reason," he said, "I could get you there."

"How much of a reason?"

"Fifty bucks, ten dollars extra if you bleed in my boat."

"Twenty-five."

"Thirty."

"Let's go."

Latham knew of a loading door that was left unlocked – the *La Jolla* used a lot of supplies when the party got rolling. Bear and I clambered from his boat into Burns' hold, and then made our way quietly to the decks above.

We caught one of Burns' flunkies in the passageway by surprise, and Bear *persuaded* him to take us to his boss' office. After the guy had knocked, called out to his boss and was told to enter, Bear left him unconscious on the deck.

Laird Burns was slim and good looking in a movie star sort of way. He sat back from his desk sharply, obviously surprised to have the proverbial 800 pound gorilla bearing down on him. The look in his eye told me all I needed to know. This wasn't some Alfar mastermind, Burns was just a human servant, an Alfar-wannabe, their human face to the human world.

"Hello, Bear," he said, as if they'd met before, but Bear showed no sign of recognition.

"You know where my Frida is?" Bear demanded.

There was a slight sound from behind a door to my right. Bear didn't hear it, but I did. I smelled flowers and earth.

"You can come out now, Mrs. Pike," I said.

The door slowly opened, and Astrid Pike stepped out. Bear turned, and when he saw her, the expression spreading across his big face made the whole story clear.

"Hey, babe," he said in a loud whisper. "Where you been? What you been up to?"

"Hi, Bear," she said.

"Go ahead, Frida," I said. "Tell him. I'd like to know myself. You conned Bear into the Met heist, turned him in, and then married Pike. My poking around looking for Frida made you nervous. There wasn't any necklace robbery, that was a setup so you could off Hilton. I figure he'd been blackmailing you. You couldn't afford for your husband to know you'd been a torch singer in a titty bar, could you?"

"Don't be stupid," she said. "It isn't my husband who must never know, it's the rest of the Alfar."

Another penny dropped.

"Baxter Wilson Pike..." I said. "I should have seen it. A pike is a kind of spear. He's the Spear. You're the Graal."

"Well, aren't you the smart human? You know what it is to become the Graal? To be always empty, a vessel craving content? And never to be filled? Sure, I married Pike because his was one of the royal bloodlines. But he's been in the human world too long. That spear won't be piercing anything ever again."

"Babe..?" said the Bear.

"Don't you get it, Bear?" I said. "The Spear and the Cup are sacred objects, she and her husband needed them to cement their power in the Alfar clans. They couldn't steal them themselves, because the objects were protected behind steel, a metal the Alfar can't touch. She seduced you to get you to steal it for them. Then she turned you in. The Alfar have very rigid traditions. No Spear without a Graal, and she can't be the Graal if she's being despoiled by the touch of a human. Once the museum heist was done, she couldn't risk anyone finding out about her liaison with you. Josie Fallon was the only human who knew that Astrid Pike had once been Frida Valentine. So she stashed Josie away using Hilton as her go-between. But Hilton started to blackmail her, so she killed him. Then she killed Josie, and tried to frame you for that."

What I didn't add was that when her Spear started faltering, humans who didn't even know of the Alfar were convenient prey for her. They wouldn't be talking to any of her Alfar kin. She might have had liaisons with any number of humans, like she had tried to set up with me, because the Graal couldn't bear to be empty.

"He's making it all up, Bear," she said. "Shut him up."

The Bear turned toward me.

"She used you, Bear," I said. "Like she used everybody else."

The Bear reached out and cuffed me. It was an offhand, glancing blow to him, but to me, it was like getting hit by a steam shovel. I went down in a heap, the gun skittering away.

Bear Cullen turned back toward Astrid, his Frida.

And she shot him.

Once, twice, three times the gun barked, and blood blossomed on Bear's garish suit.

"Babe..." he muttered, sinking to his knees, "Why...?"

She was screaming. Her hand was smoking, not just the barrel of the gun, but from her flesh where she held the weapon. Burns was down behind his desk.

I scrambled after my gun, and as Astrid turned her gun on me, I squeezed off two shots, taking her in the torso both times. There came a pounding on the door as she collapsed against the bulkhead, dropping the gun. Her right hand was a charred smoking ruin. She sank to the floor and keeled over, her head next to that of her ex-lover. The Bear was already dead.

MacNeill's voice was added to the pounding. Burns was just sitting there on the floor, peering out from behind his desk at the two dead bodies. I staggered to my feet and opened the door. MacNeill and two uniforms busted in.

"What's going on here?" he demanded.

I was swaying on my feet.

"Let him tell you," I said, gesturing at Burns. "I'm too tired."

Sitting in Pete's, I listened to the Athletics come *this close*. The Double X, Jimmy Foxx, faltered in the stretch, and the Yankees took it by a single run. I raised a glass to the guy. I knew how he felt. Bear was dead. Astrid/Frida survived, though I heard she committed suicide not long after. Her husband died about a month later. That's the story anyway. Who knows, maybe they vanished into Elfland or something. Burns was never charged with anything, and it was all swept under the carpet. I was never certain why Astrid had tried to seduce me, when there was so much risk in it for her. I doubted it was my irresistible charm. Maybe my guess had been right, and when her Spear couldn't hold the line any more, she started looking elsewhere for a stiff weapon. She'd said herself that to be the Graal was to be "always empty, a vessel craving content." Probably I came with extra benefits – she figured she could get me under her influence, and use me the way she'd used Bear. But the truth was, I'd never know for sure.

So I'd found Bear his Frida, for all the good it did the big lug. Usually, just getting the job done is enough. Sometimes it's not. There are times you wish you never took the job in the first place. But you learn to live with that.

I do, anyway.

There were other theories, but to share those with Willowbark would only foil his evil plan.

Rose Mambert teaches Italian language and cinema at the College of the Holy Cross and is Editor-in-Chief of Pink Narcissus Press.

"When I was looking for writers to contribute a piece during the early stages of this book, I asked my friend Michael Stewart, an immensely talented writer, if he'd be interested in writing the title piece for the anthology. Somehow during our discussions, 'Elf Love' morphed into 'Self Love.'

"It so happened that Michael never wrote this story, claiming that he had thought about it, but hadn't come up with an idea for the concept. Taking it as a challenge, I mulled over the idea for a few days. The last line of the story came to me out of the blue. Once I had the last line, I threw myself at the computer and '(S)elf Love' was the result."

(S)elf Love
Rose Mambert

Willowbark scrunched up his face in disgust. "Mortals do *that*? Are you *sure*?"

Dewdrop nodded his head vigorously. "Uh huh. Yeah. I saw it in one of their *moving pictures*. It was European."

Willowbark didn't know what *European* meant, but he wasn't going to say so. Besides, he was pretty sure that Dewdrop was pulling his leg. Faeries were notorious for their mischievous tricks, and – though they usually played them on mortals – it didn't stop them from playing tricks on *each other*. Plus, it wouldn't be the first time that Willowbark had fallen for one of Dewdrop's tall tales. Dewdrop was – as the mortals would say – a *prick*.

"I don't believe you."

Dewdrop coolly tossed a berry into his mouth. "Believe whatever you want, Will, but it's true."

"Gross."

Dewdrop grinned. Willowbark wasn't the youngest elf-ling in the tribe, but – by the way he acted – no one would have believed it. No wonder his folks wouldn't let him out past the veil at night. If you looked up "gullible" in the Elvish dictionary, there'd be a picture of him.

Dewdrop's grin widened. He had been saving the best

for last. "Yeah, you wouldn't believe it, Will. And then, at the end – stuff comes out."

"Stuff? What kind of stuff?"

That part Dewdrop hadn't understood. He shrugged sagely.

A shadow of disbelief crinkled Willowbark's face. No doubt he was thinking about the *stuff*. "Then you mean it isn't forbidden?"

"Guess not. Not for mortals, anyway. "

Willowbark chewed thoughtfully on one pointy finger-nail. "I don't get it," he finally murmured. "Why would anyone want to *do* that?"

"Apparently it feels really good," Dewdrop said. That had been one theory he and Moonbeam discussed after they had turned themselves invisible (using the fairy dust pilfered from their parents' not-so-secret hiding places, of course) to sneak back out of the *cinema*. There were other theories, but to share those with Willowbark would only foil his evil plan. He reached over and tweaked his friend's ear. "Hey. Maybe you should find out, Will."

Appalled, Willowbark screeched, and his face so scrunched up that it resembled a crab apple long fallen from the tree. "It's forbidden!"

Swallowing his grin, Dewdrop popped another berry in his mouth, chewing slowly, before he shrugged again. "Sure, Will. Follow the rules like a good little elfling." He ignored Willowbark's glare as he tilted his head, one pointy ear cocked compass-like north, towards his house. "My mother's calling me. I gotta go."

Perturbed, Willowbark scarcely noticed as his friend climbed up on the bedroom windowsill and sprinkled himself liberally with fairy dust. And he certainly didn't notice the mischievous twinkle in the silver eyes or the cocky, satisfied grin on Dewdrop's face as he flew away.

Alone in his room, Willowbark snorted. *Good little elfling. Why – I'll show him.*

But he didn't know how. Well, unless he did... *that.*

On the one hand, Willowbark was a good little elfling who did what his parents told him and never broke any rules. Not to mention that Dewdrop's suggestion *was* kind of gross. And even if Willowbark were to do it, it wasn't like anyone was here to see him break the rules.

On the other hand, this status was killing his standing with his peers. Unless he showed some sign of rebellion, he'd be branded a loser forever. And, in truth, as gross as it was, Willowbark – like every elfling – was curious about all things mortal. The younger fey spent whole afternoons discussing mortals and their fascinating ways, and trying to emulate them. And, finally, even though Dewdrop wouldn't see him do it, if what he said was true, then Willowbark would still be able to show him some proof.

He could show him the *stuff.*

Nervously, he glanced around. He decided it would be better to close the window – you never knew who might fly in. He jumped up, pulled the curtains shut, and then, after a moment of careful listening to make sure that he was indeed alone in the house, he snaked a hand into his pants and began doing *that* in the manner Dewdrop had described.

That felt... good.

A strange thing happened as he continued. That part of him grew bigger. Down deep in his stomach he felt strange little tingles, and he felt a strange longing for release.

I can't believe I'm doing that, he thought, as he began to move his hand with rapid, determined strokes.

Thinking was becoming difficult. He stopped thinking.

He did *that*, faster and harder. And, although he wasn't thinking, a vision of Merrybell – the sprite he'd always liked – popped up in his mind. And in this vision, it was *her* hand touching him. She was smiling at him as she held him in her soft little hand. He imagined her kissing him as she did *that*. He imagined her dropping down on her knees and doing *that* with her sweet little cherry-red mouth and then –

Willowbark began to throb and swell. Stars exploded in his eyes. His breath came out in choked little whimpers. Wave after wave of pleasure washed over him, wracking his waif-like body for what seemed like an eternity. Finally the pleasure ebbed and the stars receded, and Willowbark looked down at the *stuff* covering his hands. Silvery and shimmery, it radiated of magic.

"Oh!" he said.

And *that*, gentle reader, is where fairy dust comes from.

"You're gonna suffer for that blue blood of yours... Not honest red like a man's; there's no heat to an elf's blood." Xiao glared. "You people make me sick."

Daniel Vernaglia's "A Long Friday" is not a pretty story. Not only does it twist the love theme, but also chokes it and then throws it on the ground and viciously stomps on it a few times for good measure. In fact, after receiving this piece, someone commented that we might need to rename the anthology "Elf Hate."

As for David, he was born in July of 1969. He is still alive today and grateful for it.

His website is www.glerkofblerk.com.

A Long Friday
David Vernaglia

His blood spattered across the table and the wall behind him as the cop's fist made that familiar meat and bone sound on his jaw. Slack-necked and reeling, the elf smiled, drooling a thick cord of blood into the red pool on the metal surface before him.

"You liked that, didn't you," the cop snarled. "Made you feel like a big boy, didn't it, talking shit like a fool." His face was inches from the elf's. "You know we have enough dirt on you already," he whispered. "You're going down for this one, boy. You're gonna suffer for that mouth of yours." He paused and leaned in another inch. "You're gonna suffer for that blue blood of yours... Not honest red like a man's; there's no heat to an elf's blood." Xiao glared. "You people make me sick." The Lieutenant leaned back, returning his hands to his hips, and retreated to the far side of the table, gripping his badge.

The elf breathed heavily, his hands cuffed to the chair behind him, the light harsh on his face, pale, though for reasons in excess of his elven blood. His addictions could have colored his skin so white, but any human who looked square at him would know it instantly; he was an elf, and elves were rare these days, and the cops were psyched.

Xiao had found a patsy, and a perfect one at that: a

drug addicted, loud-mouthed elf who frequented whore houses and shady bars, fraternized with humanity's fouler folk and exercised his problems with authority regularly. To top it off, the elf had been seen with the victim two weeks before her death, and was said to have fucked her on occasion, usually after the two got high. For a cop looking to make an inconvenient murder just go away, this was a godsend! Xiao was going to get a promotion for busting this elf! He'd definitely get the summer off, and once his wife was away, he'd finally get to fuck Lao-hu in that dress he liked so much. Xiao smiled and looked at the bloody face across from him. I hate this guy, he thought. Xiao hated all his kind, especially their mothers. Thank God for the Regulations; humans had suffered too much at the hands of creatures like this for Xiao to give a shit about justice.

"Yeah. I liked it," said the elf. "Thanks for reminding me why I love this city so much, why I enjoy paying my taxes. You guys are fantastic. Choppy and Mr. Rubber fucking up an elf on a Friday night in a concrete room downtown 'cause they wanna go home and fuck the missus, drink a few brews, give her a good beating, then snore their fat asses to sl–"

Again, the meat and bone sound. More blood left his mouth and found its way to the pool on the table and the puddle in his lap. His shirt was soaked with sweat, snot, blood and drool and was definitely ruined; a shame, considering the artistry that had gone into its making. He snorted. His mother had made it for his birthday. Was it the first or second of their world wars that she was celebrating when she wove it? He couldn't remember. It was, in fact, one of the only gifts she had ever given him. He still wasn't sure if he trusted her, or if she even liked him for that matter. But thus, they say, is the way of elven mothers and their sons; difficult and not to be trusted. He smiled, thinking of her.

Xiao leaned in, smelling him. "Why'd you do it?" he whispered. "Did you get tired of fucking your mom's cold, wet pussy and want some hot human meat? You get bored with what your own kind has to offer?" He drew closer. "Was it money? Were you gonna sell her body to your elders? Was that it?" he snorted. "Did you get enough smack for your efforts?"

The elf looked up, meeting his eyes. Silence filled the room as his breathing calmed and his back straightened. "You know I didn't kill her," he said. "You just wish I did."

The cop laughed. "Sign the goddamn paper so I can go home." Xiao marched across the room, returning quickly to his side. "You had the victim's blood under your fingernails! You're going to fry for this one, fucker." Xiao looked up and smiled at his partner as he entered the room with fresh coffee and cigarettes, kicking the door closed behind him. "He's almost there, Troy. He's just about there."

"Good," said the cookie-cut, fifty-something cop with the balding head and decidedly artificial tan. "I am sick and tired of this bullshit. It's Friday night, for Christ's sake." He sat down at the far end of the steel table and offered Xiao a cigarette. "You know what I think? I think it was a crime of passion. I think he loved her, and she couldn't stop fucking every guy with a packed pipe or a juicy fix, and this asshole killed her for it. It was a crime of passion. He loved the bitch." Troy lit up and inhaled deeply. "Yeah. He loved her, then he gutted her like a fish."

There was a long pause, filled with little more than Troy's angry mutterings and Xiao's thick smoke.

"Love?" The elf laughed. "Are you serious? Elves don't love. Everyone knows that. Everyone who's not a fucking moron knows that, I should say, but since that leaves you two out, I understand if..."

Strangle gargle choking sounds and screaming followed as Xiao shouted at Troy for a long minute, trying to pry him forcibly off the prisoner. "Don't kill him, for fuck's sake! He's our ticket out of here! Lay off, asshole! I'm in charge!"

Raging and red, Troy backed off, hands twitching. "Just say the word and there'll be an accident, Lieutenant. I'll end this guy right now. I'll do it. Just say it, Lieutenant. Say it!"

Xiao picked his coffee back up and burned his tongue, glaring at him. "Get the fuck out of here, Troy. You're in my way."

Furious, Troy stormed out of the room, slamming the heavy metal door behind him and taking a seat on the far side of the one-way, glaring invisibly at the pair in the room.

Xiao turned to the prisoner. The elf was laughing softly and coughing a bit of blood.

"Love? You can't be serious. You humans think that all beings 'love.' That it's some sort of universal truth, like your god. It's pathetic! You lay your emotional laws down on those you supposedly care for the most and imprison them. You

118

enslave what you 'love,' you control and conform it to your will so that 'happiness' might ensue." The elf snarled. "You are all children, regardless of age or your history. I would never inflict 'love' on a being I held dear. Nothing could be crueler." The elf glared at Xiao with hate in his eyes.

"Love."

He spat. "Don't accuse me of that; no elf would believe you. We hate your 'love' and all that it's done to this world."

The elf leaned back, smoldering. This had gone on long enough; he knew the sound of a sinking ship. It didn't matter if he signed their 'confession.' It was over for him. But to be accused of 'love!' To be treated as if human! That he would avenge. That would not be forgiven.

Xiao stared from across the table, coffee down, cigarette up. He needed to quit, but each drag was a black lung dart that fueled his hate and kept him burning. Without it, Xiao might actually feel something for the elf, and he wasn't in the mood for that. He had found the crack he was looking for and knew what to do. He'd be out of here by 8:30.

"Yeah. Love... That's it! We're gonna label this one a crime of passion. Maybe the jury will show you some mercy and reduce the charge to manslaughter. Long suffering is always better than a quick death when it comes to your kind!" Xiao chuckled. "Twenty years of human dicks in your ass might actually set you straight, you pointy-eared prick! God knows once you get out, you'll certainly have some stories to entertain your mother with while you fuck her. 'Oh yeah, Ma! They used to bend me over, soap me up and...'"

"Give me the pen, Choppy. I've had enough." The elf was cold in all ways, as if dead, and met Xiao's eyes and stared. "I am done with this. Give me the pen."

Behind the glass, Troy sighed and leaned back, looking down at his watch. 8:21 PM. Not too bad for a long Friday. I still have plenty of time for a few drinks, he thought. Maybe I'll even get a blowjob tonight.

Back in the room, Xiao started chuckling as he released the prisoner's right hand from the cuffs. "This is going to be great," he smirked. "What was that you were telling me from the TV the other day, Troy? 'Fear of embarrassment is akin to fear of death in humans?' Looks like it doesn't work that way for elves."

Xiao's head shattered on mirrored glass one second later. The elf had whipped the chair he was sitting on up and around and through the space once occupied by the cop's skull. Five seconds after that, hands high above his chest, he turned to face the hail of bullets Troy unleashed into him as the cop burst through the heavy door screaming in panic and rage. It was over.

The elf smiled as he crashed to the floor, bullets swimming in the pool of blood that filled his chest, weighing him down, silencing everything. Elves don't love. Everyone knows that. There would be no trial. He was free.

"If sharing my fate is a curse, then you will share this with me: hidden from everyone's eyes."

Otilia Tena is a teacher and writer of short stories and fairy tales living in Bucharest, Romania. She has been writing poems and stories since childhood. A few places where her work has been published include DORLANA'S FAIRYTALES *blog,* CRUINNAIU, BEWILDERING STORIES *and* LUNA CAT.

Otilia says, "The types of elves I like to write about are the daoine sidhe and the huldufolk. Yet I always try to endow them with human psychological traits and passionate feelings, since my readers are people like me... Who knows if one day my stories may be read by some other species? Until then..."

One of the Huldu
Otilia Tena

Cooking and sweeping were not her favorite pastimes and all hard work, she let it slip through her fingers. She spent her days reading old tales or singing, though nothing of all this could compare to her grandfather's enchanting stories. He, in exchange, was very upset that she seemed to disregard her homely duties and used to scold her many times:

"You are lazy and clumsy and you expect to live only by singing and combing your hair. You do it on purpose, don't you?"

"No, grandpa, you see, something weighs on my heart, something I can't tell you about..."

"Why, Unna?"

"Because I can't find a name for it. It's more like a sort of grief... each time the music box plays... it sounds so far away..."

"Sometimes I think you were not made for this world. You are visible, you eat, you breathe, yet you don't belong here, Unna Ishildur. A child would bind you more to this life."

Their village belonged to an unknown lord, whom people referred to as "the hidden one" because nobody had seen him nor knew where he lived. This may be why they feared him so much. One day Unna and her grandfather

Hildimar and many other people saw a caravan of nomad wagons camping close to their house. A woman with milk-white skin came to Unna, carrying her two children.

"I am ready to serve you with anything, miss, I want a bath for me and my children."

"Who's next?" Unna asked. "The whole caravan? Take your children and go away!"

"No, miss, it's just us. I'll do anything you ask me to."

"Anything? Very well," Unna said, "then give me one of your children for good. Grandpa said only a child can keep me in this world."

"You can have my child and I can cook and sweep," the white nomad said.

"That's good because grandpa isn't satisfied with the work I do. You can stay."

Old Hildimar asked what her name was and the nomad woman said they called her Nuri Peperuga. They found out that she was believed to be a night murderer and that the nomads had banished her. Unna saw the hidden notches on her body while she was taking the bath. She swore that nothing of this was true and begged them to let her stay. Hildimar was pleased with her work and considered her arrival a fortunate event, since Unna had adopted the nomad woman's child and he had a new grandson.

Nuri Peperuga loved the old man's stories, since she had never heard of elves or hidden people before. One after-noon Nuri was cooking and Unna was combing her hair and singing. She ignored her grandfather and the children, as she often did.

"Who is the lord of this village?" Nuri asked suddenly.

Hildimar startled with a shiver.

"Nobody knows," he said. "People fear to mention him even without a name. So it is better not to talk about him."

"I am not a coward like you all! Why do you have to be afraid of him?"

"You and your nomads should be even more scared, since you are intruders," the old man said.

"He'd better fear us, me and my people! Nay, he'd better fear me alone! My knives can cut anyone!"

"You foolish woman! If he hears you, you are lost."

Evening came and this was the time of the day when both children had to be washed. Nuri took her child and began to look for Unna and call her.

"Unna, where are you? The boy is waiting to be washed!" She heard a faint melody coming from Unna's room. She had left the door ajar, so Nuri peered and saw a tiny music box, which Unna held in her delicate hands, close to her bosom.

"Leave me alone! Go away, I said!"

"Why are you yelling? You should fear me. I'm a night murderer."

"So why don't you kill me now?"

"It's the melody," Nuri said. "I like you, miss. Hildimar is bad. You'll never leave this place, unless you listen to me and do as I tell you." Then she sat next to Unna and whispered something in her ear.

124

The following day, Unna was home alone. Nuri had gone out to buy some food and the children were playing with their neighbors. Old Hildimar was out telling stories to the people. Unna heard someone knock at the door and opened it. She saw a tall man, his face half covered by a hood.

"Are you Nuri Peperuga?" he asked.

"Yes."

"The woman who said she is not afraid of our lord?"

"Yes, I am."

He stepped inside but his face was still under the hood. Unna offered him cookies made by Nuri. He ate and asked: "Who made the cookies?"

"I made them," she said. Then the man stood up and uncovered his face. Unna instantly dropped the tray, such a beautiful youth he was. She closed her eyes and kissed him on the lips, as if struck with fever. Then one sound slap on her cheek woke her up.

"You shameless woman!" he said. "Come! Our lord sent me to bring you to him. You will receive your punishment directly from him." He took Unna with him on his horse and she leaned her head against his back as they rode off.

"Take me wherever you want! I don't care as long as you are with me."

"Nuri Peperuga," he said and Unna startled at this. "Why do you startle? We are together on this journey but you can't be mine. I only take you to our lord."

They rode like this for a long time; the horse ran and its hooves didn't touch down. Then Unna's music box, which she had tied to her dress with a belt, fell and split in two pieces and the air was filled with an enchanted melody. The horse stopped.

"Why are you crying, Nuri Peperuga?" asked the youth and lifted her chin. "We have arrived. Look around you!"

"This is the place I dreamed so many times when I was little," Unna whispered and wiped her tears off. The soft melody still filled the air, making them silent. "Who are you? And where is this?"

"My name is Alfarr," the young man answered. "When I was a child I used to see a woman in my dreams. She was naked and covered with her long hair. And when she combed it I could see her skin, which smelled and shone like rose petals. Only I couldn't touch her. Each time I had this dream I would tell my mother: 'You were the fairest lady of all to me. Who is she, mother?' And she would tell me: 'She is your bride.' That woman is standing in front of me now. It is you, Nuri Peperuga!"

Unna looked at him and felt the cold tears down her cheeks. "But... what about the lord of the village?" she asked. "Where is he? You said..."

"I am the lord of the village, the one whom everybody fears and nobody dares to speak about. Except you! Now you are the only one who knows my name."

"Yes," she whispered, "Alfarr."

"Do you know what I am?"

"Yes," she said, "I know."

"Are you afraid of me?"

"You should say yes, Unna Ishildur!" They both turned and saw the old storyteller, Unna's grandfather. "Nobody knows about this place, except me!"

"And no ordinary man knows how to arrive here," Alfarr said.

"My granddaughter Unna has got a child to look after. He has been roaming the fields and the villages, asking about her."

"Unna Ishildur," Alfarr said, "you tell me what is the right thing I should do. Wouldn't it be right if I punished you?"

"Do as you please with me, my lord."

"If sharing my fate is a curse, then you will share this with me: hidden from everyone's eyes."

Hildimar looked at Unna and saw that she had changed. And when she looked back at him he felt that she was cold inside. Then Alfarr said: "Let the people see us just one time. I will wrap you in one hundred veils and they won't see your face until we are married."

So they returned with the storyteller into the village and Alfarr let himself be seen for the first time by the people. He passed among them, holding the veiled Unna by his side and his beauty cut everyone's breath. The words "our lord," and "the master of the village" were on everyone's lips.

"Who is the lady? Is she our Unna?" they asked, but couldn't see her face. He passed by the nomads' camp and Nuri Peperuga sprang right in front of him with both children, Unna's child and hers.

"I am the woman who threatened you!" she said. "I am

127

Nuri Peperuga!" Alfarr raised his arm to her but the children yelled and begged him to spare her.

"My new mother, Unna, she was a bad mother and left me!" one of the children said. He wanted to run to her but all of a sudden a shiver of fear froze him on the spot as he looked at her covered face.

The priest of the village told the storyteller to let Alfarr stay with Unna in their house until the following day, when they were to be married in church.

"You must not allow them enter the church, they are two of the hidden!" Hildimar said.

"We must put an end to this insane fear! They will marry in church!" replied the priest.

So Unna and Alfarr remained that day with the grandfather. At dinner they were all gathered at table but Nuri and the children couldn't see Alfarr because he had made himself invisible to them. They were afraid to pass behind Unna when she was turned with her back to them.

"He will change," Hildimar said to his granddaughter, "they all change after marriage. You'll end up breeding and cooking and washing."

The next day at dawn the couple woke up and began to get ready for the wedding. Unna wasn't in a good mood at all and couldn't find her slippers, so she began to curse and to swear at the old man. The storyteller heard her and knocked at their door.

"Is it me that your bride is swearing at?" Alfarr didn't answer, so the old man went straight to Unna and slapped her.

128

She gave him an icy glance.

"I spare you only because you were my grandfather. You won't see me again after this day," she said.

The whole village gathered inside and outside the church to attend the wedding and there were even a lot more people from the neighboring villages. When the ceremony was over and the newly married couple went out of the church, Alfarr lifted the veils from Unna's face and said:

"This is Unna Ishildur, your fairy lady!"

Everyone murmured as they passed by: "Our Unna is the village fairy, she is our fairy!"

They were so young and fair that the people begged them to stay with them, though they were afraid at the same time. The storyteller told the people that Alfarr and Unna had to leave because they didn't belong to this world. On their leave, Unna wanted to take away the nomad child but Hildimar saved him from her arms.

Just like elves — adopt technology half a century late. The Vatican's a hotbed of change compared to elvish society.

Michelle Markey Butler lives and writes in Pittsburgh, PA. She holds a doctorate in English Literature, specializing in medieval drama, and – perhaps ill-advisedly – has four children. She's begun to wonder if years trying to explain to preschoolers why they shouldn't eat gum off the ground have taken a toll on her gray matter. When not contemplating the ethics of having GPS chips embedded in the kiddos' hides, she writes short stories and novels. She blogs about parenting at www.heirraising.wordpress.com and is pleased to report that despite their best efforts none have escaped. Recently.

Her story "LITTLE HANDS" received an Honorable Mention in the Writers of the Future Second Quarter 2010. Her book-in-progress LORD GARLAND'S DAUGHTER received an Honorable Mention in Textnovel's 2010 contest.

Her website is www.michellemarkeybutler.com.

Whelp
Michelle Markey Butler

Five minutes. If he wasn't here in five minutes, I was leaving. But I knew he'd come.

I looked around the bar, remembering why I hated these places. I sipped my drink. He'd be there. Late. Not late enough to risk my leaving, but enough to suggest our relative importance. Three minutes.

I hated him and my other elvish relations almost as much as the bar. Which he knew when he asked for this meeting.

Another glance around the room. Preening men. Simpering women. Other men watching wistfully. Other women watching hopefully. Too-strong scents — alcohol, sweat, perfume — bit my nostrils. Two minutes. I scanned the room again, resisting the urge to rub my stinging nose.

One minute.

Manweard slid into the chair across from me. "Still looking for the perfect bitch?"

Nine hundred years ago, I'd have bitten him. Or tried to, at least. Seven hundred, I'd have snarled. Four hundred, I'd have sworn. Now I eyed him with the faux calm I'd learned in the last few centuries. "Good evening. Peaseblossom."

I was rewarded with a grimace. Wiped away as quickly

as it had appeared but I'd seen it, and he knew I had. "Good to see you."

Liar. But I didn't say it. "What do you want?"

He spread his hands. "Cousin. I have a lead for you."

"So you said. Doesn't answer my question. What do you want for it?"

"Not much." He pulled a photo from his pocket. "It might not pan out." He set it on the table.

I looked. A Polaroid? Where had they even gotten the film? Hadn't the company stopped making it years ago? Just like elves — adopt technology half a century late. The Vatican's a hotbed of change compared to elvish society. At least the picture couldn't be Photoshopped. As if any elf would know how to use a computer.

Against my better judgment, I set down my glass and reached for the photo. This was the sixth time Manweard had come to me with a tip. None had proven true. But I was desperate enough to listen to him. I knew it. So did he.

I studied the picture. Recent. The stench of the developing fluid still clung to it, lancing through the bar's smells to assault my nose until I gave up and rubbed it, my own scent jostling aside the chemical pitch enough to allow me to think about something other than my stinging nostrils. I wouldn't put it past Manweard to have done that on purpose. In fact, I'd have bet on it. The deep south had nothing on elves for race snobbery. Especially miscegenation. They'd never forgiven my father.

I knew better, but as I looked, I hoped. She could be.

132

The photo was small, of course, and seemed to have been taken from a car across the street from where a woman sat at an outdoor coffee shop. She was lifting a cup to her mouth. As she did, her hair, pulled into pigtails and braided at the chin, parted a fraction to reveal an ear. More pointed than it should be, tipped with short soft fuzz a shade lighter than her hair. My other hand slid uncontrollably up under my knit cap to scratch my own triangle-topped ear, the hairs tickling my fingertips.

And — she was not my sister. She could be more, I would have to meet her, but at least she was not Emma.

It was wrong — ill advised, stupid, foolhardy, downright dumb — to let hope uncurl like a spring seed and reach for the sun on so little. But it was more than I'd ever had. The last time Manweard had come to me, he'd brought a manually (and badly) doctored photo of Emma. The deception was cruel; using her image, inhuman. I hadn't seen my sister for more than a century. We avoided one another. The time before that, he had brought me a rumor — an elf had seen a woman in Spain he thought could be like me. It might have been true. Or it might have been another trick. I never found her. But I always came, because the wolf howled a millennium of yearning until I could hear nothing else.

Manweard's hand twitched, as if resisting the urge to make sure his fedora had not slipped. If it did, he'd have a bigger problem than I would. For the last two centuries or so, the elves had taken to wearing their hair banker-short; mine was longer than the woman's in the picture and hung loose under my cap. Given elves' notoriously unchanging culture I'd wondered what had brought this about, but I didn't ask. He wouldn't have told me anyway.

He gave up and touched the fedora, hand flitting back to the table when he found it still in place. Maybe the effect he'd been aiming at was Indiana Jones. What he accomplished was Al Capone.

"What do you want?" I asked.

He smiled, smugness tinged with relief. Had he worried that this time I might refuse? Interesting. I might be able to make that work for me in the future.

I realized then that I was assuming this lead would go nowhere, like the others had. I sipped my drink, holding the liquid in my mouth before I swallowed but the sudden bitter taste was still there.

"Very little," Manweard said.

I waited. I took another sip.

"An item. Something you can obtain with ease, but which would be difficult for us to acquire."

Hmm. He was nervous. His always-formal vocabulary skewed even more lawyer-like when he was nervous. They really were concerned I might say no.

There was silence again, Manweard looking at me with that eerie, unblinking stare that only elves have. I hadn't gotten that. Why didn't I get that? Emma had. The anxiety betrayed by his word choice did not show in his face, almost as creepy as his stare with its wax-like smooth, hairless skin. Looking at him made me want to stroke my beard.

This time I cracked first. I gestured that he should go

on.

His thin smile again, all smugness now.

"Mermaid scales."

I bit back my first response. His smirk deepened. They had kept tabs on me since before William the Bastard cast an appraising glance across the channel, and I was surprised that they knew about Spike's girlfriend? "I won't hurt her."

"You don't have to. They shed them all the time. You just need to collect some."

"How many?"

"A dozen or so."

"What do you want them for?"

He didn't answer. I knew he wouldn't even as the question had leapt out.

"If you're thinking of using them to capture her, or harm her, or anything else nasty, you can stuff it."

He waved a hand. "Nothing will happen to Madison. I swear. We want them for other purposes — important purposes. Which do not involve harm to a hapless," *pathetic*, his pause said, "crippled mermaid."

"I'll ask her," I said. "If she agrees, I'll meet you in two days."

Only an elf could pack so much oily satisfaction into a mere nod.

"Madison?" I knocked on the bathroom door. "Can I come in?"

"Sure, sweetie, I'm decent."

135

I peeked in. Her idea of "decent" was decidedly deep ocean. If some portion of her breasts was covered by her hair, she figured she was good to go. But today she had on a bikini top, green with white polka dots. I stepped into the room.

She eyed me. "You look upset. What's up, sugar?"

I lowered the toilet lid and sat. "Manweard."

"Oh, honey." Her tail pulsed, the large fin at its end coming up out of the water, flinging droplets. "I'm sorry."

For spraying me, or for my meeting with Manweard? I couldn't tell.

"What did he want this time?"

I didn't answer, looking instead at her fin, split and frayed in the middle; there was a corresponding gash, fading to a gray-green scar, about a foot long on the other side of her tail. She'd been hit by a boat propeller ("They always think it's a manatee. Sometimes it's not.") about six months ago. That was how she'd met Spike. He'd been fishing and found her after the accident, bleeding, unable to swim. He goes fishing a lot. Actually, all of his hobbies involve poles. I get this, Madison gets this, Spike doesn't. He's a vampire, impotent like all vampires, bit when he was nineteen and stuck now perpetually unsatisfied. Oh, yeah, I get it.

Yes, I know the press about vampires. Overcompensation, anyone? Perhaps some abject lying? With a little humiliation on the side? Anyway, who's surprised here? Vampires aren't alive, have no beating heart, no blood pressure — hence no erections. It's just physiological. It's also how I met Spike, at the gym, both of us trying to work off a little — well, a lot of —

sexual frustration on some unsuspecting free weights. It took about three minutes to realize that neither of us was actually human and about three months to figure out our mutual freakhood was companionable. So now we're house-mates, in a continual misery-fest pissing match as to whose love life sucks more. With the recent addition of a mermaid who can't swim fitting nicely into our screwball household. Even more recently, she and Spike began dating. Or some-thing. I refuse to think about the possibilities, or lack thereof, of a romance in which neither party has operational genitals.

Except it means that at the moment, my love life is certainly worse than Spike's. Because their relationship, what-ever it is, seems to be working. They have a lot in common. Naming themselves after film characters, for instance — Madison, from *Splash*, and Spike, from someone in *Buffy the Vampire Slayer*. Which suggests they both have masochistic streaks as well as too much screen time.

Madison sniffed. "Taunting you again, wasn't he?"

I shrugged. "He said he had a tip for me."

"Oh, sugar, I have a tip for you." The damaged fin quivered but did not splash again. "He's a bastard. He's not going to help you."

"He brought a picture."

She made a disgusted noise. "Fake? Again?"

"Looked real." My hands gripped one another. I resis-ted the urge to clamp them between my knees.

She tsked. "Honey, I'm sorry. I know you want this real bad. But you're better off looking on your own. Elves don't help anyone but themselves."

"He offered me the address."

Her eyebrows rose. The green undertone was noticeable only if you looked closely. I expect for most people, the giant tail taking the place of everything from the waist down would tend to overwhelm slightly odd-color brows. I'd lived with her long enough now that the tail was second nature, but the weirdness of faintly green eyebrows... I was still working on that. Of course, as far as weirdness went, who was I to throw stones? Or splash.

"That's new," she admitted.

"I know."

"What does he want?"

I looked down at my hands. Should I ask her? Manweard's promise that no harm was intended to her wasn't worth the spit on his tongue when he'd said it.

The blood beat in my ears and the wolf bayed. I asked. But I still didn't look at her. "Mermaid scales."

"Ah."

"Do you know what they would use them for?" I heard guilty desperation in my voice but she gave no sign that she did.

"Usually... healing." Her lips pursed as she considered, head tipped back against the tub. "Hmm... there's always a danger, when someone has a thing that used to be part of your body, that they could use it against you, to call upon the connection that can never be entirely broken." Her gaze darted unseeing from corner to corner. Her voice had shifted, sounding like one of the mile-deep people again, so old they made the elves look like children. "But I've never heard of elves endangering a mermaid. I do remember a few times when mermaids were captured to snatch a few scales. Nothing deadly." Her chin came down. "Some elf's hurt. Badly. Mermaid scales are part of their strongest healing magic." She shrugged, as if answering my unspoken question. *Why? I don't know. It just is.*

Her eyes met mine. The old ocean dweller was gone. "Oh, hon, I'm sorry."

I clamped my teeth, staring at my hands. It was her right to refuse. I would not argue with her.

A wet finger touched my shoulder. "Here, sweetie."

I looked up.

She took my hand with one of hers and emptied her other into it, closing my fingers around the smooth-sided, prickly-edged scales.

"I thought — " my voice faltered and stopped.

"I'm sorry they keep using you to do their dirty work. And breaking your heart." She patted my closed hand. "It's going to happen again, sugar. You know that."

"Madison." I paused, regaining control from a surge of sloppy affection for her, a mermaid speedboated like a manatee and who talked like a Mississippi waitress. "Thank you."

Three days later, I wandered the streets, not ready to go home. Madison had been right. Manweard had given me an address — of a woman who spent all her vacation days at

ComicCons, dressed up like a Vulcan. What had appeared to be tell-tale fuzz at the tips of her pointed ears turned out to be sunlight glinting off the plastic faux-skin, creating an odd aura in the Polaroid.

Damn.

The disappointment was bad enough. Sooner or later I would have to go home and tell Spike and Madison I'd been suckered by my elvish relations again.

I realized then, as I should have centuries before, that even if they knew of other elfwolves beside me and Emma, the elves would never direct me to them. Their hatred of half-breeds was too visceral to help us procreate. How much the self-deluding fool was I, to have known my cousin Manweard and not seen this sooner?

And — there were none to find. I'd searched, for a thousand years I'd searched. Emma had searched. If any more of us existed, we would have found them.

So I walked, as if these things were not true if I kept moving.

Afternoon stretched and yawned, and drawing itself back, settled into evening. Evening whiled itself away into night. Streetlights flared into life. Night grew old. And I walked.

I paused at a corner, waiting for the light to change. But when it did, I froze, not daring to cross.

Emma was on the other side, standing like she was waiting for the bus. I knew better. Her gaze had been on me before I'd seen her. Breathing deep, I could catch a glimmer of her scent, a trickle of aroma beneath the car exhaust, the billowing reek from the manholes, the greasy stench of fries and nuggets.

She slowly raised a hand and blew me a kiss. Then she was gone.

How much longer would we be able to stay away from one another, with the wolf baying for a mate? Humans — and elves — have consanguinity taboos. Wolves do not.

A minute later I heard a howl. My head fell back as I joined her.

He tasted like mushrooms and warm honey.
And worms.

Sarah Lyn Eaton was born in Niagara Falls, grew up on the Erie Canal and currently lives at the confluence of two rivers. She is a playwright and creative writer whose works are inspired by mythology, modern fairy tales and the magick of the natural world around her. Sarah Lyn hosts a weekly on-line blog, Walking with Ancestors (walkingwith ancestors.blogspot.com), featuring information on Ancestor Worship.

Sarah says, "Normally I begin writing when an imagined scene or an emotional conflict inspires me. I work from that moment, moving backwards and forwards chrono-logically, revealing the layers of the story as I go, like an archaeologist. This story was different, because it popped into my head fully formed, much like Athena bursting from Zeus' cranium in full womanhood. I knew from the beginning that this story was meant to be done as a comic script, and it was an interesting exercise in whittling paragraphs down into tighter sentences. Considering that this was my first writing collaboration, I was lucky to be working with some-one as talented as Duncan Eagleson, who expertly captured my words into a piece of visual art; he made the condensing painless.

"When Duncan and I discussed turning one of my scripts into a comic story, I started thinking about what kind of a story I had to tell. The story was inspired by my belief that magick exists in the world, and that touching true magick, even for just a moment, can elicit a change in how we

see the world around us. I like telling stories that involve the awakening of this change in people. What I know of Elves is the mythology that binds them in the World of Faerie, an old world with rules and deep magick our culture is mostly removed from. When touched by magick, nothing can remain the same. I started thinking about Elves and how I've never met one. I wondered what would happen if a modern girl were to meet an old world elf. How would the worlds collide? And what if the meeting was nothing more than a moment of convergence? What awakening would that touch of magick bear in someone? And would they be open to it?"

Duncan Eagleson has been published as an illustrator more often than as a writer, having done a number of book covers, movie posters, and magazine illustrations, as well as an issue of Neil Gaiman's SANDMAN. He has written a number of comics and graphic novels, including Millennium/Comico's graphic novel adaptation of Anne Rice's THE WITCHING HOUR, the online series ARCMAGE and RAILWALKER: TALES OF THE URBAN SHAMAN and the short story "Harkinton" for Bob Heske's anthology 2012: FINAL PRAYER.

In the 1990s, he began making leather masks, and in 1995, was voted Best of Show by the other maskmakers at the Mardi Gras Mask Market show in New Orleans. He has made masks for Wes Craven's CURSED, the Big Apple Circus, and mask magician Jeff McBride.

...AND **PAIN** FILLED MY WORLD FOR A **SECOND TIME**.

BACK IN MY APARTMENT, I FENDED OFF NAUSEA.

AGAIN.

WHAT DO I DO WITH **THIS?**

WHERE I HAD HELD AN **ELVEN RING**,

THERE WAS NOW A STRANGE **SEED**.

IT **HUMMED** AGAINST MY SKIN.

I GAZED AT THE SAME **MOON** THAT HAD BROUGHT MY **NANA** SO MUCH **MAGIC**...

WHAT I WAS THINKING WAS **FOOLISH**.

BUT I FELT **COMPELLED** ALL THE SAME.

EVERYTHING DESERVES A **SECOND CHANCE**

THE HANDS OF A DAUGHTER OF **MARZENA** HAD PLANTED AN ANCIENT **SEED** OF **HOPE** IN THE EARTH,

ON A NIGHT WHEN MY FEET HAD STOOD ON THE SOIL OF MY **FAMILY** AND THE SOIL OF MY **ANCESTORS**, HALF A WORLD AWAY.

THAT HAD TO HAVE A LITTLE **MAGIC** IN IT, DIDN'T IT?

I still dreamed of the burning metal which had carved a river of blood in my flesh, slashing tendon and chipping bone.

Michael Takeda is an American writer fascinated with all things Japanese, particularly robots.

Of all the stories we received, "Xenium" generated one of the more interesting discussions among the editors. As to the origins of this story, Michael says, "I had this idea floating in my mind for a while: a story that explored language and gender, how the two affect one another. Some linguists have theorized that language can affect not only how we perceive the world, but also how we perceive ourselves. I started with a 'What if..?' question and ended up with 'Xenium.'"

And the odd title? "'Xenium' is a word I came across recently. It means a gift for an ambassador, which made it fitting for the story. It was one of those things that came along at an opportune moment and begged 'use me.'"

"'Xenium' wasn't an easy story to write, for reasons which will probably become obvious to the reader at some point in the story."

Michael is currently at work on a post-apocalyptic novel involving famous poets resurrected in the late 21st century as – what else? – robots.

Xenium
Michael Takeda

In Cardominia, they say many things about my homeland. An arctic wasteland devoid of light, where the kingdoms
are made of ice, and where the people are pale and silvery like
snow foxes, able to change their skins at will. They call us
devils and perhaps there is the truth in those words.

Cardominia: The Immortal City. City of shadows and
mirrors. City of whores.

My arrival at the Immortal City was greeted by ink
birds whose queer laments mimicked the laughter of children.
Cloud-thick flocks threaded through the jutting spires of the
palace, dropping oily feathers in the wake of their invisible
tapestry, returning to nest as daylight waned. The nests were
shallow oval bowls, intricately woven with stolen scraps of
yarn, twigs of beech, and long stalks of yellow grass, suspended
in the branches of the trees that lined the uphill road of the
open market in the heart of the city. They were precious, these
bowls constructed by the dargum birds. Within the vulgar
flotsam they wove tiny flowers plucked from the highest crags
of the white mountains, inaccessible to all but the dargum.
Only during the conjunction of the two moons could the bowls
be cultivated by the pristine white-gloved hands of children.
The resulting rare brew of bird's nest tea was a powerful

aphrodisiac that prolonged the imbiber's life.

Such was the nonsense believed by the inhabitants of Cardominia.

As we moved like ghosts through the patterned streets under the wafting feather rain towards the palace, my Quirtal guide turned and followed my gaze to the vermillion branches of the trees. It had been difficult finding a guide fluent in both Cardominian and Verhallian, yet a relief to discover that my guide was not the loquacious sort. Only later did I comprehend that the halfbreed's silence was due to lack of linguistic skill. The Quirtal did indeed speak both languages, but poorly.

Among the branches, brightly colored scraps of paper dangled, creating an effect of festive gaiety. Although I had encountered the dargum nests in my studies, I had found no mention of this particular custom. I gestured at the paper leaves waving in the breeze. "What purpose have they?"

"*Cozen* write prayer. Celebrate the Saban. The Saban thousand year."

After near five decades of travel, I had learned to interpret the Quirtal's peculiar mangling of my native tongue. *Cozen* – a Quirtal word, which meant unholy, venerable, ancestor and master, all in one. The Cardominians were always *cozen*. And their ruler, the Saban – if I were to believe the deceptive halfbreed – was a thousand years old.

For the Quirtal, the Verhallians were also *cozen*.

I adjusted the collar of my robe with my good hand. "The Saban? What know you of the Saban?"

Wrapped bodily in thin silk, only the Quirtal's eyes

were visible, two dark caverns in a patch of sand-colored skin. Confusion flashed in them before the Quirtal spoke again, this time with uncertainty. "Saban *cozen.*"

The snow fox fur collar prickled against my neck. Adjusting it again, I stifled the urge to cuff the creature. The halfbreed had done no wrong, but the unrelenting heat made me irritable and my temper short. In truth, I would learn all I needed to know about the Saban as soon as we reached the palace.

"Never mind," I muttered. "Lead on."

Beyond the gate of bleached bone the crystalline turrets of the palace sliced the deepening sky. At the gate I was expected, and relieved of my guide. Without a word, the guards – if that is what they were – collected my baggage and ushered me inside.

I was blinded by an explosion of green in the courtyard, the musky rust of ripened fruit under the relentless sun, trees alive with the twitter of small brightly-hued birds. Among the shadows, small feline creatures prowled, unfurling long tails as we passed. In the distance, the trickle of harp-string water plucked the stones.

The courtyard – like Cardominia itself – blazed and dazzled the senses with a cacophony of colors, scents, and sounds. Even the shadows seemed bursting with life. It was chaos.

A shaded path led through another gate into the palace proper. Corridors twisted, lit with burning oil, smoky and pungent, in suspended shells. Light through windows of colored glass checkered the stone floor worn smooth by centuries of scuffling feet. Cleverly rendered flowered vines uncoiled across the walls, sheltering a menagerie of painted birds. As we turned a corner, blue flowers became crimson, then white.

In the hall of white flowers, I was brought to a cool and opulent room. Bowing, the guards retreated. I barely had time to recognize the Cardominian version of a bed, a wardrobe, and a desk before a bevy of servants swooped to attend.

I assumed they were servants. They may have been slaves. Unlike in Verhall, Cardominian society was based on caste, from royal court down to the slaves. Even worse, unlike the Verhallians, the Cardominians believed that gender determined fate. On such an inconsequential detail as this were half the people of Cardominia subjugated due to the misfortune of being born the wrong sex. And of those, the most infamous were the hakami – pitiful creatures who lived cloistered, whose only purpose was to provide sexual pleasure to the court.

On such an inconsequential detail would Cardominia be destroyed.

Oblivious to their fate, the servants made their offerings of comfort: water for washing, clothing of silk, golden platters of food, and pitchers of drink. Elegant hands danced, weaving conversations in air. To each, I refused politely, but for the drink. A painted goblet offered, with wine fruity, crisp, and pale, shockingly cold against my teeth. Hands covered

156

amused smiles. Until now, I had never seen a Cardominian up close, and I contemplated them as openly as they did me. The last Verhallian to reach the city had come over two hundred Turnings ago. I would be the first Verhallian they had seen. Unless there was truth in the rumor that Cardominians were immortal.

I had barely finished the wine when another silk-clad servant appeared, with a request in my tongue to follow for an audience with the Saban.

A waiting hand took the goblet, another my hat. Smoothing back my hair, I went to fulfill my duty: to speak with, to observe, and to judge the Saban.

Sheets of pale citrine glass filtered the light in the throne room. Water from an unseen source bubbled up below a dais. Beyond the dais, upon a throne seemingly cut from a solid block of rose quartz veined with crimson, sat the Saban.

The Saban was similar to the other Cardominians I had seen. Layered silk draped long, delicate limbs. Skin the color of sun-kissed amber. Gossamer strands of ebon hair floated unfettered about a comely, finely-boned face, but for two thin braids woven with ribbons and pearls tucked behind each long, delicately pointed ear. The only difference was that the Saban's slanting eyes, dark as night, were imbued with cobwebs of ancient intrigue.

At my approach, the Saban raised one thin hand so heavily laden with gold rings that it seemed an effort. This gesture of peace was accompanied by a benevolent greeting. "I welcome you, serah, to the city of Cardominia."

I could scarcely contain my surprise. "The Saban speaks Verhallian?"

A smile played upon the gold-dusted lips. "It amused Ser Nika to teach me. Like you, serah, Ser Nika came as an ambassador from your lands. Though that was many Turnings ago." The Saban paused. "I don't suppose that you, serah, speak our language?"

Verhallian flowed easily past the ruler's lips, and the usage of the honorific suggested great knowledge of my culture. Impossible to believe, however, that Nika – the last Verhallian to visit the city so many Turnings ago – had taught the Saban personally. Yet I, too, using the writings of Ser Nika, knew much of Cardominian culture, and responded in a befitting manner. "I claim no mastery in Cardominian, Saban."

The Saban made a small, fluttery gesture. "It is of no importance. It is rare that we have the opportunity to practice our Verhallian." The Saban indicated the advisers flanking the throne, each garbed in elaborate robes of plum and white. "Counselor Cadhla and Counselor Ailin are both familiar with your tongue, and are at your disposal."

"The Saban is too kind."

The one named Ailin spoke in a Verhallian no less eloquent than the ruler's own. "No doubt you are tired from your long journey, ambassador. We have no wish to tire you further, however we have two questions."

I nodded.

"The letter was unclear about your intentions, ambassador. In order to arrange the appropriate entertainments, we wish to know the length of your stay."

"I will only impose on the hospitality of the Saban for a decad."

Ailin spoke with surprise. "Only a decad? It seems little time after such a journey."

"I must return before the season turns," I said, and it was true, for winter travel through my homeland was – at best – a dangerous affair. Unfortunately, reaching Cardominia had taken longer than anticipated. But then, I couldn't have anticipated the difficulty of traversing the desert. The ubiquitous sand had ground the gears of the carriage into dust, and we had continued on beast, abandoning the empty metal hull to the elements.

Cadhla spoke in turn. "We know our ways are different than your own, ambassador. But if there is some need you have, or some desire you wish fulfilled, as our guest we will do all we can to honor your requests." Cadhla drew breath. "Is there anything you desire, serah?"

"Yes, Counselor," I said. "I wish to see the hakarum."

I had asked the impossible. Only the Saban's inner court were permitted into the private sanctum of the hakami. To all others, it was forbidden. Cadhla startled.

The Saban, however, raised that heavy, golden hand. "Cadhla – please escort the ambassador to the hakarum."

In that infamous collection of writings, Nika had often remarked on the "uncontrolled decadence and harmony" of

Cardominian architecture. Seeing the pillars in the hakarum recalled this phrase to mind. Decorative rather than functional, a dozen imposing towers encircled with intricate diaglyphs extended from polished floor to distant ceiling. Lithe figures seemed at the point of drawing breath, life-like in every detail excepting their monstrous genitalia. From some, arm-length phalluses sprung, straining up against the pull of gravity, while others bore swollen, gaping clefts, equally exaggerated. Briefly I wondered what it must be like for the hakami to live among these images which served as a poignant reminder to the purpose of their existence. It seemed cruel.

Yet the expressions of those figures were so serene that I could not easily dismiss them. Grotesque, yes, but beautifully wrought, and this beauty was reflected in every detail of the hakarum, creating a harmonious whole.

Besides the pillars, there were pools painted blue, and silken cushions arranged artfully under the shade of glossy-leaved trees. A soft breeze redolent with the sweet scent of fruit brought relief from the heat. In this idyllic setting lived the hakami.

Our entrance unnoticed, I glimpsed the assemblage in an unguarded moment. At least I believed it unguarded – upon leaving the throne room, Counselor Cadhla had led me here directly. It seemed unlikely that such a scene could have been created in such little time solely for my benefit.

The hakami were dressed in diaphanous silks skillfully constructed to reveal and hide their golden skin with every languid movement. Their hair was long, black and glistening like the dargum feathers which rained in the streets, either oiled and loose or else coiled up like confections. Each obsidian-eyed face was unblemished perfection. In truth, despite the differences between our races, they were not so dissimilar from the beautiful youths often seen in the gathering atriums of Verhall.

After a moment, the hakami became aware of our presence. They regarded me curiously. Then each of them, having completed their silent assessment, returned to their activities: bathing in a pool, lounging in the shade, conversing, or reading.

Surprised by the last, I turned to Cadhla. "You educate the hakami?"

"Of course."

I had not expected that slaves would be taught to read. "Why?"

"An uneducated life is not worth living," Cadhla said, then added, "It is also a pleasant way to pass the time. The hakami have few obligations. Most of their time is spent here. Reading is one way they amuse themselves. They like stories." Cadhla smiled. "The hakam in the Saban's favor at the moment also writes stories. They are very entertaining."

I wondered what sort of stories a slave could write. "Does this hakam have a name?"

"Cricket."

"And the others?"

Cadhla gestured around the room, naming the hakami. All of them had strange, absurd little names more suited to pets than to people: Lake, River, Butterfly, Grasshopper, Oriel, Nightingale, Sparrow, Moonbeam, and Starlight. The Saban's favorite – the storyteller – was not present.

Casting about, my eye fell on a pair of hakami, deeply involved over a board littered with small, iridescent pebbles. "What are they doing?"

"Ah. They are playing Stones. A simple game to learn, but it requires much strategy."

For a moment I observed as the pieces were moved in what seemed a random manner. Pebbles and fingers danced across the board, exchanging places: dark stones for light, light for dark. Intrigued, I agreed to Cadhla's offer to teach me the game.

Without lifting their gazes, the hakami watched us. I felt like an intruder. Yet I lingered. "Where do they sleep?"

"They have private rooms for sleeping."

The counselor offered to show me. Thus we walked through the grotesque pillars, the shaded recesses, the blooming vines, to where the hakami slept.

We reached a threshold. Before us was an alcove, small but curtained with embroidered silk, a sumptuous bed and other furnishings. The room was occupied. The hakam's back – half-exposed, slender, straight – was to us. A cascade of ebon hair was twisted in the golden hand, the nails painted with a purple lacquer so dark it appeared black. In the mirror of the vanity, our eyes met.

My heart ceased to beat.

I had never seen a creature more exquisite. Darkly

lashed black eyes drew me in, and yet, at the same time, pinned me where I stood. Beside me Cadhla spoke, but I could not comprehend the soft guttural sounds, lost as I was in those twin pools of night.

The hand twitched. The hair fell. And yet, the thread of our gazes – tangible, tenuous – remained entangled. I could sense the counselor's discomfort, but I was unable to tear my eyes from the mirror. I was captured, captivated and crushed by the gaze of the hakam.

Cadhla barked a brittle-sharp command. The hakam turned with a demure reply. Liberated, I could breathe again. Stiffly adjusting my collar, I looked at Cadhla. "Do any of the hakam speak Verhallian?"

"Not to my knowledge, no. If you wish to speak to one of the hakam, Ailin or myself could translate for you."

"Your offer is kind. I would like to speak to this one."

Cadhla startled again. Curious. Somewhat flushed, the counselor stammered, "Well... we... I would need permission from the Saban."

"Permission? Why?"

"Because of this hakam's status." Seeing that I did not understand, Cadhla added, "This is Cricket. The favored hakam of the Saban."

Each night I was presented with a plethora of delights.

In the theater hall the denizens of the palace gathered. Each night there was an abundance of food and wine, though no dish appeared twice. Each night, at the chime of the tower clock the lights dimmed as the entertainments began. And each night I was given the honor of sitting at the Saban's right hand, which afforded the opportunity to converse.

On the third night, the entertainments included a stage play with elaborate mechanical toys in place of living actors, another with shadow puppets, followed by an ensemble of exotic instruments cut from gourds and strung with gut. On the previous nights, there had been other music, other plays, a magic show, and – of particular interest – a group of chytik singers who sing not with words, but make a humming sound deep in the throat, a different note performed by each voice.

In the lull between performances, the Saban turned to me. "Does it not please you, serah?"

A familiar question. I had sat through all of the royal delights unmoved. That these delights were strange and beautiful was of no import. I would not be seduced from my mission. However, my attempts to sway the Saban to the proper mode of thinking had borne no fruit. The Cardominians were resistant to change, and on the subject of slavery, we were at an impasse. Discouraged, my response, though polite, was cold. "We have such entertainments in Verhall, only not quite so excessive."

Ancient eyes dissected me as neatly as the magician's assistant had been last night by the magic box, as a cupbearer replenished the jeweled goblet in the Saban's hand. "Tell me of Verhall."

The demand caught me off guard. "Certainly Ser Nika told you of Verhall."

"Have things not changed?"

In two hundred Turnings, progress had marched Verhall forward, and made us powerful. Whisperings of our strength had scattered across the world by the same method as my letter had arrived, carried by half-blood nomad tribes. "What do you wish to know?"

"I would like to see this ice kingdom of yours. Describe it to me."

I mulled over this request. To put it in terms that the Saban could understand would be like explaining daylight to someone who had spent their life in the dark. There were two seasons in Verhall, and thus two visions. In winter, from a distance, Verhall was a jagged rock of stars. In summer, it appeared white as the landscape surrounding it. Not because the city was made of ice, but because it was constructed mainly of pale stone and glass. Yet there was color within the white. The light refracted from the icy mountains and from deep within the Mare Maica glacier danced like prismatic ghosts against the expanse of blue sky. To the East rose the Dinti Balu – a large outcropping of black lava rock whose name meant Dragon's Teeth. To a Cardominian, I imagined that such a place would be bleak. "It is cold, Saban. Always covered in snow. Little grows."

To this the Saban expressed curiosity about the means of our survival. I spoke of ancient times. How once, small-tribed, my ancestors survived by fishing through the ice, diets supplemented with meat from beasts and what sparse vegetation could be scavenged, mostly edible grasses, berries, and bark. Now many foodstuffs were grown inside special houses heated – as were dwellings – by machines powered with steam.

The Saban asked many questions about our machines. I dissembled by claiming no expertise on their function, such were their complexity. Some, I said, were powered by steam, others by clockwork mechanisms, similar to those in the play we had just seen.

The Saban sat, still as a portrait but for one amber finger tracing the rim of the goblet. "And you use these machines for war?"

My hesitation was perhaps too telling, my reply too glib. "We have war machines, yes."

"And your people would bring their war machines here, ambassador?"

The Saban's eyes were as black and cold as the Dinti Balu on a winter's night, and despite the heat, I shivered.

I had been trained how to answer questions such as these. "I doubt that they could traverse the desert," I replied diplomatically, and recounted my tribulations with the carriage.

To say that my words put the Saban at ease would be misleading. Yet there was an imperceptible shift in the ruler's composure. "I would have liked to see this carriage," the Saban decided and then spoke no more, as the lights had dimmed again.

After the dance, the Saban returned to our earlier conversation. "Tell me, serah, of your people. I have seen few. Do they all look like you?"

I smiled at the innocent sound of the question. "Some are thinner or fatter, shorter or taller, but yes. More or less."

"Taller?" The Saban seemed amused. "To us, *you* are rather tall, serah. Tell me, do you have family?"

I had no siblings to speak of, so to satisfy the Saban's curiosity, I spoke of my parents: their names, their occupations, their pastimes. When I finished, the Saban brooded quietly for a spell.

I was concerned that I had unintentionally disrupted protocol and offended my host. "You look thoughtful, Saban."

The ruler's expression lightened, dispelling my concern. "Yes. I was thinking that I find your language very strange," the Saban admitted. "Is it true that you have no words for *mathair* or *pathair?* I presume you are familiar with these words?"

Indeed, I found Cardominian very odd for the fact that they employed unique words meant to distinguish one parent's gender from the other's. All Verhallians were equal – there was no need to make distinctions. I told the Saban so.

"You have no distinctions at all between the sexes?"

"There are words, Saban – male and female – but they are used only three times at most, and only for record-keeping. For each individual, they are recorded once at birth, once at death, and usually once more when choosing a permanent mate. But they are not used otherwise."

Speaking aloud those clinical-sounding words – male and female – left a repulsive taste in my mouth. Verhallian is a much simpler language, and far less convoluted than Cardominian. To refer to someone of either sex in the third

167

person, there is only one word, *erah*. A different form of it, *serah*, could be used as a polite 'you.' In Cardominian, not only the pronouns but also all other forms of speech indicated the gender of the subject.

A famous Verhallian writer had once remarked that language could either shape reality or become a prison.

Which was doubly the case in Cardominia.

"I see, serah," said the Saban, looking thoughtful again. "Do *you* have a mate?"

I plucked at my robe's collar to keep from touching the visible tips of the scars that had stolen that possibility from me many Turnings ago, and smiled politely. "No, Saban, I do not."

It had a curious effect on me, that question of the Saban's. In the days which dripped by like icicle drops at the season's turn, I would catch my reflection in a multitude of mirrors and not avert my eyes as I had before. In Verhall, we do not tolerate imperfection. Before my journey, I had imagined that the Cardominians, worshipers of beauty, would also be repulsed by my deformity, yet this was not the case. Only later from Cadhla did I learn that the Cardominians fancied the scar jagging down my face a deliberate mark like a tribal tattoo.

Ten Turnings had passed since the accident in the workshop. I still dreamed of the burning metal which had carved a river of blood in my flesh, slashing tendon and chipping bone. Left with only partial use of my right hand, I had abandoned my childhood dream of becoming Grand

Mechanist. Disfigured by hideous scars, I had fled to the isolated safety of the library. It was there I had built a new path, cobbled by knowledge.

As the Saban's honored guest, my every whim was fulfilled but one. My request to speak to the hakam called Cricket had been refused, a vague excuse proffered. Nor had I spied the storyteller again, despite the time I frittered away in the hakarum. My days were my own, and I was free to do as I pleased. Usually I took on Cadhla or Ailin as guide to explore the city, or as interpreter when I questioned the hakami. Although I knew Cardominian well enough to have no need of them, feigning ignorance was part of the obligatory charade – such is the task of the spy. Ailin was of nervous disposition and tight-lipped, so I preferred the company of Cadhla, who had taught me to play Stones, which I considered an agreeable way to pass an afternoon.

One afternoon, however, I found myself wandering the labyrinthine halls of the palace and, following a trail of purple-flowered vines, turned down a corridor previously unexplored, and came upon a garden.

From my studies, I had learned that most religions possessed a primal garden. In our mythos, the Primal Garden was the seat of creation of the First One – a perfect being, without gender. Having tasted of the forbidden fruit, the Gods punished the First One by dividing it into two beings, each a different sex, and casting them into an icy abyss. It had been prophesied long ago that only once our people had attained our original perfection would the gates of the fruitful garden

169

unlock again.

The scene before me evoked this image. Sun splashed down into the heady efflorescence, all tasted of green, while leaping koi rippled the center pool. Beside the pool, trailing long fingers languidly through the water, lay a heart-fluttering vision. Long black hair spiraled over the grass. The silken robes had slipped, revealing a tantalizing amount of perfect golden skin that stirred my blood.

I lurched forward, a ravenous beast ready to pounce on such tender prey.

As if sensing the danger, the hakam leaped like a gazelle, both hands gathering the silken robes to cover flesh, and fled.

I gave chase. I did not know what my intentions were, I only knew that this hakam had been purposefully concealed from me. I suspected that I had stumbled upon a secret to which Cricket was the key.

I pursued the hakam through several twists in the corridors. I raced down a turn, then another turn, and then around a third I pulled up short.

The corridors branched off in a myriad of directions like the spokes of a wheel. I stood in the center of the hub. Cricket had disappeared.

The pondering of my predicament was interrupted as voices floated down from a different hall.

I glimpsed three figures in plum and white. Instinctively I retreated back to the edge of the hub to better conceal myself and listened.

They spoke in hushed Cardominian. Two voices I recognized. A cautious glance confirmed that the counselors were huddled in a circle, whispering to the Vizier of the Saban.

A voice floated down the hall. Ailin. "– would resolve our problem."

The Vizier, cool and calculating. "– you propose we accomplish –"

There were unintelligible mutterings for some time. I strained to catch the words. "– always poison."

Cadhla's voice was an audible hiss. "You fool! Do you think that the ice devils will not send their war machines against us if their ambassador does not return?"

I barely heard the arguments which followed. I must admit that their talk of treachery chilled my blood. I sank back against the wall, my thoughts spinning without arriving anywhere, like a carriage wheel in the sand. The voices continued, as though each were a chytik singer, holding one single tone: Ailin angry, the Vizier calculating, Cadhla defen-sive, then, eventually, resigned.

There was irony in this. I had been thinking it a rash impulse to flee the palace when Cadhla's resistance broke. Cadhla, who had smiled apologetically when winning at Stones in those long afternoons in my chambers. The barb of betrayal jabbed deep.

I leaned in to better listen to their plotting and noticed that I was not alone in the hall.

At the corner of another branch of the hub, hidden as I was, crouched the hakam. I did not know how my earlier prey had eluded me. Perhaps the hakam had circled around the hub by means of some secret passage. Nor did I know how long the hakam had stood there, watching me eavesdrop on the nefarious triad.

If each of us were to have reached out an arm, our fingers would have touched. And yet, were I to cross the space between us, I would expose myself to the intriguists mere paces down the hall.

Cricket shifted, lifting a hand and filtering it through the gossamer strands of hair, a flash of gold against black. Dark eyes stabbed me into a thrall. Then, the hakam's gaze swung towards the others before returning to me with a conspiratorial look that spoke a thousand words.

A sudden noise, a sharp metallic clang like a dropped platter, startled us both. The mutterings ceased. Into the silence the surge of the tread of footfalls approaching. And each of us – the plotters, the Verhallian and the whore – turned in a different direction and, like fresh snow below the gust of the Northern wind, scattered.

The days were spiders, creeping stealthily past, the nights the same, unrestrained farrago of color, chaos and ephemeral delights. On this night, the octad of my visit, the delights were even more so, a goodwill gesture to the other honored guests from the East, a delegation of Yintara of whom I knew little beyond that they were of close blood-relate to the Cardominians, and who specialized in trade. I was too distracted to care about the Yintara. At the right hand of the

Saban, I brooded.

It was not long before the Saban perceived my mood. "Why such a lugubrious expression, serah?"

In the days since I had overheard the advisers in the hall, I had slept poorly, though it was meager consequence of my decision to remain. A foolish risk, perhaps, but I refused to succumb to cowardice. Still, with each sip of wine and each morsel of sustenance that passed my lips, through my head flitted the ghastly notion that it could be my last, and that I would expire, gasping on the floor, as my insides liquified. And yet, there had been no attempt on my life. The only possible explanation I could find was that Cricket – having the Saban's ear – was somehow responsible for my safety.

Despite this, the cause of my brooding was another: the hakami. "I admit... they seem happy."

No cloud crossed the Saban's face. "You speak as if you disapprove of happiness."

During sleepless nights, I had asked myself which was better: Happiness in slavery? Or misery in freedom? Yet the answer was irrelevant. To press the import of the matter, I spoke too freely. "I implore you, Saban. You must change your ways or Verhall will destroy you."

To my pronouncement, there was only the barest of flickers. The response, when it came, bore the usual in-souciance I had come to expect from the Saban. "Tell me, ambassador. If the roles were reversed, if an invader came to your homeland and demanded that you change your ways, would your people capitulate?"

I gave the Saban's question my utmost consideration. "No, we would fight for what is right."

"And how do you define what is right?"

"We know what it is, that is all."

"Why? Are you perhaps closer to the gods than other beings? Have they shared some secrets with your people?"

I paused again to consider. "The gods have nothing to do with it."

The Saban's smile was condescending. "Do you not see, ambassador? Are you not a god, the chosen one sent to judge – and with that judgment, control the fate of an entire people?"

This time, I found I had no answer.

Chimes and mellifluous trills conflated, wafting butter-fly light through the air, as drum skins skimmed my bones, announcing the next delight. Yet, when the Saban descended upon me me like a liquid serpent, I was rapt. The words of the Saban echoed intimately in my ear. "Burdened are the shoulders that bear a mantle so heavy."

A strange, melancholy understanding passed between us as I felt the stifling weight of the Saban's words and the world on my shoulders. Ever desperate, I pressed. "I cannot believe, Saban, that you could be so indifferent to the fate of your people that you would not lie to save them."

The music swelled, but my gaze remained fixed on the Saban. I waited, hopeful. In the midnight eyes of the Saban, a dangerous scintilla blossomed. "And I cannot believe that you wear your mantle with ease. Tell me, serah, could *you* destroy a thing of such beauty?"

With my gaze I followed the Saban's indicating fingers to where the clan of the Yintara clustered, encircled by lightly-stepping hakami. The dancing hakami were clouded in layers of the finest silks, jingling with chains and bells, their faces adorned with silver dust and paint. And, in the center, I spied Cricket, feeding bits of fruit to the Yintara leader, golden hand dripping juice. As I watched, the Yintara seized Cricket by the wrist to draw the golden hand closer, and licked the sticky fingers.

Something violent slithered, hissing and clawing, deep within my soul. My heart hammered painfully in my chest. My skin grew cold. My insides twisted, and I wondered if perhaps the advisers had not poisoned me after all.

I could breathe again only once the music died and the hakami whirled out of sight, as though spirited away on the fading notes of the flutes. I met the Saban's gaze.

Indifferent, polite, the Saban repeated the usual inquiry. "Did the entertainments not please you this evening, serah?"

I could barely dredge up my reply, much less the courtesy required. "Not very much, Saban."

"I see." Hints of arcane secrets curled the Saban's lips. "In that case, serah, for your final night, we shall arrange something I am certain will delight you."

I was resigned to set aside my personal feelings and to face my final evening in Cardominia in all its decadence and pomp with all the diplomatic aplomb I possessed. I had done all I could to convince the Saban of the error of Cardominian ways. History would judge me god or demon for what I had to do, and though it was my duty to condemn, my conscience, stained by so much beauty, sat uneasily within me.

I had once believed it meaningful to leave a mark of my mortal life. Yet there was no longer pleasure in the thought that I would be remembered in Verhallian history books, for in Cardominia there would be no more books, nor history, nor people.

Except that on the final night, instead of accompanying me to the theater hall, servants conveyed a light supper to my room and drew a bath while I dined alone. Silently and efficiently they attended me, whisking away the empty plates before leading me into the bathing chamber. Once I had been stripped and scrubbed, the servants withdrew, leaving me to soak in the hot, perfumed water, a delicate cup of porcelain on a gold-rimmed saucer set within reach.

Along with the cup, there was a wide, shallow brewing pot, green-glazed and cumbersome. Curious, I lifted the lid to peer inside. Nestled within the steaming brew I discovered a clump of organic matter composed mostly of twigs. A dargum nest.

The scent of this tea most rare was spicy, intoxicating and rich – cinnamon-sweet but with peppery fire, streaming pale grassy yellow as I tipped spout over cup. Because of its rarity, it was a precious gift indeed, and a great honor to receive.

I did not believe the bird's nest tea possessed those

peculiar properties claimed by the Cardominians, that it was both aphrodisiac and magical elixir of life, yet, once I had brought the cup to my lips, I hesitated to drink. Fear of poison I would have said then if asked, for the plot still troubled my thoughts, yet the truth was different. For a moment, I believed.

The tea was slightly bitter and sharp, but it left a pleasant, velvety aftertaste, lingering in my mouth even as I stepped out of the bathing chamber, fully dressed but for my fox-fur, rubbing a drying cloth vigorously over my wet head with my good hand.

My heart staggered when I discovered Cricket in my bed.

I was immobile as an ice sculpture as Cricket nimbly slithered to the edge and then stood in the penumbra, reaching for a clasp. The clasp undone, the silks slipped down in a single motion, like a sheet of water, gliding to puddle at the hakam's feet. Naked at the edge of the bed, the hakam pivoted with a soft smile, waiting with open arms.

I ravished Cricket with my eyes. Hungry, I devoured every inch of golden skin, following each curve, each dimple, each long and lissome limb. Thirsty, I drank in the hollow of the throat, the jut of delicate bones, the spiderweb thread of the cascading hair. What I felt, there is no word to describe it in Verhallian. It was not merely lust, but rather as if an invisible thread were tugging at my insides, drawing me to the waiting arms of the hakam.

Cricket's skin was strangely cool and smooth below my hands, mouth eager and tasting of honey. My senses did not return until I was already on my back on the bed, and Cricket's hands sliding beneath my shirt, soft breath and tongue in my ear. For all I knew, someone had sent the hakam to do me harm, and I had unwittingly seized the bait in the trap.

I pushed the hakam away. Confusion and hurt was in the dark eyes as Cricket gazed down upon me. "Do I not please you?"

The soft, guttural hush of Cardominian washed over my skin, spiking my blood. The hakam spoke no Verhallian. Vexed, I remained silent.

Cricket studied me, then smiled softly. "You do understand me, don't you, white fox?"

The words were a taunt, both playful and disrespectful. My expression must have betrayed me, for the hakam's smile became knowing.

"Did you not know? All the hakami call you 'the white fox.' We are like chickens in the coop, waiting to be snatched up by your hungry teeth."

I opened my mouth to protest before I realized my error.

A warm chuckle resonated deep in Cricket's throat. "Ah, you do understand me. But do not worry, white fox. I have told no one. Not even the Saban."

Too late for pretense, I relinquished the facade. I had learned the language only from books, so my Cardominian came out stilted, flat, and halting, the words tasting unnatural and ashy in my mouth. "I do not understand you at all."

"Is there something to understand?"

I posed the same question I had used with the other hakami. "Do you not want to be free?"

I had yet to receive anything other than incomprehension – real or feigned, I did not know. Yet Cricket became pensive, then smiled down at me and unfolded this tale:

"There once was a land, a wild desert of rock carved by the sun. And in this land, there came a people, drawn to the pulse of the land, people who thrived on the sun. With great magics, it is said, the people called the rock from the earth which became their buildings and streets, and water from the earth to slake their thirst, and animals and plants to nourish their bodies, minds and hearts. And yet, the life in their blood was too strong, and the people, relying on the great magics for all their needs, had no reason to work and soon became restless, and the boredom drove them to strife. The strife escalated until blood filled the streets and the people stood on the border of war.

"It seemed inevitable that the people would destroy themselves, but one had the courage to stand forth and unite them all under one rule. They called this one the Saban. The Saban believed that the people relied too much on the great magics, and they had no purpose in life. Without purpose, life was meaningless. Thus it was decided that the people would set the magics aside and everyone would be given a new role. Some would become rulers, others merchants, some would be servants, others slaves.

"Of the slaves, the most beautiful and skilled were chosen to serve in the hakarum of the Saban. They were happy, because they were well-treated and their purpose was to please. Yet, they are curious, too. One day, a stranger arrived from an exotic land, sent to condemn and destroy the people who thrived on the sun. But although this task made the stranger unhappy, the stranger was not allowed to save the people, or take pleasure in their delights, or to love them. The stranger had a role to fill, a Verhallian role, one that did not permit the heart to interfere.

"When the stranger came to the hakarum, a hakam named Cricket felt a strange, new emotion. Cricket begged permission, but the Saban refused to give the hakam's body to the stranger. But the Saban could not control Cricket's heart. The hakam was free to love anyone, to even love the mysterious white fox, if only in heart and not body. But the Saban relented and permitted the hakam to come to the white fox for just one night."

As the words wove, mesmerizing like a spell, Cricket's fingers deftly trailed out the story through my clothing – opening clasps, unwinding sashes, freeing buttons, unlatching buckles. By the end of the tale there was nothing but air between us. Cricket leaned down and sighed softly against my lips. "Do I please you now, white fox?"

The white fox snatched up the chicken in its hungry teeth, and near dawn slept, curled up in its fur, sated.

I had slept little, but my body was vibrating down to my bones as I walked briskly to the throne room. I could feel the rush of blood in my veins, and the life pulsating within me, and

I wondered, briefly, if the dargum nest tea had not been a magical elixir after all, or if this sensation were merely an aftereffect of one evanescent night spent with the hakam.

My formal farewell to the Saban was my final obligation. My baggage already packed, it waited at the front gate of the palace with my halfbreed guide.

In the throne room, I was presented with a similar tableau for my departure as for my arrival. The Saban perched regally on the crimson-veined crystal throne, flanked by the counselors in their plum-colored robes – only one detail was different. At the feet of the Saban's throne, wearing the usual revealing silks, sat Cricket.

Even now I was so enraptured by the hakam's presence that I scarcely heard the lengthy ceremonial speeches intoned by the counselors, and I fumbled my reply, though I managed to retain the minimal dignity required.

Once protocol was satisfied, I bowed to Ailin and Cadhla both.

The final word belonged to the Saban. "It is a custom among our people, ambassador, to offer a parting gift. The more important the guest, the more precious the gift. As we consider you a most important guest, I offer you my most valuable possession." The Saban paused to smile. "You may refuse, of course. In fact, Ser Nika, turned it down. However, in your case, I suspect you will have no such objections. Ser Nika already had a mate, and foresaw problems of returning to Verhall in the company of a hakam."

My breath caught in my throat. "You are offering to

181

give me a hakam?"

The Saban's hand descended to caress the hair of the hakam at the foot of the throne. "Cricket is my most valuable possession," the Saban said. "And yet, I feel there is value in letting Cricket go. No Cardominian has ever visited Verhall. Were you to show Cricket to your people, it may be of benefit to us both."

I looked at the hakam whose gaze had never strayed from mine.

I thought of Cricket's story about the hakam who had fallen in love at first sight with the stranger from Verhall in an exchange of glances in the mirror, who then overcame many obstacles to spend only one passionate night together.

Such were the romances written by the people of Cardominia. I knew them all well. Ser Nika had recorded those, too.

I believed none of it.

But this time it did not matter if I believed it or not.

I bowed to the Saban, and spoke in my halting Cardominian. "Yes, Saban, I will do that," I said, and here I faltered over an unfamiliar word – one of those words which did not exist in Verhallian, a word whose concept did not even exist – and yet, when I spoke it, looking upon the smiling face of the hakam, it did not feel strange at all.

"Prepare him."

But who could have imagined that a lover's gift would provoke legal action? What kind of world did he live in?

Bill Racicot doesn't have strong opinions about elves.

Bill has published two articles in scholarly books, and some poetry in small press magazines. His early fiction occasionally appeared in an E-zine called QUANTA. I also highly recommend his story "Mystery's Meat" available for free as part of THE CHRONICLES OF SILENCE *series on the Pink Narcissus Press website at pinknarc.com.*

The Turn of the Spoon
or Love and Bootblack
Bill Racicot

*Long ago in the city of Hamburg, there was a
poor, elderly cobbler whose arthritis made it
harder each year for him to keep up with his
shoemaking, but he is of limited interest to
this story. Our story takes place within a
hollow tree at the edge of the nearby woods.
Specifically, it takes place in the kitchen,
where our hero, an elf named Keelver, is
about to bake a batch of cookies.*

The counters in the main hollow of the kitchen tree
were stacked high with sacks of flour and sugar, pyramid-
shaped piles of eggs, and great blocks of butter and chocolate,
and Keelver shook his head. He was to bake all of these
ingredients into cookies before dawn, when the tribe would
gather and eat. With a sense of resignation, he stood barefoot
on a three-legged wooden stool and reached up to take the
largest bowl – deeper than Keelver was tall, truth be told –
from the high shelf. A cool breeze, probably the last he would
feel until the day's baking was complete, wafted through a
knothole up his sleeve, ruffling the hair under his arm. The
sensation called to mind his beloved Tommican stroking
fingers down Keelver's chest, up his sides, and down again

184

along the inside of his arms, gently, careful not to tickle, whispering quiet praise for the softness of Keelver's lavender body hair.

Bitterly, Keelver remembered his walk of shame. In accordance with the requirements of his parole, at sundown Keelver had made his angry way from the dormer tree to the kitchen tree, twigs and mulch and pebbles and tiny worms from the forest path squiggling up between his hairy toes, making him think once again of his forbidden love, a shoe-making elf, an outsider. Perhaps he should have been more discreet about the fine hip-high boots Tommican had made for him, a gift exchanged for two dozen kisses and two dozen of Keelver's secret special macaroons. But who could have imagined that a lover's gift would provoke legal action? What kind of world did he live in?

Standing rigid now on his stool in the kitchen tree, Keelver angrily cracked eggs into the great clay bowl, resenting the sultry drafts that had begun to emanate from the heating oven. *Crack! Plop. Crack! Plop. Crack! Plop.*

Each *Crack!* reminded him of the judge's gavel.

Crime was rare in Hollow Tree Village, and hard to define, but His Honor Judge Silverbeard had decided that "trading cookies for favors from outsider elves" was embezzlement. He had sentenced Keelver to a week's parole, demoted him from Master of Recipes to lowly baker, and confiscated Tommican's wonderful boots.

Shoeless now, Keelver struggled across the kitchen under the weight of a ten-pound bag of sugar – heavier than

Tommican! He poured the entire bag into the bowl. Who did old Silverbeard think he was, anyway? Probably didn't remember what love felt like, if he ever knew at all. Who would stroke *his* tangled hair? Keelver grabbed a wooden spoon taller than he was and with both hands began to blend sugar into the slimy mass of eggs.

Earlier, when walking to the kitchen tree, Keelver had imagined the whole tribe of baker elves peering at him out of knotholes, frowning and muttering. Something wet hit his cheek, but perhaps it was just dew. An owl had closed one eye, cocked its head, and booed at him. Despite all of them, Keelver walked proud. He had done nothing wrong, and he would not crouch and he would not apologize. He had aimed his nose at the owl, and stalked under the roots into the main hollow of the kitchen tree. He would show them. He would not cringe and he would not give them the satisfaction of his refusal. He would bake these final cookies to feed the tribe at the next meal.

Remembering his trial and his barefoot walk reinforced Keelver's conviction. He added butter and flour to the bowl. The wooden spoon, slick with butter, slipped around the sides of the bowl, so like his hands across Tommican's sweat-slick belly. Resentfully, he stirred the batter another turn. He would not spit in the mix, because the secret ingredient today was not saliva. He would not add dirt or stones or marmot-soil with the chocolate chips. These were not the secret ingredient either. The secret ingredient was exquisite.

Another turn of the spoon, and Keelver recalled how his

186

so-called friends, green- and blue- and magenta-haired elves with whom he had shared nectar and pastry for so many years, had restrained him, their hands on his shoulders and arms and hips, a foul parody of Tommican's touch, as Silverbeard's bailiff had dragged the black, shining boots from his feet. It was just yesterday, and he remembered the event vividly. No elf was innocent, except possibly Keelver.

He stirred in the secret ingredient, shiny and black, then dropped balls of dough onto baking sheets, squinting to protect his violet eyes as he placed each sheet into the hot oven.

They had confiscated his boots, yes, but they had left him his rags and polish. What else was he to do with so much shoe polish! Another turn of the spoon. No elf was innocent, but Keelver must feed them cookies. No, the secret ingredient was not spit or guano or stones, and it was certainly not love. And after this evening's meal, Keelver and Tommican, alone in the hollow dormer tree, would be free to love as they pleased.

"See ye, kinsmen, what bale these troll-folk have worked upon us?"

Rev DiCerto has worked as a medical editor for several years and has written numerous newspaper and magazine articles. This is his first publication of fiction.

"The Saga of Anund the Berserk" is an excerpt from an unpublished novel called ON A WINDY TREE, inspired by the period literature of the Viking people: the Poetic Edda and the sagas, especially the tales of Sigurd the Volsung and the Yngling Saga from Heimskringla. He says, "As someone who has studied Viking literature, history, religion, and magic for many years, I thought it was about time that someone wrote a tale of Vikings in their own world that did not deal with the conversion to Christianity or recount existing sagas.

"I'm a big fan of the Alfar. They are beloved by Freyr and Freyja, and are said to know things beyond human comprehension. There certainly must be great potential for misunderstanding and conflict between human and Alf, but since they live on a higher plane than ours and feel their connection with the earth more strongly, there is a lot to be gained from knowledge of them. I do not subscribe to the idea that the 'writer' of the Saga of Anund the Berserk seemed to be putting forth that it is always perilous to interact with the alfar; but we all know that throughout history, not everybody has had the right idea about things."

The Saga of Anund the Berserk
Rev Di Certo

There was a mighty sea-king hight Guthorm. Guthorm was son to Ingvi, who was son to Yngvar, who was son to Yngling, who, it is said, was son to he who is hight Yng, the mighty Vanir-god Freyr.

Guthorm was king at that time over Mirksund. The mightiest of kings was he. Seventy huscarls[1] he could boast, and this at a time when a man could walk from Mirksund to the Ringvik and meet perhaps twenty bonders.

Living in Mirksund at that time was a jarl[2] hight Anund, and he owned three farms and two hundreds of cattle. But he had thralls to see to his land, and spent his days in the hall of Guthorm. Anund was the mightiest of berserks, and it is said that the All-Father gazed through his eyes. He had slain Halfdan the Dane in holmgang[3] years before, and offered his blood to Odin.

A ship also had Guthorm, which it is said was a gift

---

[1] *Full-time warriors who live in a king's hall. His bodyguard or private troops. Literally, "house-carls."*

[2] *A lord or tributary king under a higher king. In England this word was Anglicized as "earl."*

[3] *A one-on-one, formal duel. Often such duels were fought on a small island, called a "holm."*

from Týr the one-handed god. This ship was proof against sinking, unless it should be burned to the water-line; no spike could pierce its skin: nor rock nor spear nor bearded prow of dragon-ship. Many another ship had Guthorm, besides.

Skuli was the name of a king who ruled a folk district in Sweden. For long years Skuli and Guthorm had warred with one another, and much scathe wrought they one upon the other; for, many years earlier, Egil the father of Skuli had been slain in a viking raid by Guthorm. But for some time the war had lain thus: that neither king had done scathe to the other, nor harried in the other's land. A daughter fairer than spun flax had Skuli hight Alov, and Guthorm sent Anund to Skuli to pledge the troth of Guthorm's eldest son, Granmar, to her in the hope of sealing the peace between the kings. Alov said that she would be pleased to wed Granmar, so famous a warrior was he and so well known for his good looks and the promise of his skills and wise ways.

When the time came for Granmar to take Alov as wife, he sailed forth with Anund upon the ship unsinkable. The ship was fully manned with warriors fully weaponed. They got a fair wind, and reached the coast of Sweden without scathe.

But Skuli was a wily man and a hard, and he laid a trap for guiltless Granmar. Twelve ships of Skuli's surrounded Anund and Granmar in their one; and a fierce battle was held.

Then when Granmar's ship was cleared save for Anund and Granmar, the two thegns[4] were bound and taken to Skuli's

---

[4]   *Warriors of rank, though not of a noble class. In Viking literature all terms referring to warriors were interchangeable depending on the situation.*

hall. There before the door of the hall the huscarls of Skuli gave Granmar the blood eagle[5]. Granmar died shameless and fared to Valhol. Anund they bound, and they brought him before Skuli.

"Anund," quoth Skuli. "No harm to me hast thou done. Wilt thou have peace?"

Anund looked darkly at Skuli, and the king quailed. "Aye. Peace I shall have, Skuli, when my kinsman's blood hath been bled from thy throat," said Guthorm's thegn. Then the huscarls of Skuli bound Anund and left him on a skerry that vanished with the incoming tide: for fear was in Skuli, and he saw the Valfather's eye in the gaze of Anund, and dared not visit harm upon him by his own hand or those of his huscarls.

Hreithmar was hight a huscarl of Skuli, and he was troll-wise and learned in the lore of the runes. Hreithmar left a horn of ale leaning beside a stone, as the carls bound Anund upon the skerry. But ere he left, he cut Anund's bonds with his scramasax, whispering, "Do nothing, for they will surely slay thee." Shame was in the heart of Hreithmar at the evil deeds of Skuli. Yet no choice had he but to leave Anund there; and in washed the tide.

Anund had use of his hands, and though it was too far to swim to shore, there were pieces of driftwood upon the skerry. Taking the cut bonds from his wrists, he lashed together the driftwood. Then ere it was engulfed by the incoming tide, Anund drained Hreithmar's horn, and found that

---

[5] *A method of execution when enemies were given in sacrifice to the gods. The ribcage was opened from behind and the lungs pulled through to lie on the back, like bloody wings. The victim died of asphyxiation.*

strength-runes had been scraped into that draught. As the tide rose to his neck, Anund took hold of his raft, and he began to stroke toward the mainland. In two nights he stood panting upon the strand, not far from the hall of Skuli.

Gazing down the strand Anund espied the ship of Guthorm. Some men saw he around that bravest of boats; and yet he knew the face of Hreithmar. Swift as a wolf Anund strode along the strand, until he stood before the company. Unarmed he faced them.

"Hreithmar, carl of Skuli, I hail thee," quoth he. But the eyes of Hreithmar glinted with a smile. "I come the goodly vessel to reclaim."

"To ward the goodly vessel were we set," Hreithmar said. "And yet to ward a thing is to keep it from harm. Is it not a harmful thing to be had by the honorless?"

Then hope sprung up in Anund's heart. "Indeed, to be honorless, I ween, is an evil thing. Wilt thou not then fight me?"

"We will not," Hreithmar said. "We will sail with thee." Then Anund took Hreithmar within his arms, and the two mingled their blood as warriors, and swore to be brothers ever and ay.

Anund wished straightway to seek vengeance upon Skuli; but Hreithmar spoke against this rede. "We are but fifteen," he said, "and are too few to lay the district beneath us."

"I list not to set myself upon the high seat of Skuli," quoth Anund. "His life alone I crave. But if we sail from this place, we may die ere we can return. Guthorm and Granmar are my kinsmen, and I will avenge the slaying of Granmar ere I leave this strand."

So they fared to the hall of Skuli, and came there in the night, when Skuli was feasting with many warriors around him. They were all deep in their ale.

Then Hreithmar and Anund piled wood about the hall and before the doors, with the aid of the men who were with them. For though Hreithmar had sworn oaths to Skuli, long had he watched that king fall into dishonor and oathbreaking, and he held it no evil thing to break an oath to a mainsworn man. Then they set fire to the fuel.

As the hall began to burn, Anund heard a commotion within; and he heard the voice of Skuli swearing oaths of vengeance upon whomever had done this deed. Then standing nigh the doorway, Anund cried out: "Hail, Skuli! Dost thou find now the might of thy high-timbered hall less of a comfort than when peace thou offered the red gold-wearer?"

"What cur calleth thus upon the Ylfing king?" Skuli cried.

"Guthorm's jarl am I, Anund hight, Asbjorn's son," called the atheling[6].

"Grim was the hour I gazed upon thee, Asbjorn's son," cried Skuli, "and Bolverk I name thee." Then the hall collapsed, and Skuli spoke never another word. Some few huscarls who still lived ran from the ruin; but Anund and Hreithmar slew them all, and gave them to Odin and to Týr; and for their part,

---

[6] *A hero, a warrior of skill, often possessed of magical or spiritual lore. In Viking literature all terms referring to warriors were interchangeable depending on the situation.*

the carls of Skuli died manfully.

Anund and Hreithmar returned then to the ship, for they dared not stay nigh to the hall when they were so few. Again it was the rede of Anund that they should go straightway to Guthorm with the tidings of Skuli's treachery. And again troll-wise Hreithmar counseled otherwise.

"To come before thy king empty-handed with word of his son's slaying, though avenged he be, will bring thee small honor," he said. "Come to him, rather, with gold rings and willing warriors, hardened by the harrying of far strands. So might thou bring the comfort of wealth to Guthorm to soften the blow, and thus bring honor upon thee." In this rede Anund saw wisdom.

Many days they sailed, and much did they harry. Nine ships, 'tis said, they sank, and cleared all their decks of the shield-oaks; though ever and ay this warrior or that would forsake his allegiance and join their band, until their company numbered thirty.

They wintered in the north, guests of Ulf the jarl, a hoary warrior who had fought beside Guthorm against Skuli many winters past. In the spring they sought to return to Guthorm with their cargo and the Ylfing crew. But the going was difficult, and when they drew nigh to Mirksund they were turned aside by stormy weather and ran for four nights before a wild wind, and at last they abandoned their hope of coming home and let the brine-stallion ride as he was led.

Already as they neared Mirksund they were none too well furnished with food, and now their stores had run bare; so they began to search for land. In three nights, they found a small isle of which none of them had heard. They beached their wave-steed, and went ashore to seek water and game.

At the first this isle seemed barren of folk. Then Angrim found a house, though he saw no folk thither; and soon Anund came upon a timbered hall. Gilded were its gables, and carved were the posts, such that this hall was more fair than any they had seen before. Smoke rose from the louver and fire was upon the hearth, yet no folk could they find.

Then Hreithmar sate within the hall, and he drew forth his pouch and his runes, and he bade Anund bring him a hare: for he wished to learn to what strand they had sailed. Hreithmar slew the hare, and he sang a song to the Allfather and cast his rune-tines upon the ground, while the warriors steaked the game and set to their drinking.

But ere Hreithmar had read the runes wholly, Anund cried out, and drew his brand, and dashed toward the door. Then he reached out; and when he drew back his arm, he clutched in his hand the long locks, silver-sheened, of a woman. He dragged her into the hall.

"Who art thou, and what hall is this?" cried he; but the warriors shuddered, for fairer than any maid was this woman, and a madness and a dread mingled with lust crept into the hearts of those thegns.

"Harm me not, Anund Asbjorn's son," quoth the woman. "I mean thee no evil. 'Twas the casting of the runes drew me hither."

"How knowest thou my name?" the warrior asked; and

yet in that moment, all of the men saw that the woman had the flashing eyes of the alfar, who it is said are the folk most dear to the Vanir-gods. Then in amazement Anund released her, for it was plain that the wind that had blown them hither had taken them to Alfheim, or to some isle that bounded it. But the alf-woman's beauty pierced Anund's heart like a spear, and the dread and lust grew within all of the carls.

"I am Asta hight," the woman said. "Queen am I of this isle, wife to Dag Keen-Spear the king. Among my folk I am wisest in runelore and other magics." In silence the vikings stared at her. "I wished to see how the Midgard men read Ygg's runes," she said. Fear was in her eyes. Hreithmar stood then in amazement, and he stepped toward her.

"Teach me, then, madam," he said. But his breath came fast and heavy, and Asta's face went white. "I would gain thy wisdom," Hreithmar said. His hands shook as he strode forward.

Then there was a sound near the door, and more folk entered the hall. No mail wore they, nor weapons bore. Men there were, and women, and children eke. Of them all one alone bore a brand. Of piercing loveliness were they all, and strange were their flashing eyes, and soft their voices; and they gazed in awe upon the vikings, even as the Midgard-men gazed in awe upon them: for fierce and warlike were the Ylfing warriors and their twain chieftains, whereas wise and quiet and lithe seemed the alfar.

"Anund Asbjornsson, Hreithmar Ketilsson, I give thee Dag Dagmarsson, king of Freyrsstad," quoth Asta.

196

Then Dag, who alone bore a brand among the alfar, placed his hands upon the heads of the two children beside him. "Dagvi, my son," he said, "and Dagni, my daughter. Dagni, bring our guests mead. Dagvi, see that this meat is finished." The alf-girl appeared no older than five winters, as Midgard folk count them; her brother, perhaps twelve. "Welcome to Freyr's Isle, chieftains and heroes. Feast with us and tell us thy tale," quoth Dag.

"It is a bloody one," Asta said, and she gazed upon Anund with a black look. But fire leapt within the chieftain's heart at her gaze.

Then a feast was set, and all the vikings were seated at a table amidst the alfar, and fed with the finest fare. Long did they dine, and fine was the ale, and finer the mead; and soon the warriors' heads were aswim with drink. As they feasted the madness and lust, and dread of the alfar, grew within the vikings, such that they could hardly withhold from acting rashly. But Hreithmar questioned Asta of the runelore and the troll-wisdom of her folk; yet he could not conceal the lust in his eyes, and ever did she cast a searching gaze toward Dag, and a gaze of fear toward Anund.

Then Anund saw where a sleepiness had come upon the warriors with passing suddenness, and he sipped anew at the mead in his horn; and pouring it out upon the table, he saw where a thorn had been cast within the mead, and that there were shavings of wood in-blent with that draught, so that he knew that sleep-runes and the sleep-thorn had been dealt to them. A great wrath took him, and drawing his brand he leapt

197

to his feet, and snatched up the sleep-thorn, and showed it to Hreithmar.

"See ye, kinsmen, what bale these troll-folk have worked upon us?" cried he. "Wotst thou, Hreithmar, the scathe we are done?"

Then Dag rose to his feet and drew his sword; but Anund straightway leaped upon the table and struck him a blow to his neck with his brand. This proved to be the death-blow of Dag; and the women-folk shrieked and the bairns of Dag and Asta wept and cowered. But Hreithmar seized Asta and tore the gown from her breast. The other vikings straightway drew their arms, and began to slaughter the men in the hall; but they would not suffer the women to leave.

Then Dagvi the king's son took a knife from the table and thrust it into the back of Hreithmar as he wrenched at the weeds of Asta, and the lungs of Hreithmar were pierced, and that was his death-wound. But Anund wheeled and thrust his brand through the boy, and left him dying upon the floor. The youngest child Dagni shrieked, and ran to the corner to hide; but Asta stood by and wept, and the lust of Anund overcame him. He took Asta then and had his way with her, while the vikings slew the men and ravished the women in their lust and madness. But Asta did not cry out as Anund took her, so when he had finished, he slew her with his brand. Then the warriors fell into a sleep.

When finally they woke, Anund wished straightway to leave that place, for despite the treachery of Dag, there was remorse in his heart for the slaying of Asta, and he felt grief at the loss of Hreithmar. But the berserk had not yet left all the carls, and many of them listed to despoil the hall of its goods, and to make of it a pyre for the alfar who lay slain within, in the hopes of appeasing the wrath of Freyr. In this Anund let them have their way. But they brought there Dagni, who had been shivering in a corner unmoving the long night through, before Anund, asking whether she should be taken as a thrall. Anund looked upon her and saw that she was broken, and bade them leave her where her own folk might find her and care for her.

Then they brought the girl outside and sate her in the grass within the garth, and they burned the hall, and sailed away with the goods of the alfar. But when they were come some miles from shore and gazed behind them, they saw naught: nor island nor hall, no tree nor stone, only the open sea. Smoke, however, they smelled, and they hastened forth. But the goods they had taken from the alfar they found had turned to ashes.

A fair wind they had then, and it was not long ere they returned to Mirksund. Then Anund came before King Guthorm, and he told him of the treachery of Skuli, and of the death of Granmar, and of the aid of Hreithmar. Anund presented Guthorm with the warriors and the goods from the ship, and the gold's foe was glad, and rewarded Anund and all the Ylfing warriors with weapons and with gold torcs and rings. And when Anund told of the alfar and their isle, Guthorm praised his deeds; for in those days, even more than now, men feared the alfar, and rightly so.

"You certainly know how to speak kindly of a dead elf," she quipped, "especially at his funeral. Leave it at that and be nice, or I'll tell your mother what you said."

Here is the sequel to "A Long Friday," David Vernaglia's other story to appear in this anthology. Although not nearly as bloody, it still isn't what I would call a pretty story.

David believes in elves.

And Their Mothers
David Vernaglia

The tiny silver bell over the bookstore door tinkled as the last patron of the day left Out of the Mothballs and returned to the city rain. Porpra walked over and locked it then began blowing out the lights. I know, he said to himself, I shouldn't use oil lamps in a bookstore! I just love the quality of light they shed.

He walked back to the scarred wooden counter, pulled out the cash box and started tallying the day's take. Not bad; he smiled. He knew he'd sell his first edition of *Haalak's Beastiary* eventually; it was a terrific piece, and the Venerable Mr. Mao had exquisite taste. A great week overall, even though it had not stopped raining once; too bad he had to go to a funeral in the morning.

Life had been kind to Porpra since he last saw Gris, back when the humans wrote their "Declaration." He never really liked the guy, though he had pretended to at times. They used to hunt together in a band of friends, exploring the wild and populating it with imaginary beasts when no real ones surfaced. Gris had often lead the hunt, or Adaan, but Porpra thought Gris was an arrogant leader; he was too sure of himself and his skills, cocky. And he certainly thought himself handsome, the conceited prick! Porpra snorted. Enough of this, I need to get home and press my shirt.

Porpra locked the door twice as he huddled beneath his umbrella on the slick city street. Out of the Mothballs was in one of the older parts of Providence where the streets were still cobbled. Porpra had scored a fantastic deal on the building during the Bleak Years, and had maintained it through numerous human presidencies, wars, financial disasters and witch hunts. He had always kept his head low, charged fair prices, and made the right kind of friends amongst the humans, and so had succeeded in their world. He had money, a fine townhouse and business, he was out with his family and friends and they were all relieved that he had finally dropped the human convention of heterosexuality. Life was good, even if he hadn't found another elf he really connected with yet. Besides Rosa, that was. They had been friends for years and the crazy bitch had always kept Porpra on his toes. He might go so far as to say he loved her, though that was far too human and she'd probably get angry if he said so. What was he thinking? Elves don't love. He chuckled, and walked home in the rain.

"Fancy seeing you here," Rosa sneered as Porpra walked up the hill and joined the crowd around the pyre. Gris's body lay high upon it under a shroud. He was not fit for viewing; the cops had shot him over a dozen times in the face and chest and the drugs had not been kind to him either.

"Well, I knew you'd be here and would never let me forget it if I didn't come, so here I am. Happy?" Porpra looked a bit awkward and uncomfortable, as if he was worried about what people were thinking of him or who he might bump into at Gris's funeral. He had arrived ready to leave.

"I am," said Rosa. "I always understood why you didn't like Gris because I'm your best friend, but none of us really know why you cut him out as completely as you did. What the fuck did he do to you, Porpra? His arrogance and affection certainly made my life miserable, as you know quite well, but I was fucking him at the time so I didn't let it bother me too much. You certainly did. You two used to be friends!"

"He was an asshole, intellectually insecure and unkind. I bet he was gay." Porpra put on his trademark goofy smile and shuffled about a bit. "Who else is here?"

"Wow. I can't believe my ears, Mr. Projector! You certainly know how to speak kindly of a dead elf," she quipped, "especially at his funeral. Leave it at that and be nice, or I'll tell your mother what you said. Or I'll tell Gris's for that matter. The bitch will be here soon enough and I would love to torture her with just such a whisper. I'd do it, too, but I don't want to get you killed. Too bad; it would be fun."

The blonde elf turned her back and swirled her long black coat up around her body, covering the silver beauty of her clothes and shape beneath. Porpra had always admired Rosa; her face was that perfect pale beauty that the humans endlessly write about in their poetry. Her eyes were bright, yet strangely soft, and her mouth and tongue were red and sharp and full of fire, as the gentle bookkeeper knew from centuries of personal experience. He was glad she had pulled herself away from the drugs. In light of the body on the pyre, it looked like Gris hadn't been able to.

"What happened to him?" Porpra asked.

"Later," she hushed. "It looks like the Grande Dame has arrived. It hasn't been long enough since I saw that vile succubus last. Check this shit out." Rosa took a drag off her cigarette, smirking from the perimeter as she watched the scene on the hill unfold.

An elven woman of great age and stature was making her way up towards the pyre, dressed entirely in black and as beautiful as the moon. Strong eyes, strong skin and a tall bright aura surrounded and protected her from all that could occur, whoever or whatever it might be. Ama had weathered far more years than any other elf present. She turned and met Rosa's gaze perfectly, then returned her face forward as if ignorant of Rosa's identity and unimpressed by her presence; Ama had never given Rosa anything ever before and was not about to start doing so now.

Gris's mother walked directly to the Officiator, ignoring all those who had gathered about the pyre to pay their respects and spoke with him in low tones. A few seconds later, she picked up a torch and walked over to the pyre, throwing it down and lighting the mass of wood and bone and body. She checked the time, turned and left, speaking to no one as the flames roared behind her with a woosh that took the air away. The crowd began to disperse.

"Bitch," Rosa spat. "She always has to take center stage, doesn't she?"

204

"Yeah, I guess she does," offered Porpra. "I know how it is with elven mothers and their sons, but what the hell did Gris do to deserve that? It doesn't even look like everyone has arrived yet and she lights the thing up and leaves?"

"Shut the fuck up, Porpra," Rosa snapped. "Now that you see how his mother acts you suddenly feel bad for the guy who never really did anything to you except bruise your fucking ego? Crawl the fuck out of your shell and admit it! You never liked Gris because you wanted to be more like him! You really piss me off, Porpra! Or was it that you just wanted to fuck him, but that was before you had the courage to act like every other elf and not give a damn about gender roles? Sometimes you act like a human," she spat. "I'm out of here." She threw her cigarette to the ground.

Rosa stormed off down the hill, avoiding the remainder of the crowd, knowing or liking few if any of them and angrier than she'd been in years. She remembered all too well how bad things were for Gris when he was young. A psycho and a puppet master for parents; at least his father had had the decency to off himself years ago, though who knows the horrors behind that story. She felt like screaming.

The rain swallowed Rosa and her wet, golden hair as she disappeared from Porpra's sight, leaving him alone where he stood. He felt awkward and uncomfortable, knowing no one save the burning deceased, and terrified at bumping into someone he actually did know. It was time to leave. Why did Rosa always have to get so nasty? Probably because it's Thursday, Porpra quipped. If it had been Tuesday, things might have been different. The elf smiled. She'd kill him if she knew what he was thinking. In all actuality, Rosa was probably right, if it really mattered any more. For an elf that had so much, who had achieved his dream and was living happily ever after, Porpra realized that he would never get a chance to put his shit aside and make peace with Gris. It was too late for that. Gris was dead and Porpra, for an elven moment, felt sorry. That's what you get for reading too many human stories, he said to himself: feelings.

Porpra needed a stiff drink and a blanket. The rain was getting to him. Maybe I should write something about this, he mused, and burn it up as an offering to Gris. He shrugged. Rosa's right, I really need to start reading more elven books. The dead can wait. Life is hard and I have work to do. I hope this rain stops soon.

Porpra wandered off, aiming for home. Behind him, the pyre sizzled and burned, later sputtered then died, and the Officiator cleared the remains away. Only a few arrived to see it.

"So, Mr. Elf, why are you in my room? Looking for the one ring?"

Born and raised in New England, Joe Mogel studies engineering and creative writing at college. His interests include martial arts, rock climbing and psychology.

"The process I have for stories always begins the same way: research. For this story I researched elf mythology and folklore. Once I identified the aspects from history that I felt would make the best character, I composed my first character. From there I built his foible and based the plot around those two main figures. I build each story in a different manner, depending on the emotion of the plot and the nature of the leads. The funniest thing about this story is I found that the old mythological elves were badass! They kidnapped, treated humans as prey and were nasty to tangle with."

Editor Josie found Joe through a post on a local writers' board. After a few e-mails, he offered to write us an elf story. I didn't expect anything to come out of this exchange, but Joe came through with "The Mischief Makers." We're certainly glad he did.

Joe has previously published two other stories, available on-line: "The Devil's Advocate" *in the* NATIONAL GALLERY OF WRITING *and* "Outlaw's End" *on* ROPE AND WIRE.

The Mischief Makers
Joe Mogel

A light breeze blew across the shrub-lined side yard. The full moon highlighted every leaf and twig. A small, two-story, English cape style house sat back from the rough road. A lone birch stood sentry, its side branches tickling the windows of the upper story.

A tiny shadow moved with the wind, from the shrubs to the birch. The shadow grew as it slipped up the tree. The branches twitched ever so slightly as the dark figure moved along them.

Alice's bedroom window was open. She lived in the small house with her parents and younger brother. Her room was resplendent with all the trappings of a teenage girl. Stuffed animals and youth literature were scattered over the mahogany furniture.

Alice was sleeping lightly under her frilly bedspread on a large, ornate bed. She was a blond seventeen year old with light blue eyes and a pretty face.

The shadow on the branch stole through the window. Once inside he stood upright. He was medium height and lithe. His skin was very pale and his long blond hair was pulled back into a loose ponytail over his pointed ears. His small, dark eyes darted about the room. He wore a green tunic, leggings, pointed shoes and a thin leather belt.

As he started to tiptoe across the room a gasp came from the bed. He froze. With the most careful movement he turned to face the four-poster. Moonlight glinted off his hair and skin.

Alice was sitting up in her bed; her hands were over her mouth.

"Are you...?" she started.

"Oh, fuck," he muttered under his breath. "Yes, I am," he groaned.

"You're a vampire?"

"Huh?" he honked. His shoulders dropped and his face contorted into a stunned expression.

"You're shiny, beautiful and you're watching me sleep. You're a vampire!"

"But I'm not..." he croaked.

"Do we kiss now?"

He looked around in terror then bolted through the window. He scampered down the tree, zoomed across the lawn and vaulted a hedgerow.

"Wait! Come back!" Alice cried, leaping to the window. "We haven't fallen in love yet!"

He tumbled to the ground on the other side of the shrub.

"Shit!" he exclaimed. "Fucking fangirls are making my life fucking hell."

He reached into his tunic pocket and pulled out a sheet of paper. He ran his finger down the list of names.

"Alright." He tapped the sheet. "Let's try you."

Jessie was sprawled across her bed, one leg under the covers, the other hanging off the side. Her short, dark hair was as messy as the bedroom she slept in. She was fit, lean and snoring lightly. Softball equipment was strewn around the room. The window was open, the curtains pulled back crookedly.

Pale, lithe fingers gripped the windowsill. He pulled and heaved himself onto the sill. Once his chest was through he paused, half in, half out of the room.

"Seventh story," he panted. "No balconies, no trees, just brick. I hate these shitty apartment buildings and fuckers who make them."

He pulled himself through the window and flopped onto the floor, where he lay for a moment. After a deep breath he clambered to his feet. With a brief scan of the room, he spotted a half-open closet door. He slid through the mounds of clutter to the door. As he started to peer in, a rustling came from behind him. As he turned around, a large, white object slammed into his forehead. His head rocked back and bounced off the closet doorway. He stumbled forward, trying to raise his throbbing, contused head. He lifted his right hand and index finger and opened his mouth as if to speak. "Ow," was all he could manage before falling over.

He rolled onto his back, his eyes swimming in their sockets. He groggily lifted his head. Jessie was standing over him holding a softball bat, her face in a snarl. He let out a high pitched scream and covered his head. She squeezed her eyes shut and winced in pain.

"Are you kidding me?" she grunted. She stuck a finger in her ear and wiggled it about. "There's a ringing in my ears."

He started to scramble away. Jessie grabbed his ankle and pulled him back.

"What kind of burglar are you?"

"I'm not a burglar!" he protested, shielding his head. "I'm an elf."

"You're a what now?"

"An elf. You know – woodland folk."

She lowered the bat and looked him over. "Sure you're not a fairy?"

He furrowed his brow. "Don't say shit like that, my uncle is gay."

Her eyes widened. "How can they tell?"

His face puckered. "He wears purple."

Jessie burst out laughing.

"Stuff it, bitch!" he roared.

"Call me bitch again," she said, raising her bat, "and it won't just be your screams that are high pitched, got it?"

He lowered his hands from his head to cover his groin. "Perfectly."

"So, Mr. Elf, why are you in my room? Looking for the one ring?"

"No, and don't call me Mr. Elf. I have a name, you know."

"And what would that be?"

"Rinaldo," he muttered.

She stared in silence, one eye half closed, an eyebrow arched.

"Rinaldo?" she parroted. "Are you an elf or a ninja turtle?"

Rinaldo's mouth puckered. "Shut up, bit..."

She raised the bat.

"Bi... Bi... Beautiful, crazy woman with a large club who doesn't want to whack my head open." He gave an anemic smile.

"That's better." She lowered the bat to her shoulder and put one hand on her hip. "So, why are you in my room?"

"I'm an elf; I'm here to make mischief."

"Really? I never would have guessed," Jessie said sarcastically.

"Listen," Rinaldo started, getting to his feet and dusting himself off. "It's the job of elves to make mischief. We hide TV remotes, steal sunglasses. You know, that kind of stuff. Ever lose a sock in the dryer? Yo!" He jerked both of his thumbs towards himself, giving a cheesy smile.

"So does that mean you're responsible for all the lost clothes I've had to replace?"

Rinaldo bit his lip. He whimpered, "Are you going to hurt me if I say yes?"

"You're not as dumb as you look."

"Gee, thanks."

They stood there a while, awkwardly silent.

"Okay, so why do you make mischief?"

"Huh?"

"Why mess things up?"

"Because," he stated, with an air of superiority.

Jessie stared at him.

"That isn't an answer!"

"But it's what we do! We make trouble for humans!"

"But why?"

"I don't know, it's just what we do!"

"That's just stupid!"

"Hey, don't pick on other people's culture! Would you make fun of a Hindu person for being nice to cows or a Christian person for trying to forcefully convert people?"

She narrowed her eyes.

"Ok, sorry, sorry! Bad example."

"So I was your target this evening?"

"Well, you're on the list."

"There's a list?"

"Yeah, I have to fill my quotas."

"Quotas?" Her arms dropped and her jaw went slack. "You have no idea why you mess with people and you have quotas?"

"Yeah, well..." Rinaldo threw his arms up and sputtered for a few moments. Jessie groaned and pinched the bridge of her nose.

"Show me the list." She reached out her hand.

Rinaldo looked her over, and then looked at the bat. Reluctantly he reached into his tunic.

"Alright, here you go."

He handed her the sheet. She snatched the paper out of his hand. After a quick, cold glance at Rinaldo she scanned the paper.

"This is a joke," Jessie snorted. "You have to screw with Alice Johnson?" She leered over the paper. "I would pay you to watch that brat suffer."

"Really?" Rinaldo arched an eyebrow. "Why would that be?"

"Beside the fact that she is an ever-peppy spaz with the IQ of plantfood? Perhaps because she shoves her craptastic teen novels down everyone's throat? Little snot has been bugging me since the semester started."

"Well..." Rinaldo blinked. "That was... informative."

"So," Jessie's eyes lit up. "How did you stick it to that little snot?"

"About that..." He scratched his head and gave an uneasy smile. "She kind of scared me off."

"She has that effect on people. Her mindless obsession with bad literature has lost her plenty of friends."

Rinaldo nodded vigorously. "I need to get some back up."

"Say no more!" Jessie exclaimed. "If it means making Alice and what's left of her lousy pals miserable, I'm in!"

"No."

"Huh?"

"You're not an elf. It would be against the rules."

"There are rules now?" Jessie snapped.

Rinaldo rolled his eyes. Jessie grabbed his collar and

yanked him in.

"Listen, twinkle-toes, you need help and I'm offering it, so chuck the rules and take it!"

Rinaldo's eyes widened and the corners of his mouth pulled back. "Um... OK."

"Fine." She let him go. "Sorry."

"No real damage done, I think." Rinaldo brushed his clothes smooth, then paused. "Say, this is an apartment building. Aren't your neighbors or family going to notice?"

Jessie snorted.

"My family are the only people under eighty in this building and they wouldn't care if there was a T-Rex in my room. I'm the daughter that's a boy so they don't care."

Rinaldo's head tilted to one side, his jaw slack and open.

They stood there quietly in the dark for several seconds.

"If we're going to work together we'll need a plan," he said.

"I think I might have an idea," Jessie hissed, touching a finger to her chin.

The high school bell clattered. The teenage hoard swarmed into the hall. The various cliques nucleated off to their respective territories. The fangirls chattered away in their designated zone.

Out of this, a single figure in jeans, a sweatshirt and a tee-shirt with a khaki knapsack slipped away. She scurried down the hall, careful to keep the bag from bouncing.

"Are you sure this is a going to work?" Rinaldo said, from inside the knapsack. He clung to several loose threads to keep from falling into the pencil sharpener.

"Yeah I'm sure it'll work," Jessie said then paused. "Remind me, how did you do this again?"

"What, make myself tiny?" He guffawed. "I told you, we elves are–" he sarcastically emphasized the word "–*magical* beings. We can do shit like this."

"Un huh," Jessie grunted.

She sauntered up to an out of the way locker, the door of which was covered in bright pink stickers. Jessie lifted the knapsack up to the slits in the door. Rinaldo slipped out of the bag and through the slit, dragging a gold sticker behind him.

"Put it in the same place as the others stickers," Jessie whispered.

"What's going to happen when the broadcast comes over the intercom?" Rinaldo queried.

"Hopefully a riot," Jessie snickered.

The lunch bell rang. The school radio crackled to life. The principal's voice growled through.

"Announcements: the three bean salad in today's lunch has been replaced by a baked potato. There is a blue SUV parked in the handicapped space by the side entrance that will be towed if it isn't moved, so, Mr. Johnston, get in gear. Finally there is a note here about a movie contest. Apparently to select for the upcoming movie adaptation of the popular vampire novel 'Evening Shade; Nighttime Sun,' inside the front covers

216

of the book there is a gold sticker. The sticker with the numbers 4 2 3 8 is the winner."

After a brief moment of contemplation, the fangirls stampeded into the hall. Lockers were ransacked, doors slammed, bodies hammered into one and other. A first scream of victory "I won!" was echoed by other screams. Jubilation morphed into fury as every gold sticker had the numbers 4 2 3 8 on it. Within minutes a bleach-blond riot was whirling through the school.

"I think this will work for total mischief," Rinaldo chuckled.

He stood on Jessie's shoulder as she leaned against the wall.

"It's beautiful, just beautiful," Jessie said, brushing a tear from her eye.

"What do we do from here?" Jessie asked. She was strolling back home from classes. The police had been called in to break up the chaos. Jessie and her elven companion had slipped away while the authorities were trying to figure out what had actually happened.

"What do you mean? We got them all, the stickers were genius and the school radio was great." Rinaldo poked his head out of the knapsack.

"Well I mean I'm still on your list, right?"

"Ahhh... I forgot about that," Rinaldo hummed. He snapped his fingers. "I have an idea. Go over to those bushes." He pointed to an unkempt lawn.

Jessie wandered into the gardenia jungle. Once she was completely entombed in the foliage she put the knapsack down and Rinaldo scuttled out. He somehow expanded to full size. She gave him a dull look and raised her eyebrows.

"Magical!" Rinaldo said with a manic grin and jazz hands.

"Whatever," Jessie snorted. "What is your idea?"

Rinaldo fished through his pockets and pulled out his list. He ran his finger down the page.

"Here." He pointed to an entry. "Read this."

"J. Wilson, why?"

"Do you have any relatives with J names?"

"Yeah, my dad, Jeremy."

"All I have to do is screw with a J. Wilson, not a specific J. Wilson. I can mess with your dad and fulfill the list."

"One problem," Jessie said, holding up her index finger.

"What?"

"You could drop a bowling ball on his crotch and he wouldn't blink."

"Oh, that's a problem." He covered his mouth. "What about people around him? Some people are more affected by things happening around them. What if we do something to another member of your family?"

"The only thing that might get him off his butt would be if he couldn't make jokes about how masculine I am."

Rinaldo's shoulders dropped. His face puckered as he looked down. He scanned the bushes as if searching for something, then his eyes lit up.

"I've got it!" he exclaimed. "Take us to the forested area behind your building."

"Why?"

"You'll see," Rinaldo snickered as he shrank back into the knapsack.

Jessie crunched through the underbrush. Shrubs and low hanging tree branches grabbed at her.

"We're almost there," Rinaldo said.

"Gee really? I can't wait," Jessie mocked.

Rinaldo gave her an oblique glance. He stood on her shoulder, holding onto her collar.

She tromped on for a while, until Rinaldo tugged on her sweatshirt.

"We're here!"

Jessie looked around. There were several trees, bushes and moss covered rocks.

"We're nowhere," Jessie said.

Rinaldo hopped off her shoulder and expanded to full size.

"Put your pack down," he stated.

She put the knapsack down and Rinaldo took her hand. She looked at his hand, then at his face. He was smiling.

"Come on," he chuckled as he pulled on her arm.

Jessie grunted as she was yanked along with unexpected strength. What started as a trot grew into a full run.

"What the hell?" Jessie snapped.

Trees, bushes, rocks, grass were all growing larger. The

distance they traveled seemed to decrease.

"What!" Jessie shrieked, digging her heels into the ground.

The dandelions were now at shoulder level. Rinaldo let go of her hand.

"What did you do?" Jessie screamed. She looked around, frantic.

"I shrank us."

"How?"

"Magic!" Rinaldo waved his hands around with a goofy grin.

"Why?"

"Because of that," Rinaldo pointed to the base of a knotted pine tree. Small spots of light flickered at points on the tree. Rinaldo started picking his way forward. Jessie trotted up behind him.

"Do you live in a tree?"

"Yup." Rinaldo nodded. "My entire village lives in there."

"Do you make cookies?"

"Shut the fuck up!" he growled.

Jessie scowled and kicked him in the ass. Rinaldo jumped and yelled. He spun and snarled while rubbing his butt.

"What was that for?"

"Do you always have to cuss me out?"

"I like swearing, fuckin' deal with it!"

"Fine," Jessie sniffed. "Lead on, O Sparkly One."

Rinaldo stomped his foot and hunched his shoulders for a moment, and then he wilted.

"Follow me," he said though clenched teeth.

The small door squeaked open. It was hidden between two root growths and camouflaged into the bark.

The main hall was warm and cheerful; its irregular shape was gouged with stairs and walkways. Side doors to individual apartments honey-combed the walls. The happy hum of activity burbled everywhere. Gaggles of little elflings ran about.

"We need to see my boss," Rinaldo said.

"Let's do it quick, this place is so sweet my teeth are starting to hurt."

The pair found their way across the main hall to a series of doors. Rinaldo led the way into a back room. A group of white-haired elves milled about. They shuffled papers from shelves to desks to filing cabinets. At a large desk filling out the far wall sat a fat, smiling, old elf.

"Santa!" Jessie squealed.

Rinaldo turned to her with a blank look.

"What? He's a jolly old elf!"

All the elves in the room turned to the old man behind the desk. The fat elf blinked.

"Rinaldo, why did you bring a human here?" he inquired.

"Well..." Rinaldo said, tapping the tips of his index fingers together. "This is part of my mischief."

"Really?"

"Yes." He pulled the name list out of his pocket. "The name on the list is J. Wilson, her father is Jeremy Wilson." He handed the paper to one of the old elves, who in turn handed it to the jolly old elf.

"She's good at making trouble and her father is a putz. So I thought..."

"That we could let her join?" the old elf finished his sentence.

"Well... yes."

"Wait, what?" Jessie spun to face her blond companion.

"I asked them if they could make you an elf."

"What?"

"Why not? You saying it wouldn't work?"

Jessie tackled Rinaldo. The pair flipped to the floor, Jessie sitting on Rinaldo's chest, her hands on his neck, shaking him.

"You were gonna try and make me a pointy-eared fruit cake like you?"

The old elves started chuckling.

"So that's why Rinaldo wanted to have her join!" One of them snorted. "She's exactly his type!"

Jessie looked at the elves, then slowly turned to Rinaldo.

"I'm your type?"

Rinaldo flushed. "Yes."

Jessie screamed.

* * * * *

Two small shadows slipped along under the moon light. The shadows darted through the side lawn and up the tree beside Alice's bedroom window. Rinaldo stepped into the room first. Jessie struggled through the window, her growing belly getting in the way.

"Need a hand?"

Jessie gave him a dirty look. "I'm pregnant, not crippled."

"Sorry, shit!"

Jessie scratched at the growing pointyness of her ears.

Alice rolled in bed. Rinaldo and Jessie glanced first at her, then at each other. They grinned evilly.

The last thing I heard before the darkness claimed me was Darian screaming my name as his faithful guards spirited him away.

Rose Mambert's fascination with book publishing may be directly related to the volume of toxic fumes she inhaled while running a variety of printing presses in the early 90s. Since then, she hasn't been able to remain more then three meters away from a book without experiencing withdrawal symptoms.

"This story began with an image of a man waking up in an unfamiliar room and realizing that he is being watched by a dubious stranger perched upon the back of a chair. The story built itself up around that image. However, I knew, too, that I did not want to write a story where everything existed on the surface. Instead, the reader is limited to the narrator's point of view: his perceptions, his feelings, his assumptions. He sees the world in black and white, but all around him are shades of gray. He thinks he understands what's happening – but does he? As the writer, I have my own ideas, but I leave the readers to make their own interpretations."

To Kill the Oak King

Rose Mambert

Darian du Montague, heir apparent to the throne of Ersilia, near choked on his ale when I expressed my sudden desire to pillage his new guard's codpiece.

Moreover, I began to question my intelligence as Darian's face turned an alarming shade of red. Killing the son of one's liege – even accidentally – was a terrible idea. One that led to being clamped in irons and subjected to prolonged torments at the hands of the King's able torturers. At the least, I should have saved *that* comment until after he'd finished drinking. But good judgment had vanished several pints ago.

Fortunately, Darian soon ceased his sputtering. He slammed the tankard down on the table, ale sloshing, tossing back his head as he laughed heartily. His face was still flushed pink when he finally caught his breath. "Michael! I can't believe you said that!"

I grinned down into my tankard. *I* certainly couldn't be blamed for noticing the young and quite handsome new addition to the Crown Prince's ever-present entourage. The guardsmen had followed us to the tavern, of course, but observed from the far side of the room, allowing Darian the illusion of freedom. There was no way they could have heard our conversation from that distance.

I wiped my mouth with the back of my hand after another swig. "Well, cousin," I said lightly, "if my mother would stop hiring only female servants at Château du Tremontaine, then perhaps my bed wouldn't be so empty." I smiled slyly. "And, I must say, that new guard of yours *does* fill out that codpiece quite sufficiently. It leads me to speculate what *else* he could fill with it."

Darian laughed again, so hard he had to cling to the table to keep from falling out of his chair. Finally he regained his composure. "Michael, you're incorrigible." He sighed, wiping the tears from his eyes. His expression suddenly grew grave. "If my brother-in-law ever heard you say such things..."

I grunted. The mention of Lorne du Beaumont was enough to sour anyone's mood. Mine in particular. "Fortunately for me, then, that he resides at Château du Beaumont, far, far away."

Darian had the bad habit of twisting a lock of his long, raven-black hair around his finger whenever he had something disagreeable to say, which is what he was doing now. "Ah. You haven't heard the news, then."

"Don't tell me..."

"He's here. With my sister."

I groaned. *"Why?"*

Darian looked at me, half hazy from drink, half perplexed. "You really haven't heard?" When I shook my head, he continued. "Ah, that's right, you were a-hunting when it happened. There was trouble down in the slave quarters. A revolt."

That caught me off guard. "The *elves* revolted?"

Darian squeezed his tankard with both hands, leaning across the table, his voice low. "It was over a fortnight ago. My father –" here Darian grimaced, "– well, you can imagine what happened."

I shuddered. "A slaughter."

"A slaughter." Darian sighed, running a hand through his heavy hair before letting it fall back to his tankard. "They say the streets of the elf quarter were washed with blood. The instigators were caught, but my father considered it... *prudent* to summon Lorne to quell any further rebellion."

That the elves in Ersilia were slaves was their punishment for warring – and consequently losing – against the humans. Except that the Elf Wars had been fought centuries ago, and the poor wretches now enslaved were several generations removed from the events which had merited that punishment. On the injustice of this matter, the prince and I were in accord, but we belonged to the silent minority.

I didn't like this turn in the conversation. I forced a cheerful smile. "Well, when you take the throne, perhaps you can do something about it. Grant them a royal pardon, if you wish."

Darian did not laugh as I expected. Instead, his face grew pale and he crossed his fingers as he tipped them towards the floor in a gesture to dispel evil. "Be careful, cousin," he warned. "You speak too freely. If you do not learn to control your tongue, you will be drummed right out of court."

I had drunk too much to care if I'd shocked the prince.

After all, he had been my best friend since childhood, and was, in all likelihood, too deep in his cups to remember our conversation in the morning. I chuckled, then drawled, "Court, Darian? That dull place? Why, I *long* for the day."

Darian sighed. "It's late, cousin. We've tarried long enough."

I realized just how drunk I was when the room spun as I near tumbled from my chair. Darian was having similar difficulty maneuvering around the table. Laughing once again and using each other for support, we staggered gracelessly out of the Silver Dragon. No doubt we made quite a spectacle of ourselves. Fortunately, disguised in our worn down boots and threadbare hooded cloaks, we easily passed for commoners in the slums.

Out in the street, it was cold, with scarce light to guide us back to the coach waiting around the corner. After the smoky lamps of the tavern, stepping outside was like being enveloped in a black velvet mantle.

What happened next was just a blur. Darian lost his footing, stumbling against a stone, dragging me along with him as his arm was still locked about my neck. As I reached out to steady us both, out of the corner of my eye I glimpsed a movement to our left.

A flash of silver blade cut through the dark. All at once it seemed I was shouting to Darian even as I shoved him away from me, groping for my sword. A clang of steel rang through the night as I raised my blade to meet that of the attacker. Unprepared, I staggered back, my arm numb from the fierce blow.

I saw no faces, only dark shapes of men and their advancing blades. I clumsily parried, dodged, then thrust. A weak thrust, easily turned aside, but I was not concerned about winning, instead focused on preventing them from reaching the prince.

The prince fared better than I, however. Blade drawn, he twisted away from danger like a cat, spinning to slash at his opponent. A pained yelp from below a hooded cowl confirmed a strike.

I hastened to block the blade sweeping towards my face, but my hilt became entangled in my cloak. Unseen hands pulled at my arm, causing me to trip over my own feet, and collide against a body which was not Darian's. Then something hard cracked against the back of my head and the ground rushed up to meet me.

Stars bloomed in my vision as I sank, helpless as a worm in the dirt. There were noises, but muffled as though coming from a great distance: the musical clank of plated armor, the slither of swords, the shouts of the guards as they poured out of the tavern, the harsh kiss of steel, followed by hurried footfalls growing faint. The last thing I heard before the darkness claimed me was Darian screaming my name as his faithful guards spirited him away to safety.

I woke with the strands of my thoughts twisted like a cat's cradle and slowly realized I was not dead. Although, considering the agony in my head, being dead may have been favorable.

Details of the previous night's events were muddled. But I remembered that Darian had escaped unharmed. Convinced of the Prince's safety, I sat up and turned to more pressing matters. The most pressing of which being that I was on a strange bed in a small, dingy room I didn't recognize and that I wasn't alone.

This last realization jolted me to full consciousness. There was nothing like danger to start the blood racing first thing in the morning. And the danger was clear, for the man so casually perched on the back of a chair near the window was not a man at all.

He was an elf.

Elves were not allowed freedom of movement beyond the walls of the slave quarters. If this elf were a slave, he was already a lawbreaker, and thus capable of other crimes. And if he weren't from the elf quarter... then he posed an even greater threat.

For a moment we studied each other in silence. I do not know what the elf thought, for his expression was as blank as a moon mask.

He was a shadow, a vague outline dressed in black clothing cut in the latest Ersilian style. A dark cloak lay in a heap on the floor nearby, carelessly discarded and half covering a worn traveling pack. By the light of the window, I could make out his features plainly enough. Like a typical elf, he possessed all the aspects that court ladies longed for: slender of limb and body, eyes wide set and light in hue, a fine-

230

boned face marked by a high forehead, a narrow nose, and full lips, all of which was crowned by an abundance of long hair shiny and fine as corn silk. The only difference between a lady's ideal and the elf was the fact that the elf's skin was the color of golden wheat, and that his hair was an unusual shade of silver which shone lavender in the sunlight, and that his ears, pierced through with silver clan rings, ended in fine points close to his head.

Despite the lack of color in his clothing, by the fine cut of them, along with the quality of his boots and the forbidden rings, he did not seem a slave.

My wits had recovered enough for me to realize that if the elf meant me harm, he could have easily killed me as I slept. Still, I only felt a bit more at ease when my gaze came to rest on my sword, propped against the wall near the bed, within reach.

"Who are you?" I asked. When the elf responded with stony silence, I let some temper color my tone. "What do you want from me?"

"I saved your life last night."

I don't know what surprised me more: his words, or the way in which he had spoken them. He had what my mother called a honey voice – one of those voices that was slow and sweet and sticky and would just get caught in your ear and make you forget your own name.

I remembered men in cloaks with long blades. There was the glint of a knife hilt in the elf's boot, but he wore no sword. That did not mean that the elf had not been somehow involved in the skirmish. *"You* saved me?"

"I assure you that it was entirely unintentional." The cold and calculating look he gave me nearly frosted my skin. "But, regardless of my intentions, there is a blood debt to be paid."

I had no reason to trust him. And, despite any sympathy due the elves for their plight, I could not deny my duty. Montague blood flowed in my veins, and it was with the King that my loyalty lay, and the elves were still our enemy.

I lunged for my sword as I bounded from the bed. I had hoped to catch the elf off guard to disarm him, and yet, in the blink of an eye, I found myself against the wall, the sword forced from my hand and a knife pressed against my throat.

His face was still a mask, but the way his breath whistled short and rapid through his nostrils betrayed his unsteady state. He snarled stale breath into my face. "Would you like to try that again, human?" he demanded. "Or can you give me some reason to let you live?"

This close I could distinguish the color of his eyes, cold, pale amethysts, unflecked. By the look in them, I believed him capable of slitting my throat.

As we stared at each other, I considered my options. Given my disadvantage, the options were few. I sighed, resigned. "The blood debt," I said reluctantly. "What would you have of me?"

His eyes narrowed. "Fool," he muttered. For a moment I believed the insult was leveled at me, but he continued to murmur under his breath. "That I thought I could trust a human..."

"Then we are in the same bind. I do not trust you."

The elf regarded me, wary. "*You* attacked *me.*"

"A poor decision, in retrospect," I admitted. I watched the elf thinking, weighing his own options. I guessed the obvious. "You saved me for a reason."

"If I let you go... no doubt you will bring the guard down upon my head."

"If there is truly a blood debt between us, then I will give you my word on my honor as a knight that I will repay you," I said, though I was quick to add, "as long as your request is reasonable."

"Your word as a knight means little."

"If that's what you believe, then you know not what a knight is."

"Oh, I know what a knight is. I know about your promises to serve God, king, and country. Your oath to protect the weak. The weak being women and children." He sneered. "But only if they are of noble human blood."

Under the elf's relentless stare, I cast down my eyes. I could not deny what he said. I could only think of Lorne du Beaumont and feel ashamed to share the same rank and blood with a man such as him.

The knife suddenly withdrew. Glancing up, I saw the elf take a step back, tucking the dagger into a sheath hidden under the loose sleeve of his tunic. On his face, the same resignation I felt. Reluctantly, his gaze flickered to meet mine. "I need you to do something for me," he said.

My cloak pulled tight around me, I trudged off to yet another herbalist's shop.

In the merchant quarter, there was no need for the disguise. Still, I did not wish to risk being recognized fortuitously by a passing acquaintance. By now, word had already spread about last night's adventure, and, all things considered, it was likely that the guard was trying to determine my whereabouts. And, though the thought of Darian worrying over me was a troubling one, I did not wish to be distracted from my task.

Although none would hold it against me were I to break my promise, I had been sincere in giving my word to the elf. In truth, I was motivated by something other than the dubious claim of a blood debt. Apart from the occasional outings incognito with Darian, life at court truly *was* dull. Encountering the elf had been the most interesting thing that had happened in a very long time.

The task he had set me, however, was neither dangerous nor difficult, and scant repayment for a blood debt. As if I were a mere servant girl, he'd sent me out with a list of items scratched out on a scrap of parchment. What he needed them for, he'd refused to say. Some I recognized as herbs, but the rest were unfamiliar. I had asked him if he meant to brew some magical concoction with them. Although use of magic was forbidden on the point of death, there were rumors that the elves still practiced it in secret. However, I mused, if the elves truly did possess magic, then it was too weak to do them any good.

What seemed like an easy task turned out impossible. Every shopkeeper I queried was unable to recognize all the items on the elf's list, much less aid me in finding them. Finally admitting defeat, there was little else to do but return to the elf in the upstairs room of the inn not far from the Silver Dragon where I had left him.

My first thought upon entering the room was that the elf was gone. I didn't realize he was standing behind me until he spoke. "Did you bring everything I need?"

Startled, I turned. His face was still a mask, but I noted a tension around his mouth. I sighed and told him how I had fared.

The elf made a small noise of disgust. "I set you a simple task, human," he growled. "One that even a child could have managed. You're useless."

I bristled at the insult. Reaching into my tunic, I drew out the scrap of parchment. "Eye of bluebells? Dragon drop blood? White maiden tears?" I waved it in his face. "What are these? Ingredients for some poisonous elixir?"

The elf glared at me.

I crumpled the parchment in my fist. "If you know magic, elf, then why don't you just cast some spell instead of wasting my time? Turn yourself invisible and take what you want. Or... or... or conjure the ingredients out of thin air!"

Anger sparked in the elf's eyes. "You stupid human," he growled. "You understand nothing of magic."

"Is that so? Explain it to me, then."

"You wouldn't understand. You... uh... huh..."

The elf trailed off, his words turning into a groan as he suddenly pitched forward.

Instinctively I moved to catch him. Darian stumbled much when he was drunk, so I'd had years of practice. Unlike Darian, however, as my hand skimmed over his waist, the elf emitted a whimper of pain. Surprised, I slid my hand back under his ribs. This elicited another whimper as sharp nails dug into my shoulders. Lifting my hand, I saw that it was wet with blood. "You're injured."

The nails burrowed deeper into my flesh as the elf panted in my ear. "I'm... not... don't... uhhh..."

Carefully I maneuvered him the three paces to the bed. Leaning over him, I wasn't really surprised to note that the cold mask from before had completely disintegrated, that his face was a wide-eyed mix of pain and fear. "I'm going to take a look."

The elf made a noise which I interpreted to be permission.

Peeling the tunic away from his body, I was surprised that he'd been able to hide his injury for so long. He'd been caught by the edge of some sort of blade, which had left a nasty gash that began a finger's width from the edge of his breeches and curved all the way up to the edge of his ribs. And, worse, the wound was festering. The sick smell of it near turned my stomach. "When did this happen?"

"Last... night. While... trying to... escape."

That it was festering this badly and so soon seemed

impossible. But men knew little about elf physiology. Nonetheless, I knew that *something* had to be done, and quickly. "It's bad," I said. "It will need to be stitched shut. And you'll need to cleanse out the wound because it's infected."

His hands clutched at the sheets as his face twisted in agony. "I... uh... I need..."

"You need a healer."

"No!" He jerked in the bed, a move which then left him gasping in pain. I put my hands on his shoulders, easing him back down. Below my hands his skin was feverishly hot. "No healers."

"If you don't get a healer, you'll probably die."

I had spoken plain truth. The elf was quiet for a moment. I imagined we were thinking the same thing. A King's Hands could save him, perhaps, were he to turn himself in, but the best he could hope for was a quick death if they believed him a runaway, rather than a slow and painful death if they believed him a spy.

Fevered, half-delirious, his eyes had taken on a glazed appearance. His honey voice had gone soft. "Eye of... bluebells. Dragon drop... blood. Need them... for a healing salve."

I thought. "Perhaps the herbalist has something. I could go..."

"No. Human remedies will not... work."

I leaned back with a sigh, running a hand through my tangled hair, trying to think, and half-hoping that the elf wasn't going to suggest what I suspected he was going to suggest. And, of course, he did.

"You have to go... there. Find... Grandmother Clock. Tell her... it's for me."

I didn't have to ask where "there" was. And I didn't bother to ask where to find this "Grandmother Clock." But there was one other problem. "I don't even know your name."

The pale eyes closed. Lying still, he looked almost peacefully asleep. But then he sighed softly. "Gray."

"Well, Gray," I said. "Do you really think I can just waltz in 'there' and get what you need?"

He answered without opening his eyes. "Of course," he said softly. "Because you... are Sir Michael the Fair."

The streets of the elf quarter were unusually quiet.

At one time, the elf quarter had been the poorer part of town, so it had never been a luxurious or beautiful place. Hundreds of years later, though, it was a shadow even of the slums. Roads and buildings were in disrepair, statues and archways eroded by time, stone and wood sun-bleached. Other than the people who lived here, all colors were variations on gray.

Gray. An odd name for an elf, and probably an alias. He had not revealed to me how he knew my name, and I had not pressed him. Instead, I had set my concerns aside and had hastened to the elf quarter.

Despite the lack of activity in the streets, I managed to find Grandmother Clock with ease by asking the first elf I found. He led me to a small hovel at the end of the street, where a silver-haired elf cautiously listened to my plea. Within moments, I had procured the rest of the ingredients for Gray's balm.

In my haste, I had not considered the price of this exchange. In the elf quarters, coin was worthless. Foodstuffs would have been considerably welcome, yet I had nothing but my purse, my blade, and the clothes on my back.

I offered my cloak. Although threadbare, it would be treasured here, particularly with winter coming soon. She took it with a faint smile, and I was out on the streets again, more puzzled than before.

I was certain that Grandmother Clock had recognized Gray's name. And yet, if he were not a runaway slave, then there was no logical reason for her to know him. That my own name was recognized by the elves was no surprise. Although the elves were forbidden to leave the quarter without a work permit, men were free to come and go as they pleased. The first time Darian and I had ventured here, we had been motivated by boyish curiosity. Seeing the miserable conditions in which the elves were forced to live, however, our interest in their fate had evolved. To keep abreast of the situation here, Darian used me as his eyes and ears. Later he set me the task of distributing much needed goods – food, clothing, blankets and the like. Not allowed to reveal the Prince's name, I had developed the reputation as generous benefactor among the elves.

I was nearly at the gate when I heard the screams.

A small rational part of me thought to turn away. If the King's guard were here, I had little reason to interfere. Furthermore, if the Prince had given orders to have me seized, there would be nothing I could do to keep the guard from dragging me back to the castle. And yet, even as I thought this, my feet were drawing me towards the sound.

Turning the corner, I found the source. Two guardsmen held a female elf between them, laughing viciously as they played a cruel tug-of-war with her limbs. Another elf was being dragged from a hovel by her golden hair, her clothing in tatters. Within the hovels, hideous screams mingled with telling grunts. Along the street stood more guardsmen, the sun beating down on the glistening white enamel and steel scale of their armor, as red blood dripped from their blades.

In the shadows I glimpsed the children, torn from their mothers' skirts, and the sight of them, more than anything else, filled me with rage.

I strode forward, my hand itching over the pommel of my sword, speaking with my father's voice. "What in God's name is going on here?"

It was a voice that roared, that voice of the Duke of Tremontaine. One that permitted no disobedience. At the sound of it, all who stood before me cringed. All was quiet but for the soft sobbing of an elf as she slumped to the ground.

The soldiers stared at me. One murmured my name. And then, as if a signal had been silently sounded, the soldiers' eyes turned towards a man whose back was to me.

He was a tall man, slender-bodied, narrow hipped, but broad of shoulder, wearing a long coat of embroidered red velvet, down which coursed a river of heavy black hair captured by a loosely tied red ribbon. I had not expected to see him here. "Darian?"

As he turned, my heart sank. It was not Darian at all.

It was Lorne du Beaumont.

I cursed myself for my error even as Lorne approached me, wearing a creamy smile not dissimilar to the one that a cat wears as it traps a mouse beneath its paw. "Sir Michael. What a pleasant surprise. Come to enjoy the festivities?"

"Sir Lorne," I said in polite acknowledgment. "What are you doing here?"

"Quelling the rebellion," he said. His gaze swept over me as his fingers twitched artlessly around the lace cuffs of his sleeves. "You know, cousin, I was about to ask you the same thing. Running around the elf quarter, with all the trouble that's been going on... what were you thinking?"

I knew what Lorne thought of me. At best, a foolish courtier. I threw myself into the role by giving him my haughtiest smile. "I was bored, really," I drawled, and then sighed. "All this talk at court about the revolt. Well. I decided to see for myself what all the fuss was about."

Again the dark-lashed green eyes swept over me, assessing. "I suppose matters of state would be boring to someone like you," he said, trying to bait me. I did not rise to take it, so he continued. "Well, since you are here... perhaps we can devise some entertainment for you."

I suppressed a shudder at the thought of Lorne's idea of "entertainment." As a boy, he had taken great delight in tormenting small animals before moving on to serving girls, wenches, and numerous other victims. As to the nature of

Lorne's torments, I knew them all too well.

Before I could form a polite refusal and make my excuses to slip away, Lorne snapped his fingers at the nearest guard, who scuttled towards us, dragging an elf girl by the arm. Gracefully, Lorne seized the girl, tearing her shift, then thrust her towards me, holding her at arm's length. An offering.

An elf's age was hard for humans to judge, but the girl seemed precisely that. On a small frame, her budding breasts quivered as Lorne twisted her spine. Over her shoulder, Lorne smiled at me as though he were offering me a dram of tea. "Does this one please you, cousin?" he purred. "I assure you, she's scarcely been used."

As the guards laughed, I bit my tongue. Lorne had always been adept at playing the swaggering braggart among the soldiers, but I was in no mood to participate in that game.

He stepped forward, trailing one gloved finger across the girl's cheek. "She is a rose, cousin, ripe for the plucking. Does she not set your blood on fire and your staff at attention?" Lorne paused as the guards laughed again. I remained silent. Lorne looked at the girl, then his eyes met mine. "Of course if she's not to your taste, perhaps we could find you a pretty little elf *boy* to take behind the stables?"

In those words, a memory. Suddenly I was twelve years old again, the victim in Lorne's sadistic game. My tongue had still been between my teeth, and now I tasted blood and bitter rage. I hated Lorne du Beaumont with a hatred I had not known I possessed. I wanted to kill him.

I wanted to kill him. But I could not. With the scrap of

self-control that still remained, I smiled at Lorne and spoke through gritted teeth. "Not at all, Lorne. I am merely not interested. The elves, they're so *dirty*. Probably diseased, as well. Truly, I find the idea of even touching one quite distasteful."

Lorne studied me for a long moment. Then he shrugged. "Suit yourself, Sir Michael."

In all haste, I took my leave. Though I still felt ill, my breathing had steadied by the time I reached the gate. I was halfway to the slums before my rage finally abated. And it was only when I passed by the Silver Dragon did I recall the words Gray had spoken about a knight's oath to protect the weak, and I did not favor myself very much in that moment.

I forgot all about Lorne and my self-pity when the elf damned me to hell.

After the damning, he heaped insults upon me. The insults were followed by an impressive string of curses – some of them new to me and colorful enough to make a hardened soldier blush. And, finally, once he had run out of curses I could understand, he hissed and screamed in what I presumed to be his native elfin tongue.

I could not blame him. The gash was long and the bone needle thick and the pain must have been excruciating. His cursing and insults did not distract me from the task of sewing him back together. However, his constant thrashing did.

I lost my patience. "I cannot fix you if you don't hold still!"

Gray muttered a feeble curse.

Sighing, I rubbed my fingers, stiff from holding the needle so tightly. "Listen, Gray," I said. "We are halfway through the stitching. I cannot continue like this. I must insist. The binding or the elfweed. Choose."

An hour had passed since my return from the elf quarters. In that time, I had tended to Gray, cleaning his wound, preparing and then applying the healing balm. None of it had been pleasant, but he had borne it well enough. When the moment of the stitching arrived, however, I had suggested he allow me to bind him to the bed. Or that he ingest the elfweed I had brought.

That Gray had refused both did not surprise me. Although he needed me, there was not enough trust between us that he would agree to being bound. The same applied to the elfweed.

Elfweed was used for two reasons. For one, it dulled an elf's senses and kept him submissive. Second, it was quite effective in banishing both pain and fatigue, thus an injured or exhausted slave could be made to work longer and harder. Elfweed was the elves' version of man's poppy. And, like the poppy, an elf who was given too much elfweed soon developed a sickness for it. This sickness was so common that it had earned the nickname "the weed demon."

Gray grew still and his breathing slowed as I waited for his answer. Pale and exhausted, he seemed halfway across death's threshold. He stared at me for a long time. Finally he squeezed his eyes shut, making a strange little noise, and when

244

he spoke, his voice was faint. "The elfweed."

It was a good choice – for me at least. Once the elfweed had taken effect, I was able to finish the stitching in no time, and I was certain that the patient no longer felt a thing. Soon I had knotted the thread into place, applied some more balm, and loosely bandaged his wound.

I had been sitting on the edge of the bed and was about to rise when his hand upon my arm stopped me. His voice floated up from far away. "Arisal..."

I looked down at Gray. The elfweed had left his body limp and his eyes heavy-lidded. The previous tension had drained from his face, leaving it smooth like porcelain. With his mouth slack and his strange silvery hair spilling across the bed, he reminded me of a woodcut of a most beautiful dying mermaid in a book I'd owned as a child.

"Who's Arisal?" I asked. An elfin name, male. He did not reply. His hand remained on my arm. Though, given the amount of elfweed I'd shoveled into him, I was certain he had just forgotten it was there.

This thought led to another. An unfair thought, to be sure, but, given the situation, I had no reason to be fair. "Gray? May I ask you a question?"

His eyelids, already heavy, drooped. He made a small non-committal hum.

"Tell me. How did you know my name?"

That honey voice of his was soft and dreamy. "Hmm? Oh. All the elves... know of you..."

"The elves in the slave quarter know of me. You're not a

slave. Where are you from?"

"From... *Sithcythril.*"

The way he spoke it, in a whisper like a caress, his voice accent-thick, I near didn't recognize the word. But it was a name I knew well from the history books. Sithcythril: from whence the elfin army swooped down on their demon steeds in an unholy crusade against the Montagues. Sithcythril: seat of an ancient kingdom, and home to the free elves of the world. Sithcythril: a name forbidden to speak, so that even the elfin slaves called it, as the common people did, Elfland.

"You're far from home, then. Why are you in Ersilia?"

"Sent here... a contract..."

"What sort of contract?"

One amethyst eye cracked open briefly, then closed again. "You ask... too many questions."

"I'm a very curious man," I said. Elfweed did much to loosen an elf's inhibitions, but as a serum of truth-telling, it was not always reliable. I studied Gray, thinking about how expertly he had disarmed me, how quick to draw the knife, and the murder I had read in his eyes. Although I did not want to hear the answer, I asked the question all the same. "Gray, this contract... are you an assassin?"

The eyelid flickered again. Gray grunted softly. "You're too curious," came his hazy voice. "Now... leave me alone."

"Fine," I replied lightly. "Just as long as it wasn't *me* you were sent to kill."

"No... not you."

It took me a moment to fully understand the implications of those words. If not me, then... well, then someone else. I was not certain if I wanted to know the name of the assassin's victim. I was far too involved with the elf as it was. On the other hand, Gray's presence outside the Silver Dragon last night, at the very moment in which Darian and I were attacked, was suspicious. If I had believed that Darian was the elf's target, I would have slain him on the spot.

I did not believe it. I remembered the hands which had pulled me out of harm's way. The elf had saved me. If Darian had been his target, he would have gained a perfect opportunity to kill him were I to have died before the guard's arrival.

At the end of my silent debate, I decided it would be better to know. "Gray?"

My only response was Gray's quiet breath. While I was wavering in indecision, Gray's hand had slipped from my arm, down to the bed. The elfin assassin was asleep.

I spent the following days nursing Gray back to health.

Other than taking leave for provisions or to avail myself of the public baths, I spent most of that time in the room. The elf passed the days asleep or in an elfweed haze. The former was rather dull, yet no more boring than court, but the latter was interesting indeed.

Although I wouldn't have said so to him, I preferred the drugged, submissive version of the elf better than the tough, menacing one. In that unfeeling state, he spoke freely, responding to most of my questions. Certain ones he refused to answer – such as his age. Elves did not age as humans did, showing their years on their faces, and for this it was once believed they were immortal. The silvered hair was the only indication I had, and I supposed him the age of my father.

Despite the fact that much of what he revealed was vague, I was fascinated by his fairy tale like accounts of Sithcythril, the free elves, and magic. Not all elves could do magic. Only those gifted were permitted to train with the wizards. The wizards also served the purpose of reading a child's gifts at birth, an act which determined his or her fate. Gray's gifts were known as the "triple dark." Those born with this rare combination were given the name "shadow children" and trained as spies, assassins, and concubines.

That a male had been trained in the pleasure arts intrigued more than his training as a spy and assassin concerned me. In Ersilia, those were common enough. Even the King had his own reserve of assassins, referred to as a "necessary evil." Although the noble houses were all bound by blood, our history was replete with usurping brothers, uncles, sons, and, on one occasion, at least, a tenacious second cousin.

For four days I tended him, conversed with him, and told him tales from Ersilian history which seemed to amuse him, as much as anyone in an elfweed haze could be amused. And in that time, in our private pigeonhole, a tenuous trust built up between us.

Reality crashed into the pigeonhole on the fifth day.

On the morning of the fifth day I had gone, as was my habit, to the baker's for sticky buns, then to the Silver Dragon where the tavernkeep's wife would sell me a dram of strongly-brewed black tea, and carry all back to the inn. Gray was usually asleep when I returned, but on this morning he was awake, and lucid.

He refused the usual elfweed but accepted the offer of tea. With my help, he managed to sit up in bed and take the cup, though he held it unsteadily with both hands.

I sat down in the room's only chair and watched as Gray slowly raised the cup to his lips. I chuckled at the sour expression he made. He scowled down into the cup as though its contents had insulted him. "What is this?"

"It's tea," I said. "The same tea you've been drinking for days, in fact."

Gray's look was skeptical.

"Well, it's all we have, so drink up. It's certainly strong enough to put some much-needed hair on your chest."

"Elves don't *have* hair on their chests," he mumbled, but drank the tea anyway.

The sticky buns, soft and still warm from the oven, were good at least. We gobbled every crumb, washing them down with the rest of the tea. Then I set the cups aside and turned to consider the elf.

Amethyst eyes met mine. "Why are you looking at me like that?"

In truth, I had been wondering at the fact that, after four days bed-ridden with no comb in sight, in that long abundance of silk hair not a single tangle appeared. My own was the impossibly thick mop of unruly black curls typical of the nobility, and I felt a pang of envy. And I had... well, in all truth,

I had been wondering how it would feel to run my fingers through those luscious, silvery strands.

Instead, I said, "I should look at your stitches."

He leaned back as I knelt before him, unwinding the bandages. Carefully I prodded the edge of his wound. Gray made a small hiss of pain, but otherwise remained still, which I took as a promising sign. Though not completely healed, the previous swelling had diminished and there was no longer any sign of infection.

Next I fetched the healing salve and fresh bandages. Meticulously I applied the salve to the wound and at the edges of each stitch. Examining them again, it struck me that the elf had healed quickly, and that stitches could come out in a few days.

My eyes and hands were focused on the task, but my thoughts were elsewhere. Without raising my eyes, I asked, "Gray? Who is Arisal?"

There was a pause before he spoke. "I said his name?"

With surprise, I looked up at him. "You don't remember?"

Gray sighed, lifting a hand to rub his face. "No. I remember." His mouth tightened. By his expression I could see his quiet struggle. And the clear pain there made me sorry I had asked.

"You don't have to tell me."

"No, it's just..." He twisted each of his clan rings before lowering his hand to the bed. "He was my son."

I drew back, wiping the traces of the sticky balm from

my fingers. "I'm sorry."

"Sorry?" Gray laughed, a dry, hollow and pained sound. "You can't understand. No one can understand how it feels to lose a child. Not unless he has lost one himself. Only then..."

"How did he die?"

Gray's voice was flat. "He was killed."

I knew not what to say. What could one say in the face of such tragedy? Also, his revelation had surprised me. I had not expected an assassin to have a family. Perhaps he had other children waiting for him in Sithcythril. A wife.

I felt like a fool.

Gray sighed. "Michael. Please. Let's talk about something else."

None of what he had revealed changed how it felt to have that honey voice wrapped around my name. It was like a caress, like wax melting below a flame. It rankled me how he could do that so easily, unaware. "Certainly," I said, using my courtier voice – airy and indifferent. "Why don't we talk about your contract, then? Who are you supposed to kill?"

He studied me, his expression guarded. "Why are you asking me this now?"

I shrugged, then picked up the bandages, retuning to my task. "Perhaps I wanted to give you the chance to have a clear head when I asked."

Gray was quiet as I wound the bandages around him. I was certain that he was not going to answer, but then he did, in a tone both soft and deadly.

"He must pay."

I leaned back on my heels. "Who must pay?" I asked, though one thing was clear: only the wealthy could afford an assassin's high price. And the victims were rarely commoners. "What nobleman? What House?"

Gray, silent, did not meet my gaze.

I thought I'd put all previous doubts to rest, yet now they surfaced. I snapped at him. "Why?"

Gray stared down at his own hands, pale-knuckled, twisting the sheets. It wasn't so much that he spoke as forced out the bitter words. "He must pay... for what he did to the elves."

I had an epiphany. It seemed to me that my heart ceased to beat, and that the space in my head had suddenly grown too large, making me dizzy. I choked on a weak laugh. Gray's head jerked up, and on his face an expression of surprise.

"I know who you must kill," I said. "It's Lorne du Beaumont."

Scarcely were the words out of my mouth that I took my leave. Abruptly.

I could not stay in the room, yet I could not go home. My arrival at Château du Tremontaine would be unexpected. Once I had made my decision to tend the elf, I had written to my mother to inform her that I would be staying with a friend until the Winter Masque, and had paid an urchin to deliver it.

Without a destination, I wandered the streets, my thoughts tumbling like acrobats. I hated Lorne du Beaumont. I had even wished him dead. But despite my feelings, Lorne was still of noble blood, husband to my cousin, and son-in-law to my liege, the King. To allow him to be murdered in cold blood would be treason.

To murder him in any blood would be a community service.

I passed the day with inner turmoil as my only company. It took me some time to admit, even to myself, that much of that turmoil was caused by the fact that Gray, injured, had little chance to succeed. In his current state, he could barely walk, much less kill a man. And time was running out – Lorne would be returning home long before Gray's injuries healed. These thoughts also troubled me and I struggled to convince myself to the contrary. There was scant reason for me to help him. The blood debt had been sufficiently repaid when I saved his life. He was little more than a stranger. He was an assassin. He was merely an elf.

That last thought surprised me. My father's voice again, but in my head where it did not belong. "Merely" was not apt to describe Gray. Despite the dulling effects of the elfweed, there had been hints of a keen intelligence and sharp wit below the haze. That he was an assassin spoke little of his character – a decision made for him at his birth.

It was after a third pint of ale in a tavern at the edge of town that I finally resigned myself to the possession of this knowledge.

When I entered the room, Gray was sitting in the bed with his back to the wall and his legs drawn up, a dagger ready in his hand. Recognizing me, his face flooded with relief. Seeing that clear need I suddenly felt bad for having abandoned him for so long. Outside, daylight was already waning.

In silence, Gray watched as I pulled out the feast I'd brought: meat pies, honeycakes, cheese, fruit, a jug of wine. He did not speak until we were halfway through the meal. "I didn't think you would come back."

"I almost didn't."

We spoke no more as we ate. After, I cleared away the crumbs, set aside the remaining honeycakes for the morning, and poured us each some wine. Then I withdrew the final item from my sack: a deck of cards. Sitting down on the bed opposite Gray, I shuffled the cards and began to deal them out.

Gray cocked his head. "What are you doing?"

I set the deck on the space between us and turned four cards face up. "I'm teaching you how to play Spit."

The elf looked at me, clearly puzzled. "It sounds unsanitary," he decided. "Why?"

I gestured at him to pick up the hand I'd dealt him. "Because that's what men do when they need a distraction from the harshness of life. They drink and play cards."

Gray gave me a skeptical look, but picked up his cards.

I spent some time teaching him how to play. In Spit, there were a lot of trump cards, but Gray memorized them quickly. Once he had a grasp of the rules, we played a few rounds open-handed and then I reshuffled the deck.

"What kind of game is this?" he asked as I dealt the first round.

254

"The kind that's played in taverns. Normally, the loser must drink. The game ends when the players pass out. Given your condition, however, I suggest a different penalty."

"Such as?"

"The loser must answer any question of the winner's choosing. Truthfully."

Gray's eyes glittered with interest as he considered my proposal. Then his lips curled into a cunning smile. "I agree."

We played cards until late in the night, and thus it was near midday when I woke. I left the honeycakes for Gray and decided to break my fast after a visit to the public baths.

Upon my return, I found Gray out of bed. Using the wall for support, he was slowly inching around the room. Given his expression, either the movement pained him or his mood was just foul, so I spoke cautiously. "Gray? Have you eaten yet? I brought you some tea. There's some honey in it this time. And what are you doing?"

"I'm sick of being in that bed," he said. "I need to get up and move around to regain my strength."

"I was always told that a sick man had to stay in bed to regain his strength."

"I'm not a *man*," Gray muttered.

"If you're not careful, you're going to reopen your wound. In fact, you could make it worse. And don't expect me to be able to stuff all your guts back in if they happen to fall out."

He snorted. "You sound like a nursemaid."

"I thought elves didn't have nursemaids."

"No, but you told me all about yours during that silly game last night." He shifted his hand against the wall, the other thoughtfully twisting the rings in his ear. "Do all humans spill their secrets as easily as you do? If so, that would make my job much simpler."

The quip on my tongue dissolved as a knock came at the door.

Gray and I both froze. Judging that he would not be seen from the hall where he stood, I gestured at him to stay still, then I moved to the door, opening it a crack.

A young boy thrust a folded bit of parchment at me. I recognized him as being the same boy I had sent to deliver the letter to my mother a few days ago. "Letter for you, Sir Michael."

Having sent the boy away with a coin, I sat down on the chair, turning the folded square of parchment over in my hands. I recognized Darian's elegant script even before I broke his seal.

The letter was brief. After his apologies for having left me in the fray came a severe chastising for my subsequent disappearance and causing him concern. This was followed by his relief the next day when his brother-in-law informed the court of my presence in the elf quarter. Then he finished the letter with a demand that I tell him everything at the Winter Masque tomorrow night, which I was obligated to attend.

Below the decadent slant of his signature, he had added in postscript a clever insinuation about my new "friend" and his codpiece that caused me to laugh.

If only... I thought.

"Must be amusing that letter."

I looked at Gray. He had arrived at the window and was leaning against the frame, looking out. He had swept up all his hair and was holding it aloft, revealing the bones of the long, delicate nape of his neck.

I had a sudden vision of myself rising from the chair, crossing the room, and kissing the back of Gray's elegant neck. So vivid was this vision, I could feel the heat of his body to mine, and taste his skin on my lips.

Gray turned to meet my eyes. For a moment he stared at me as if puzzled.

I promptly folded up the letter, tucking it into my tunic. "Shall we play cards?"

For the rest of the day we played, stopping only to sup. Instead of playing Spit again, I taught him Devil's Maw, another tavern game, and Queen's Knight, a game popular at court. Although we did converse, Gray did not ask me about the letter. Nor did we speak of Lorne du Beaumont.

Instead, as we played, we philosophized about truth, love and beauty, recited what poetry we knew in our respective tongues, recreated the Elf Wars with our words, and talked at length about food. Also, as we played, I would often catch him casting me a strange, questing look that I could not decipher and he would not explain. And then the hour grew late.

I set aside the cards, put out the lamp, and stretched out on my usual place on the floor. Yet I could not sleep, thinking about the Winter Masque. I had made no arrangements for my costume, but it was probable that my mother had arranged it months ago. I would have to go home then to change before heading to court. I would have to remember to leave Gray enough provisions before I left. I would have to –

Gray's voice broke into my thoughts. "Sleeping like that – it can't be comfortable."

I leaned up on my elbow and looked to the bed. I could just barely make out his face by the moonlight coming through the window. "It's not, but you're the injured one, so you get the bed."

I heard the sound of sheets sliding as Gray shifted over. "There's enough room for two."

I considered his offer. I was too tempted to accept it. "That isn't a good idea," I said. "You don't know... what I am."

"I know what you are."

I was certain that he had misunderstood me. I tried again. "You don't know what you're asking."

"I know what I'm asking."

I frowned. "Gray..."

"I was trained in all the sexual delights," he murmured invitingly. "Would you like me to show them to you?"

A shiver ran through me. Suddenly I understood the meaning of that look he had been giving me all day. That honey voice got all caught up in my ear, making my thoughts impossible and sticky. Before I knew it I was sitting on the edge of the bed, leaning over Gray, looking down into those strange, elfin eyes.

His light hand danced over my face, then my lips, moving as if sketching out a magical spell of aching and longing. Then his hand trailed down my chest, slender fingers expertly unknotting the laces on my shift as they traveled, exploring.

In a moment of clarity, I moved to stay his hands with my own. "You're injured."

His eyes were like smoke. A seductive smile played upon his lips as his hands curled up around my shoulders. His voice was a teasing caress. "I'm not that injured," he said, and pulled me down to the bed.

There was a painstaking care to what we did that night. Yet his skill was such that those acts were no less the pleasurable for it, and each delight he showed me hinted at the possibility of even greater pleasures yet to be revealed.

I didn't know if the thought of what he *could* do were he uninjured alarmed or intrigued me. Entangled in his velvet limbs as his sweat cooled on my skin and night drew to an end, I only knew the truth in my heart.

"Gray," I swore, "I will be your blade. I will kill Lorne du Beaumont."

I arrived late at the Winter Masque.

From past experience I knew that preparations for the Winter Masque had been taking place for days. The Great Hall was lit with both torches and lanthorns, festooned with the last of the season's flowers, painted silk banners fluttered from the ceiling beams, and the floors had been cleared of rushes for dancing. In one corner a miniature village made of corn husks had been constructed to delight the young, and there was music, food, and drink in abundance for all.

I arrived late enough that most of the revelers were deep in their cups, and the more promiscuous members of the court were occupied with flirting their way into a reckless tryst. My arrival thus garnered little attention, as intended.

Earlier that afternoon, Gray had told me of his plan. Costumed, the assassin would attend the Masque, lure his target to a shadowy place to kill him, and then slip away in the night. I had thought it an impossibly simple plan until he unraveled all its details before my eyes.

It would begin, he said, by walking through the palace gate.

The Long Night was celebrated by all Ersilians in the same manner, with feasting, dancing, and costumes. The only difference between the commoners and the nobility was the amount of excess. At the castle, everything was far more elaborate, particularly the costumes. It was a long-standing tradition in court that each year's costume not only outshine everyone else's, but outshine one's own costume from previous Masques. In fact it was common that the day after the Winter Masque, certain court ladies – and quite a few lords – would begin planning the costume for the following year's festival.

There were no invitations required to attend. In fact, the costume served to hide the identity of every guest. Anyone could gain entrance simply by appearing at the gate in an appropriately decadent masque.

When I expressed my skepticism, Gray instructed me to open his pack. Reaching in, my fingers touched upon something soft, and I pulled it out.

Feathers had been in vogue at court of late, so much so that Darian had amused me with a quip about the sorry lot of so many bald birds in Ersilia, so the robe I pulled from Gray's pack was thus the height of fashion. Long, green feathers, deepening in hue, swept from the collar down to the floor. More feathers adorned the hood, framed with the eyes of peacock tails. The sleeves and collar were trimmed in cloth-of-gold, with tiny roses stitched in silver thread. It was exquisite. Exquisite, too, was the face mask, painted gold, with hooded eyes and jutting down to the chin, hinting at a bird's beak. Soft boots the same color gold as the mask completed the ensemble.

The last thing Gray did before I took my leave was to fasten the sheath of his hidden knife on my arm, and teach me how to draw it without catching the loose sleeve of the feathered robe.

In this disguise would I need to find Lorne and lure him to his death. Except, as I quite bluntly pointed out to Gray, he would also be disguised, and thus, it would be impossible for me to recognize him.

To that, Gray smiled a strange little enigmatic smile. "You must kill the Oak King."

Using legends was a common theme at the Masques, and I did not question the fact that Lorne would choose such an ancient, powerful, and blatantly virile god as his masque. I did, however, question Gray's method of acquiring this information. A costume for the festival was a coveted secret, revealed only at the end of the Masque itself.

Gray sneered. "Whose hands do you think stitched every feather of your cloak until they bled? Elven hands, Michael. Who do you think breaks their backs tilling your fields, building your walls, and polishing the floors of your halls? Who cooks your food, scrubs your chamberpots, and spreads their legs for the nobles' lust? Elves, Michael. Whose ears hear all your dirty secrets and lies because you think them deaf and dumb and unworthy of your notice?" His eyes flashed murder. "And who washed the streets of the elf quarter with the blood of the innocent? Raped our wives and murdered our children? *Men*."

His venom shocked me. "Gray! I'm on your side."

The hatred drained from his expression. He hung his head, staring at the cup of tea trembling in his hands. "I know that," he said softly. "I know you're different. That's why I..."

He trailed off suddenly, leaving me in an anxious state. I could sense the import of the words he'd left unspoken. And yet, a part of me did not want to hear them. Not when a missing piece of the puzzle had just clicked into place. "You saw it, didn't you? You were there during the slaughter."

Gray explained. He had been hiding in the elf quarter for months, plotting and making his arrangements. Where better for an elf to hide than among elves? But he refused to speak of the horrors he had seen, and I had not pressed him.

262

Instead I had gone home to fetch the costume my mother had arranged. Once Lorne was dead, I was to quickly change from the feathered cloak into the other costume, at which point "Sir Michael" would make his appearance, and the "assassin" would have disappeared.

Having entered the Palace, I had stashed Sir Michael's costume in a dark niche near the Great Hall – a particularly good place I'd often used when Darian and I had played hide and seek. Then I made my way into the Great Hall, and cast about my gaze.

I saw him across the room, conversing with a woman all in white, a silver goblet held casually aloft in one hand. He wore a long coat of green velvet, craftily adorned with leaves and twigs. More leaves were entwined in his long black hair, falling loose about his face fully covered by a deer-horned mask of brown leather.

I stopped a servant and bid her deliver a note to the Oak King.

I watched as he took the note, unfolded it, and read it. Upon the note I had written:

> *Cousin,*
> *I must speak to you urgently about a private matter.*
> *I will await you at the next hour strike behind the stables.*
> *Tell no one.*
> *M*

He lowered his hand and directed a question at the serving girl. Following her gesture with his eyes, he found me. For a moment he looked at me as if puzzled. Or rather, I imagined his puzzlement – from where I stood, I could only see the blankness of his mask.

Sending the note had been my contribution to Gray's plan. Although I had worded it carefully enough so that Lorne would not be able to use it against me, there was still the possibility that he could ignore it, or – if he choose – use it to unmask me.

Yet I was counting on him to take no such action. I was putting myself in his hands. Knowing Lorne, I doubted that he could resist such a temptation.

A moment passed and then he folded up the note, secreting it away. And to me, he raised his glass.

I slipped from the Great Hall and made my way to the stables where I crouched in a shadow cast from the palace wall.

I knew not how many times I adjusted my mask, or reached to touch the hidden blade, or jumped at the smallest whisper of noise while I waited. My senses seemed unusually sharp. The night sky was a palette of indigo but for the moon, a perfect circle framed by two of the castle turrets, casting spindly black shadows among patches of gray. In my nostrils stung the odors of wet earth, horses and hay. The breeze tingled against the skin of my hands. It was strange – waiting to kill a man, I had never felt more alive.

After what seemed an eternity of waiting, the Oak King arrived. Alone.

Hidden as I was, he did not espy me among the shadows. He took a few tentative steps, searching about. Following him with my eyes, I let my hatred fill me.

His back was to me as I stepped from the shadow. I

made no attempt to silence my footsteps as I approached. A twig snapped, loud as a whip crack, below my boot, and he turned. As he turned, I plunged the knife into him.

It was fortunate that his heavy coat was open in the front, offering no resistance to my blow. The knife sank up to the hilt. Twisting it halfway out, I thrust again as Gray had instructed me, angling the blade up below his ribcage to pierce his heart.

He made only one noise – a pathetic thing halfway between a gasp and a cry. It struck me that he was dying. Killing a man was pitifully easy. I had expected there to be more blood. Mundane, perhaps – but such were my thoughts as I withdrew the knife.

Hands clutched at the wound as he wavered on his feet, sounds coloring his jagged breath. He took one staggering step towards me, arms outstretched in silent supplication, long white hands spattered with blood. Then, as if he were no more than a puppet whose puppeteer had cut the strings, he crumpled at my feet.

As the dead man hit the ground, the mask slipped out of place, and by the moonlight I clearly saw his face, and it was not the face of Lorne du Beaumont.

What happened then was strange. I did not suffer rage or sorrow; instead a calmness descended upon me, along with a silence that was pure and absolute. In that moment I had only one thought: *My God, I just killed Darian du Montague.*

A moment – no more, no less, yet it seemed to stretch on endlessly, an inexplicable paradox.

Then the silence was broken by the footfalls of the faithful guard as they came thundering down upon me.

Her beauty intoxicated, though I didn't let that stop me. I would not be elf-drunk!

Jon Bishop is currently a senior at Assumption College and double majors in Political Science and English. He divides his time between Wilmington, MA and Worcester, MA.

"Elves are cool. I wrote this story in hopes of putting a twist on the prompt given. Honestly, the inspiration came from some of the individuals I met while attending a tabletop gaming convention a year or so ago. I was hoping to write a funny piece."

Jon's work has appeared in BOSTON LITERARY MAGAZINE, and Assumption College's L'ESPRIT.

David and Gerty
Jon Bishop

My name is David, but in the game – the fantastical world of online role-playing – I am known as Harbender. All fear my Ogre-self. Though today was an event that would cause even the mightiest of half-breeds to quiver and tremble. Even a powerful Ogre like me found it nerve-racking.

I'd get to meet her today. The thought always sends me into pure bliss.

I had to get ready. I got myself out of bed and brushed my teeth. I combed my hair neat and put on shorts and my favorite shirt: the black one that read "They're action figures. Not dolls." I cracked my knuckles – I had to relieve some soreness after a long night of gaming – and put on my glasses.

I lumbered over to my desk, sat down, and turned on my computer. I loaded the game. There she sultrily stood, her pixels pulsating with primal beauty. My elfin princess. I typed her lovely name to message her and it echoed in my head: Ravenda. A lovely name – it rang of the poetry present in old Marvel Comics. Like Fin Fang Foom, the dragon-beast, but better.

We met long ago, in the peaceful age of low-cost gaming subscriptions. I entered the woods to kill goats to up my ranking. Someone else had the same idea: her. She radiated beauty. Her long, flowing blonde hair danced in the wind. She had perfectly pointed ears. She wore a sparkling white dress. Her porcelain skin made me utterly weak. But, regardless, I wouldn't allow anyone – let alone an elf female! – to take my kills. I attempted intimidation: I shook my fist and waved my massive bat in her face. She didn't budge.

How intriguing! Yet how attractive! I immediately noted her as a possible partner with which to breed and converse.

"Greetings! I am Harbender. Scourge of the Great Land."

"I'm Ravenda. Nice to meet you!" She giggled. Or I imagined she did – this was all text. My imagination enjoyed pulling these scenarios out from the screen and into reality.

We did everything together following that encounter. We frolicked through meadows with fairies dancing around us with the tree-walkers smiling. We tricked townsfolk into giving us their gold and laughed at the noobs who had no clue. We defined perfection. Ravenda and Harbender – together. Like a super-powerful computer, we'll be on forever.

But now sweat slid down my skin. Question time – the moment I'd been agonizing over for weeks.

Her beauty intoxicated, though I didn't let that stop me. I would not be elf-drunk! I pressed onward in the conversation!

"Um, Ravenda?"

"Yes?"

"Shall we, say, meet up in person? I'd really like to meet

you. I'm sure you're just as ravishing as your elfin avatar."

"I'd love to!"

Goody! I felt my hair. Greasy and wet – I must shower! I must put on my nicest clothes. But where to eat? I'm sure an elfin goddess like her would only prefer the finest cuisine.

"Would you like to meet at Steve's Pizza Emporium?"

"Sounds great. I'll meet you there?"

"Yes. Harbender, out."

She began walking away.

"Wait!"

"Yes?"

"Does six o'clock sound good?"

"Yes."

"Today?"

"Sure."

"Okay. See you then! Harbender, out."

I signed off. The time: 3:26. I had about two point five hours to prepare myself for a most excellent meeting.

Who knows? Maybe she would be willing to breed with me in real life. And we could conquer this town – crush those who dare stand in our way. The possibilities excited me. I stretched and rubbed my head as I considered them.

I arrived at the restaurant with a few minutes to spare. You're good, David, I kept telling myself. She is a female and plays online games with you. She is Ravenda and you are her king. I exhaled and exited the car.

I entered the restaurant and immediately knew it was her – the plump goddess. She sat in the booth afar, the sunlight shining on her and the wooden seat. Her craggy blonde hair rang of the Great Forest: a cornucopia of ragged trees, rocks, weeds, and dangerous creatures. One must conquer this to become a true warrior. Her glasses spoke of her intellect. Her face pockmarked like that of a battle-scarred knight. Her upper-lip glistened with saliva, the fuzz matted down – she must have literally licked her lips in anticipation.

I walked over and bowed before sitting directly across from her. She sniffed, making a snort. I stared. She did as well.

What to say? What to say?

"Um—"

She sniff-snorted once more.

"Hello. You may know me as your terrible scourge and partner, Harbender. But I am David. What is your name, sweet Ravenda?"

"Gerty." A phlegmy, yet angelic voice.

"How intriguing."

I stared at her.

She sniff-snorted.

Two minutes passed. Four minutes. Eight.

I breathed heavily.

A heavyset bearded man wearing an apron with the name "Lance" etched onto a tag approached the table. He held a notepad.

Gruffly: "What'll it be?"

Silence.

"Well?"

Me: "What'll it be? Hopefully a higher level! I'm looking

to level up."

"Ugh. I'll be back in a few minutes."

Gerty: "I like your shirt."

"Me too. It's my favorite."

"I like t-shirts. They are funny."

"I also like pizzas. I ordered a pizza two days ago. It was great gaming fuel."

"Pizzas are tasty."

Silence again. Lance returned.

"Well? Have you guys made a decision? What can I do for you?"

"..."

"You're both looking a little sickly. All clammy and stuff. You okay?"

We looked up at him. Another sniff-snort from Gerty. We rose and left the table. I hurried to my car and sped off. I had to return to the game.

I jumped out of the car and flew my house. I dragged over to the desk and pulled my computer out of standby. I eagerly resumed my game.

And there she was – sweet Ravenda! – waiting for me.

I typed:

"Greetings Ravenda! Never mind the being David you encountered. He is quite strange."

We left for the forest, with the sun's glorious pixels setting above us.

She had not died. She was simply resting and would wake when the sun crossed her face. There was no blood soaking the white, sparkling snow.

James Thibeault is a middle school English teacher for Venerini Academy.

"I notice my best work is when I'm given a circumstance which is unusual and not typically what I write about. Elves being in love was not an idea I ever considered, but I decided to give it a try. However, I was stuck for a couple of weeks – not having any clue into what Elves do or how they feel. Then one day at work I suddenly thought up the line "He could not see the way she nestled in the snow." Soon after, I thought up a story of Mikaloi and his recently deceased companion Kaléma. At first I felt sympathetic for him, but soon it switched to frustration – constantly rereading his incompetence which cost Kaléma her life. But then I realized this was love's universal appeal: a relentless passion neither sharp nor wise. Soon after, I understood all love acted the same way, but it was only a matter of how we wish to see it."

James' work has been been featured in several literary magazines, including: NEW HAMPHIRE WRITERS, WRITE PLACE AT THE WRITE TIME, FEWERTHAN500, THIS MAGAZINE and FREIGHT TRAIN MAGAZINE.

Unseen
James Thibeault

Mikaloi could not see the way she nestled in the snow. The forest loomed, a thick canopy of branches and pines above. Darkness clouded her image. Occasionally, the winds bent the trees, creeping in rays of sunlight. But Mikaloi would not beg for any luminosity. The light would not breathe the air or take space near the silhouette – this lovely shadow of Kaléma. Yet, he needed to know and only illumination's authority would reveal it to him. But he wished for the light to lie. Let it, just once, fib in his face. When the glow finally warmed through the black and silent trees, let it slander. Only for a while, let this hope of a mistake be true. She had not died. She was simply resting and would wake when the sun crossed her face. There was no blood soaking the white, sparkling snow. No, he could not prepare for the light. If he had to anchor the trees from the wind, hold great pines in place, he would. He could not let light come.

But as the winds blew down the mountainside and nudged the trees below, a faint light crept through to stalk the face of Kaléma. He saw her auburn flowing hair tangled and ripped from the scalp. A black hoof mark, which covered from chest to her waist, crushed into her body. Mikaloi did not notice the blood on her tunic, the lacerations or bruises.

Neither did he see her pointed ears, almost cleaved from her head, dangling like wind chimes. He gazed into her clear blue eyes, open wide as if awake. Her eyes stared back at Mikaloi, saying to him, "I did not see the men as they trod upon me." He would not acknowledge her silent voice. Mikaloi ached for the old, dark uncertainty – before the trees released the light and the fate of the elf remained a mystery. He yearned for lies and knelt beside her. Mikaloi begged Kaléma to lie and say she was fine – that in this darkness, men did not trample over her like brush on a trail; there were no screams from her voice as they crushed her bones. *When the light leaves your face we'll walk as we did through frost and thick snow. I'll kiss your hand and stroke your hair, laugh at memories and masquerades and love you as I do now.* But she did not speak. Mikaloi kissed her lips, seeking one more thought or dream or pleasure. Yet nothing remained but dried, cracked lips.

Mikaloi touched the blood on her cheeks in the fading sunlight. Although Kaléma was trampled, her limp body merging into the mud, he worried about the blood staining her face. He ripped cloth from his tunic and dabbed the deep, stark color away. Her face, preserved for now in the light, reminded Mikaloi how soft her cheeks were. And yet, the light bore emptiness on her face. Mikaloi cradled her in the empty trail and apologized for the snowball he'd thrown.

Mikaloi wrestled with Kaléma at the outskirts of the forest. The sweat from her brow glistened from the light. She snuck herself from off the ground and laughed. When Mikaloi

275

rose, she lightly slapped his chin.

"You'll have to be faster if you wish to pin me."

"I believe you once thought differently."

Strong for her small stature, she pushed Mikaloi back into the snow.

"Your games are done. We have work to do."

But still he rose, ready to grapple.

"We still have time in the light."

"But I need you in the dark."

"It's too dark in the woods, lest I topple over you."

She coyly smiled and brushed away the long hair covering his face.

"I thought it was your wish to topple over me."

"But I must see how to aim my sword at the beast."

"A beast, I am?"

"How else can I explain the wild passion which comes?"

She held his hands and tried tugging him toward the woods.

"So then the beast beckons you into the dark."

Yet Mikaloi held his ground, despite the strength she mustered. She persisted.

"We have to see if the hole I made on the lake froze over."

"Kaléma, there is snow everywhere. The freshest water is chilled for us!"

"But the fish, Mikaloi, the berries you picked won't last long."

She departed into the woods, her appearance darkening with each step. Mikaloi remained where he stood. Before he knew the thoughts conceiving in his head, he dug into the snow and pressed a solid white ball and threw. She crashed into the snow, sobbing.

"What was that Mikaloi?"

"Kaléma, quit crying. It was only play."

She stumbled up while stunned from the pain and hobbled into the woods. Kaléma disappeared and never looked back – her tears piercing the snow.

Oh god, he had made her cry. He cast away the elf he loved into the solitude. He left her alone to walk the blackish trail. Even when he saw the four men barreling down the trail, with nothing but the dim light guiding, he punished her. It was only when he thought of Kaléma and the sound of hooves, did Mikaloi run. The men would see the trail, but no elf. They would hear the horses' hoofs rattle, but think of no reason to stop. They would imagine a branch, in the worst case an animal. Mikaloi forced himself into the stubborn woods, crashing through sticks and rocks, falling and rising, pushing through thick black, to warn Kaléma. And it didn't matter. Mikaloi dug his fingers into Kaléma's cold flesh. Was there a smile on her face when the horses arrived? Perhaps her rage subsided? Was she calm walking the snow? No, he was a fool to think she found her peace. He killed her. He could have stopped her one more time from crying, ceased one more moment of pain. Mikaloi could have grasped all the joy from his soul and cast it away if it could cleanse the death from

Kaléma's body. But it didn't matter now. There were no more attempts to give her happiness. The trees closed in on the light and Kaléma was dark again.

The elf waited at the other side of the forest, where the light shined with confidence. The men stopped their horses and shouted.

"We have no quarrel with you, creature. Let us pass."

Mikaloi drew his sword, the length of a human's forearm.

"But now you can see, and see a quarrel."

Mikaloi killed them all and their horses. He did not bury them or give them sacred rights. They would rot, not forgotten by time, but remembered as wasting bodies. Those arriving at the outskirts of the forest would see the slaughtered men, the sunshine revealing the ugly, brutal mess Mikaloi left behind.

He buried Kaléma miles from the trail – down where the light never shined. He told her stories about the melting snow and how the grass peeked through to see the sights of spring. Mikaloi laughed at the jokes he told for both of them. He said how he loved her. Every day, he was here. He loved not what was buried below, but treasured the unseen. It was here she remained beautiful. In the darkness he could conjure back his finest love, without the light's objection.

"The Feather Clan are not to be trusted. Deceit is written in their bones. Cruelty in the heritage of their quills."

Joanna Fay is an Australian poet, short story writer and budding fantasy novelist. From an early age she loved to create her own storyworlds, which grew into a lifetime habit. She has an honors degree in Fine Arts and worked as a tapestry weaver before turning to "serious writing." She has many published and awarded poems, and her short stories have shortlisted in a number of competitions. Joanna currently works as a natural therapist, homeschools her son by day, and writes epic fantasy by night.

"'Feather Fall' was actually inspired by the theme 'Elf Love'. It sat in my head for a while, percolating. Then, when I was glancing through a novella set in the storyworld I most obsessively write in, I came across a scene of a woman (with elvish traits) finding the body of a man on a beach. And I asked myself 'What if he was alive?' and 'What if he was an elf?' and the new story just unfolded from there."

Joanna's first published short story is "Threadsongs," a science fiction story included in the SHADES OF SENTIENCE anthology, a collection of finalist stories from the inaugural competition of the same name.

She blogs along with four companion aspiring fantasy novelists at egoboo-wa.blogspot.com.

Feather Fall
Joanna Fay

Kieri walked alone, not bothering to shield her skin and clothes from the rain. Past Tanem's wet shoreline, the border-spells' blue geometry swirled like a wall of oil. Kieri looked away from their shifting patterns. They no longer seemed beautiful to her. Sand crumbled between her toes. Her gown caught in the wash of a stealthy wave, velvet dragging behind her feet. She wished the ocean's slide would take her memories with it – she didn't want to think about her father and brother any more. Or the "mission" being forced on her.

Kieri drifted to a halt, losing herself in the sea's hushed voice. Tears clung to her lids. Looking north along a crescent of sand, she thought of the distant mountains where the Snow Clan lived, and wished she were there.

But not in the way my clan wants of me, spying out their frailties.

The thought sickened her, as did the fear rising with the idea of leaving her home. In her brief two hundred years, Kieri had never been allowed outside the protection of Tanem's shielded bays.

Protection! Bitterness hardened her mouth. *How many times in my short life have the shields been breached?*

She looked up along the border-spells meant to withstand the aerial attacks of the Feather Clan. Their rolling oil-shimmer glowed under the rain.

But the shields aren't strong enough – now even my brother is gone.

Kieri hugged herself, against the darkness of her thoughts rather than the lowering light. Even so, the prospect of night frightened her, alone on the beach. Turning from the sea, she started across the sand, the straight russet of her hair matting into damp ribbons. She reached a line of silvered tussocks, and stopped. A sound too close to the tenor of her thoughts sent her heart into stutters. Directly overhead, the sky rippled – and cracked.

High above her, a fissure appeared in the shield ringing the bay's dim sky. Sparks of white bounced at its edges. Densely-woven defences began to unravel. Kieri raised her hands to her mouth, poised to run and sound the alert. But instead she remained motionless, her eyes fixed on the blazing hole, closing as fast as it had opened. The border resealed with a ringing snap, and a glittering object plummeted toward her from the sky. In a stream of black feathers and hair, a man's limp body hit the sand at the water's edge with a jarring thump... and didn't move.

Speechless, shivering, Kieri took a few uncertain steps toward him. Then she broke into a run, wet cloth gripping her ankles. Ignoring the rain spattering her face, she knelt by the man's side. Her fear vanished at the shock of perceiving his injuries. An acrid swirl of nausea rose in her stomach. Was he past healing?

Why would I even want to?

Her eyes moved over the tortured wounds lacing his body, still welling blood of a thick, gleaming amber; they appeared to have been inflicted and cauterized, wrenched and reopened countless times. She sucked in a steadying breath. Her gaze settled on the beauty of the still, expressionless face, the sugar-white skin framed with hair like black silk. The ears as pointed as her own, sign of their kinship. Water trickled in tiny rivulets across his brow and cheeks and down his neck, mixing into the tawny pool around his body.

Kieri didn't move. Thoughts splintered through her shock. She forced herself to take in the extent of the man's wounds. His spells must have disintegrated; she'd heard often enough of the powers of the Feather Clan – used too often in aggression against her people – to think he could be this badly damaged otherwise. Questions spun in her head. The memory of a teaching jolted through her; *elves of the Feather Clan can't heal without light.* Kieri assessed the sky. Darkness would wrap the island in half an hour.

Undecided, she reached down a tentative finger, stroked back a strand of jet-black hair. *What am I doing?*

Her stomach tightened. *My father and brother died fighting these savages.*

Acid swirled into her mouth. She should kill this man – gods, for all she knew, he might have killed Trien. Her brother's last sombre salute formed in her vision. She blinked it back and focussed on the man at her feet. At the very least, she should wrap him in spells of binding, summon those who

282

dealt in death. The defiance that had driven her to the sea's edge surged up again; she kept the mental links to her clan tightly shut. A long pinion shivered against her toe. Kieri stumbled to her feet clutching at a hair that had come away in her hand. Backing away, she broke into a run.

Stop!

The word sent ice through her head, the sensation of falling through cloud. She froze.

Help me.

Kieri looked back over her shoulder. The man was pulling himself to his feet, watching her. Even from this distance, his eyes were as grey as her own, but hard in his white face. He seemed to pick up on her thought, and softened his expression. Then he staggered and clutched at the longest gash in his thigh, losing blood in an amber string.

"Please."

His voice drifted to her across the sand. It was low, and it shook. Kieri paused, torn. She turned and stared at the man. He stared back, and she took one step toward him. His beauty wouldn't be enough to hold her, although *that* was breathtaking. But the naked vulnerability in that one word – *please.*

He didn't move. Perhaps he didn't want to startle her, scare her away. He needed her. He was the enemy. He *needed* her.

Kieri sucked in a breath and walked back across the beach, until she stood within a few paces of the man. This close, the lines of pain at the corners of his mouth, the tight self-restraint of his posture, the repression of any sound or

283

gesture that might show his weakness, were much clearer.

She became horribly aware of how exposed he was, how exposed *her* sudden act of complicity was, on the open beach. And the light was failing.

From the lift of his gaze, he was measuring it too. Fear swept from him on the breeze, tingling against Kieri's wet pores. She stood quite still, moved against her will. The gulf of a few footsteps hung between them, filled with darkness, violence, the blood of her people and of his. He swayed, the blackness of his eyes clouding. Behind him, jet feathers splayed awkwardly into the sand. His wings repulsed her, symbolized everything she loathed about his kind, and yet...

On reflex, Kieri leaned forward and gripped his arm. "You've got to heal yourself *now*," she said.

Holding him, she muttered a string of words, fortifiers, clarifiers, comforters. The warmth rising around her spells brought a faint colour to his skin. The man shook his head. Wet black locks flipped across Kieri's arm. She didn't flinch, or feel revulsion. Instead, something altogether different prickled up to meet the slide of his hair. Kieri absorbed the sensual shock, and glanced back at his face. His eyes were closed, his head slightly tilted back. Trusting her with his life, he had let himself slide deep into the healing trance of his kind.

Its warmth resonated through her senses, not so different from the mending craft of her own people. Kieri found herself wanting to touch his bared throat, let her fingers follow the hard line of his jaw, slip through rips in the black fabric fitted snugly to his frame. Her shock sank deeper, laced with fascination, a connection that pulsed through the hard sinews of his forearm into her fingertips. Her grip must have tightened. The man's eyes opened, and they were contemplative.

Looking down, Kieri realized he'd already closed most of his wounds, although his clothes were drenched in blood, and he was still leaning into her grasp.

"Who did this to you?" she managed.

The man's head tilted in unconscious arrogance. "Who could get close enough to inflict these kinds of wounds other than my own people?"

His voice held a sharp edge, although Kieri sensed it was not directed at her. Questions crowded her head, but this wasn't the place to voice them. She looked back along the rough-grown edge of the beach. Still no figures hovered in the closing darkness, but urgency now filled her and she tugged at the man's arm.

"Come. We mustn't stay here."

Adrenaline pushed Kieri into a half-run. She'd have to steer a course clear of the houses lying over the mound of hills past the beach, for her own sake now, as much as this man's.

This man's.

She stopped and his lean body lurched into her. "I don't even know your name. I'm Kieri," she offered.

The man regarded her from slate eyes, then gave her a faint smile. It changed his face, took away some of its chiselled harshness. When he spoke, his voice was gentle. "My name is Rathen."

"Rathen." Kieri rolled her tongue around the hardness and softness of the word, and took his hand. His fingers were slippery with rain – and blood-loss.

Come.

She pulled him into a fast walk, praying he could manage it. Rathen's hand pinched tight in hers, speaking mute effort, but he said nothing and kept up with the pace she set. He didn't question her, and Kieri bit back the words her prejudice wanted to fling at him. His silence spoke a trust she couldn't encompass. Chaos threatened her mind. She pushed it back and focussed on the stiff sea-grass catching at her wet skirts.

Up ahead, the dark twisted shapes of trees became visible through the water, offering cover. Rathen stumbled on a tussock. Black feathers spilled down Kieri's side for a second until he righted himself, leaving a splatter of amber on her dress. She glanced at him, reassuring herself of the wholeness of his skin. He would live.

You want me to live.

The words floating into her head were not a question, but they were tinged with something – a wonder, a plea, that made Kieri draw closer to him. Wet leaves slapped her cheek, breaking the enchantment. Returning to her task, she looked for clues in the darkness, the shadow of a tree limb, the silvering of a rock, to guide her onto the trail she was seeking.

The night's shade deepened. The white hand in hers gave off a faint glow, the sign of latent spells. Latent. Kieri didn't want to think about how this man had used his spell-craft. The Feather Clan had no gentleness – not even, it seemed, to their own kind.

That's not completely true.

Rathen's soft voice ran into her thoughts.

Kieri choked on a scornful laugh. "Then why did they do this to you?"

"Because I refused to keep fighting. I left the war-party. They – incapacitated – me, and left me here for your people to finish." Rathen's voice was calm, detached.

The tremor in his fingers signalled quite different emotions and Kieri's mood softened. Pushing between thicker boughs, shaking cold droplets loose, she absorbed what he'd just said, and gasped. "You betrayed your clan."

Rathen didn't answer.

The ground dipped under Kieri's feet. At last. She moved as silently as she could through the clinging leaf litter and surveyed the slatted walls of the wood-hut. It was the only place she could think of that might be safe. Ordinarily, no one came here before spring's late chill. She clenched her fingers around the bolt on the door and prised it loose.

The door whined. She had to push it hard. The single room was dry and, to her relief, empty. Releasing Rathen's hand, she crouched by the stack of wood piled along the far wall, careful not to stub her toes in the darkness. Picking up a long splinter, she worked it into a gap in the timbered floor and cupped her hands around the tip.

Focussing her mind and words, she pulled the few particles of light in the hut around the stave and set her spell.

The tip glowed into a yellow ball, driving shadows back into the room's corners. When she turned, Rathen was standing very still, watching her.

"Why are you doing this, Kieri?" he said softly.

Kieri held his stare. "I think you know what I'm feeling, Rathen of the Feather Clan." She wondered if he could see the flush mounting in her cheeks. "There's something more though, isn't there? I sense – a likeness between us."

Rathen didn't move. "You're betraying *your* clan too. For me."

Kieri nodded. The shock gripping her had shifted into stillness so deep she could hardly comprehend it. Fears, questions, outrage, accusations prowled at the rim of her mind, but in its centre was a warmth brighter than her spell's sheen. She shivered, and realized her dress, still damp, had chilled. And Rathen, too, was trembling where he stood.

"We need to dry our clothes," she said.

Rathen nodded and started to strip out of his jacket, reaching back to undo straps and clasps around the base of his wings. His boots and torn trousers followed. His pale skin was smooth, its remaining bruises and scrapes striped by the shadows of long feathers. Kieri felt her skin heat, and averted her gaze.

"You don't need to look away." Rathen's voice was soft.

"I –"

Warm breath stirred against Kieri's cheekbone. She hadn't even heard Rathen's approach. His hands landed on her shoulders. "Come. I'll help you out of these."

His fingers began to pry the ties loose down the front of her dress, and Kieri registered that the gesture was easy, well-practised. She shivered, although she was no longer cold.

"You're not shy, are you Rathen?" she muttered, trying to keep her voice even. It didn't work.

She met Rathen's eyes, and saw amber swelling through their grey. He smiled.

"No," he said. "It is not the way of my kind." His busy fingers paused at her bodice. "Is it yours?"

Kieri took a breath, and held his gaze. "It's a long time since a man has seen me unclothed."

What have you been waiting for?

The silent question carried so much more resonance than Kieri was prepared for. But then, she hadn't been prepared for any of this. Rathen's hand brushed down her ribcage, taking the velvet of her gown with it. His fingertips closed around her left nipple, already so hard it ached. His mouth dipped toward her lips, questioning, not yet de-manding. Long black hair slid over Kieri's neck and breast. She shivered again, and pulled back.

"Rathen." No pretence of steadiness in her voice now.

The amber glow muted in Rathen's eyes. He stepped back and let her peel the rest of her gown down off her hips, onto the floor. She had never been so conscious of the creamy shade of her skin, the fiery lights in her hair. Rathen took her dress and spread it on top of his own garments, keeping it off the floor's dust-film.

Kieri watched the supple curves of his body, limned by

the low light. Sensations uncurled beneath her skin, sent unsettling tingles down the soft inner flesh of her thighs. Her stomach knotted, then grumbled. Worry broke through her body's more pleasurable responses.

We have no food.

She knew how to find forest food, but unclothed? In the wet darkness surrounding the hut?

Rathen's hand closed over hers, and drew her close. "Sleep with me, Kieri. We'll find what we need in the morning."

The morning. Kieri tensed, thinking of the next day. Too many problems.

Leave it, Kieri.

Rathen sank onto his knees on the bare floor. Kieri looked around hopelessly for something to soften the grimy slats. Rathen shook his head, and pulled her gently down into a crouch. Fatigue quivered through the muscles bunched under his luminous skin. In a fluid movement he was on his side, one black wing spread across the floor. Kieri followed him and landed on warm feathers. She breathed in, and smelt the tang of ocean mixed with a subtle, cloudy musk. Jet pinions slid over her ankle, then she was folded under a snug quilt of down. She sighed, and nestled in closer to the body meeting hers.

Rathen's skin was as warm as his feathers. Against the dip of Kieri's lower belly, he stirred and hardened, but didn't attempt to do anything more than slide his arms fully around her and press his face into her hair. Kieri closed her eyes, and listened to his breathing even out. The hard lines of muscles

290

and lean flesh eased along the length of her body as Rathen coasted into a healing sleep. Very softly, Kieri kissed the side of his mouth and felt it curve faintly in his slumber.

Images fragmented her own drowsy lull; black wings beating, the white peaks of the Snow Clan, impossibly far, tainted by the deceits she sought to resist. The sharp, clear sensation of hope and trust built in a point between her breasts. Kieri could have laughed aloud with the rapture of it. Instead, she curled her fingers in the hollow of Rathen's throat and let sleep take her.

Silence. The rain had stopped. Kieri yawned and stretched against a body that already felt disarmingly familiar. When she opened her eyes, morning light was spilling through chinks in the hut's walls. Rathen's intent stare was fixed on her face. So much flickered through his gaze in a few seconds that she couldn't speak. Loss chilled the rims of his irises, but the velvety orange around his pupils was tender.

"Your mind is very open, Kieri," he said softly.

Allowing herself, Kieri pressed her lips into his and drew the breath from his opened mouth. *What did you see?*

That you don't want to follow orders. That you don't care for this deception and ambush your people plan, or using your mind gifts to spy out the weaknesses of your foes.

Kieri studied him. *You would have no love for the Snow Clan, surely?*

Rathen's thumbs stroked along her cheekbones. His expression became ironic. *No more than for the Sea Clan. The*

Snow people drove us from the mountains, but yours deny us the smallest area of land.

"The Feather Clan are far from blameless," Kieri said, more sharply than she intended. "Even so, *you* don't want war."

"Even so." Rathen's feathers brushed across the side of her head. "My son was killed, Kieri."

Kieri didn't answer, but pulled her arms tighter around him.

And you've had losses too.

She nodded, and conjured an image of her house, her mother sitting bowed by the window, eyes in a hollowed face looking out on ghosts. "I've dreamed of travelling into the mountains, begging for a heal-spell for my mother." She gave an unhappy laugh. "Instead, I'm supposed to help my people *steal* the Snow Clan's spells."

Rathen's lips grazed her chin, then he tensed. The exposed expression on his face became harder, and guarded.

The sound of voices, male and female, crept through the hut's walls.

"Kieri."

The turmoil Kieri had been shutting out crashed over her.

"Kieri. Kieri."

Rathen's feathers quivered on her arm and hip. Panic spiralled up into her throat.

What are you going to do?

Kieri thought of the demands of her people, what they

were forcing her into, just as Rathen had been forced. An image of her mother, fragile and alone, tore at her. She couldn't leave, not yet, not like this. But she couldn't desert the man in her arms, this enemy who had opened himself to her with gentleness, and courage.

She pulled herself into a sitting position, and Rathen's wing slid from underneath her. He was on his feet in a single movement, holding out her dress. Kieri stepped into it and dragged it up over her hips, fumbling at the laces. She hardly noticed her own clumsiness as Rathen's deft gestures broke through her terror. A wonder more powerful than fear pulled her towards him as he adjusted the splits in his jacket.

"Let me," she murmured.

Despite the dangers closing outside this tiny sanctuary, Rathen smiled and turned around. Kieri took the straps he passed over his shoulders and threaded them through the back of his coat, deciphering the row of clasps on either side, under his shoulder blades. Overcome, she leaned in and kissed the places where silk feathers sprouted from his skin into sweeping arches. Rathen's breath hitched. Turning back to her, he pulled her close.

One breath. Two. Three, in unison, like the swell of the sea.

"Kie-ee-ri."

Kieri lowered his arms, and walked to the door. The handle was cold under her fingers. *Rathen, if you head north, I'll follow when I can. I'll try to divert them long enough for you to run – but their senses are keen. I don't have to tell you, do I?*

"I won't run or hide, Kieri." Rathen's smile faded. "I was meant to die here."

"That doesn't mean you have to," she snapped back at him. The harshness in her voice surprised her, but the thought of losing him was already terrifying.

Rathen didn't react to her tone. His eyes were warm. "And I don't want you to tie yourself to secrecy, or lies. If we're going to be together, Kieri, we need to stand together, don't we?"

Kieri sucked in a breath, ready to deny his words. But he stood calm, so self-controlled she couldn't argue with him. He believed what he said. It was that simple to him. No doubts. No regrets, although his losses were layered, she sensed, beyond what he'd yet shared with her. Was she prepared for such loss? She had no illusions about how her own people would view *her* treachery.

Kieri shivered and braced herself against the door-frame until the chills running chaotically under her skin settled. *Perhaps – I can make them understand.* "Give me a moment with them first then, Rathen. Please."

Rathen nodded. Kieri. *This is – strange for me.*

Kieri laughed. "Strange." *Is that the best you can do?*

A lop-sided smile met her. Amber sparks shot through Rathen's eyes. Kieri wanted nothing more than to make them shine brighter. Gathering herself, she turned and headed out the door. Leaves whispered under her feet, and she knew the sound would be heard. She scanned the dawn-lit gaps between the trees, saw shapes flit through a warming, humid mist. The closest form she recognized: Arkan, second clan leader of the east bays. She opened her mindlink wide to the people she'd been shutting out.

Kieri?

"Arkan."

Kieri waited, unable to force her feet forward. Arkan's tall figure closed on her through the veiled air. If she could have chosen a different person to discover Rathen's presence, she would have. Arkan had been a warrior for more years than Kieri had lived, and his flint eyes were already narrowing, his dark red locks swinging with the sharp motion of his head.

He came to an abrupt halt, and sniffed the air. A hunting wulver wouldn't have scented Rathen, but Arkan's trained senses were alert, even inside Tanem's boundary spells. His hand whipped down to the spell-casters slotted into his belt. In a blur, his arm flicked out. A carved cylinder ex-tended from his fingers, its tip beginning to glow.

Wait! Kieri hurled the word into his head, breaking his focus. She knew he'd almost forgotten her presence.

"Arkan, this isn't what you think."

Arkan's gaze swivelled from her to the hut, to the man now standing in its doorway framed in jet feathers.

"Feather Clan." The words hissed through his clenched teeth. "Kieri, get back."

"No."

The clan's second threw her a glance that shifted rapidly from amazement to condescension. "Kieri, you're no fighter."

Kieri found herself smiling. "Truly, Arkan. And this is no fight."

She walked to Rathen's side and slipped her hand into his. *Together,* she said.

Arkan didn't move. Kieri opened her mouth, but the shriek crossing the woods wasn't hers.

"Kieri!" Her mother stood beside Arkan, a crumpled leaf on the wind. Blank shock wilted into misery on her gaunt features.

Oh, my daughter. What have you done?

The internal scream tore through Kieri's head. Wetness blurred her vision. She was dimly conscious of the approach of other figures, a cautious, tightening circle around her and Rathen, but her mother held her transfixed. Anger had painted the thin cheeks Kieri cherished to rose, feverish life blazed in the faded gaze pinned to her. But it was the crushing *shame* in her mother's mental voice that buffeted Kieri's resolve.

Mama.

Kieri trembled, and felt Rathen's hand settle in the small of her back. Steadying, she looked around the bristling ring of onlookers, meeting blank horror. She must speak now, before that initial reaction descended into judgement.

She held out her hand, palm up. "Let me explain..."

The high whine of arming spell-casters cut through her voice. Rathen stepped in closer to her, the muscles in his thigh stiff against the side of her leg.

"Doesn't he have a voice?" a woman snarled.

Rathen lifted his chin. "Would you listen to me?"

Kieri raised her voice over the humming glitter of aggressors. "Rathen isn't our enemy. Look at him." She gestured to the tattered state of his garments. "He was attacked by his own people, punished and cast out for his refusal to battle us. I found him close to death."

Arkan's gaze levelled with Rathen's, measuring. "And why, exactly, are you *here?*"

Rathen's mouth twisted. "My clan didn't drop me through your border-spells out of kindness."

The hardness in Arkan's face shifted under the implication of Rathen's words.

"Liar!"

Kieri shuddered at the shrill accusation in her mother's voice.

"Liar. You came here to *steal* from us."

She longed desperately to fold her mother's frail body into an embrace, but she didn't dare leave Rathen exposed.

Another man, Adien, added, "Or to *spy* on us. Isn't that right, Rathen? Good try though, the outcast story. You'd like us to believe you have no value as a hostage, wouldn't you?"

Rathen didn't answer. He held his composure, but Kieri sensed he never thought this conversation would go any other way. The circle pulled closer around them, and began to move in that graceful inward spiral which meant an attack. Only Kieri's mother stood still, arms clasped across her ribs, eyes an angry green.

"You're wrong," Kieri protested. "Rathen's clan don't

want him back. I promise you, it's true."

Arkan's expression shadowed. His gaze darted to Rathen, back to her.

"Arkan, you must believe me." Kieri struggled to hold her strength under the pressure of building spells.

Arkan's tone was dark. "I see *you* believe him, Kieri, but don't you think your judgement's been affected by your – partiality – for him? The Feather Clan are not to be trusted. Deceit is written in their bones." His eyes shifted to the glitter of Rathen's wings. "Cruelty in the heritage of their quills. We'll test this Rathen's truth for ourselves."

The spiralling figures locked into position, spell-casters blossoming into light.

"Stand aside, Kieri."

Kieri gritted her teeth until they ached, and slid her arm around Rathen's side. He lowered his head, as if already defeated. Arkan's wrist flicked downward, and his spell-caster released a scarlet plume of disablers. Rathen's breath hissed between his teeth. A hook arced through the muscle of his forearm, its barb deeply anchored. Rathen spread his fingers in a counter-spell and broke the stream of fire attached to it. But its tail lashed around his wrist, burning deep.

"No," Kieri sobbed.

Spells whined around her. On reflex, she swung in front of Rathen's body, her back to the sparkling flares. Fire burned up her spine. She muffled a cry against Rathen's chest. His heartbeat thudded under her cheek. His undamaged hand swept down her back, the ice of an air spell chilling the pain.

298

The void of spell-craft stopped Kieri's breath before wind rushed inward, balancing the energies unleashed.

Keep him on the ground! Adien's urgent cry grated through Kieri before the man hazed in the corner of her sight, spell-caster flailing. Rathen's head snapped up, and he ducked sideways. Instead of shearing through his pinions, the spell hit the upper surface of his coverlet feathers. A cloud of black down swirled into the air and he gasped.

Rathen, fly.

His eyes met her for an instant, asking. Kieri answered him with a tiny nod.

Hold onto me then. Tight.

The earth dropped from under Kieri's feet, tumbled into a dizzying tilt. The whine of projected aggressors leapt after her. Her right ankle stung. The toes of her left foot curled away from a sharp, burning sensation. Black wings cut the sky around her in powerful arcs.

How could she betray us like this? Her mother's agonized question echoed in Kieri's mind.

Lili, he healed her. Did you see – that he healed her? Arkan answered, his mental voice awed, disbelieving.

She betrayed us. She betrayed the memory of her father, the memory of her brother.

She's betrayed us all. Adien's voice, almost un-recognizable. Others joined him. The words drummed through Kieri in a furious litany. She held the wonder in Arkan's tone close, and pulled her focus back to Rathen. He'd already torn the hook from his arm, leaving an ugly gash. His wing-crests were touching a ceiling of cloud over a pearl-coloured sky. Air ran like silk over Kieri's body, stranding her hair into a long banner. Rathen's limbs were shaking, his breath ragged. She brushed her hand gently over the wound in his arm, over the circle of burns at his wrist, drawing on the air's dampness to form a heal-spell. The gash began to close, the blistered crimson stripes smoothed into pink bands.

Rathen broke through the cloud-roof into pale daylight and spread his wings on a strong current. He closed his eyes. The breath he'd been holding expelled in a loud grunt, then he sucked in a great lungful.

"Thanks, Kieri," he managed, "but by the gods, you need hollow bones."

Kieri laughed helplessly. She laughed until water streamed down her face, fell in droplets to a bed of cloud. She felt light-headed on the thin air, on sudden liberty, on love. Rathen's deeper chuckle ran into her flesh, woke a different fire in her spine. His mouth closed over hers, gently. Kieri responded with a fierceness she couldn't hold back, riding on a white arc of desire – and the sky's invisible support.

Rathen pulled back a little, laughing again. "Careful, my love. This isn't the time to break my concentration."

His flight feathers angled, adjusting to a curve in the wind. *Later, I promise.*

Kieri shivered. Rathen veered towards the brightening light. "Where are we going?" she asked.

Rathen nodded forward. Kieri watched the picture projected from his mind. A picture of mountains. She drew in another dizzying breath. "The Snow Clan."

Rathen's eyes grew grave. "I know the stories of the mountain people too, Kieri. I too have dreamed of the healing they possess, far beyond the skills of your clan or mine." His finger ran slowly down the side of Kieri's face. "And your mother will not last long, in her wasting. I know the signs."

Kieri watched the images chasing each other through his mind, people weeping, notched black feathers scattering from high cliffs. Kieri didn't want their mourning, but it was Rathen's too. A new feeling pooled behind her breastbone, a resolution. She thought of the brutality her own clan were capable of, the role she had refused. She thought of seeking the mountain people freely, asking their aid, not forcing it.

"Feather and Sea coming to the snow folk as one." Her mind stilled. "It might be enough."

Rathen nuzzled at her hair. "It's a start, Kieri." He was smiling, and his eyes were flooded with amber. *Together then.*

Kieri stretched her gaze to the horizon, through curls of soft moisture. The tips of two white peaks floated on an ocean of cloud. She pressed her fingers over the hand Rathen had clasped around her waist and let the light fill her.